OFFICER DOWN

Acclaim for Erin Dutton's Work

"*Designed for Love* is…rich in love, romance, and sex. Dutton gives her readers a roller coaster ride filled with sexual thrills and chills. *Designed for Love* is the perfect book to curl up with on a cold winter's day."—*Just About Write*

"*Sequestered Hearts* is packed with raw emotion, but filled with tender moments too. The author writes with sophistication that one would expect from a veteran author. …A romance is about more than just plot and character development. It's about passion, physical intimacy, and connection between the characters. The reader should have a visceral reaction to what is going on within the pages for the novel to succeed. Dutton's words match perfectly with the emotion she has created. *Sequestered Hearts* is one book that cannot be overlooked. It is romance at its finest."—*L-word Literature.com*

"*Sequestered Hearts* by first time novelist, Erin Dutton, is everything a romance should be. It is teeming with longing, heartbreak, and of course, love. …As pure romances go, it is one of the best in print today."—*Just About Write*

In *Fully Involved* "…Dutton's studied evocation of the macho world of firefighting gives the story extra oomph—and happily ever after is what a good romance is all about, right?"—*Q Syndicate*

With *Point of Ignition*…"Erin Dutton has given her fans another fast paced story of fire, with both buildings and emotions burning hotly. …Dutton has done an excellent job of portraying two women who are each fighting for their own dignity and learning to trust again. The delicate tug of war between the characters is well done as is the dichotomy of boredom and drama faced daily by the firefighters. *Point of Ignition* is a story told well that will touch its readers."—*Just About Write*

Visit us at www.boldstrokesbooks.com

By the Author

Sequestered Hearts

Fully Involved

A Place to Rest

Designed for Love

Point of Ignition

A Perfect Match

Reluctant Hope

More Than Friends

For the Love of Cake

Officer Down

OFFICER DOWN

by

Erin Dutton

2015

OFFICER DOWN
© 2015 By Erin Dutton. All Rights Reserved.

ISBN 13: 978-1-62639-423-0

This Trade Paperback Original Is Published By
Bold Strokes Books, Inc.
P.O. Box 249
Valley Falls, NY 12185

First Edition: September 2015

Credits
Editor: Shelley Thrasher
Production Design: Susan Ramundo
Cover Design By Sheri (graphicartist2020@hotmail.com)

Acknowledgments

I've spent the past sixteen years working at a 9-1-1 center in various capacities. Despite all that time, I still remember the early days, when I was young and working second shift with the people who would become some of my closest friends for years to come. I recall hearing the veterans talking about how things used to be done and how much had changed over the years. But I was young and fresh and not even certain I wanted "dispatcher" to be a career rather than a job. So it never occurred to me that one day I might be one of them. Sixteen years later, I can't deny that I am. Because I remember the days when the police officers didn't have computers in their cars and the only way they knew what was going on was if we told them. I remember when the number of calls from landlines far outweighed those from cell phones, in fact, we even had our fair share of calls from payphones.

The technology and the policies have changed and evolved, but at its core, the job has stayed the same: serve the citizens of our county, render aid, and do our best to keep the first responders safe and informed. Remembering that and delivering on those promises, can go a long way toward making the stress of the job worth it.

Though my own job responsibilities have evolved with the years as well, I try never to forget the sense of responsibility, commitment, and awe I felt in those early days. And I appreciate and respect those qualities when I encounter them in another dispatcher.

Turning to my other career, I must give my thanks to my publisher, Len Barot. It hardly seems possible that it has been over eight years since I signed my first contract with Bold Strokes Books. I believe your number of published books was already in the teens by then, and I remember thinking about how unreal it felt that I would have one book published, let alone reaching double digits. And now, with my tenth book, I suppose I've officially reached that point. Of course, you're in the forties now, aren't you? It has been an amazing ride, and I'm thrilled with the vast array of intelligent, talented, and incredible women that I've met since my association with BSB.

Dr. Shelley Thrasher, I cannot thank you enough for teaching me and helping me to shape each and every story. Thanks to Sandy Lowe for seeing the potential in my attempts at story proposals and for the insights that add depth practically before I've begun writing. To Cindy Cresap for keeping everything on track and running smoothly. To everyone who touches my stories as they move through the process, helping to refine, package, and support the finished product.

I must say thank you to the readers. I hope you enjoy this tenth one as much or more than the previous nine. Thank you for your e-mails, tweets, and Facebook messages. So much of writing is just me and my laptop that it's sometimes difficult to be objective about my work. Hearing what you liked, and yes, even what you didn't like, about my books means so much.

Dedication

To my dispatch family through the years.
And to those working in centers all across the country.

CHAPTER ONE

Olivia Dennis pushed open the heavy door and strode across the vestibule, slowing only when she stepped from sound-dampening carpet onto hardwood. The click of her heels echoing up to the soaring ceilings announced her late arrival. She eased open the door to the cathedral and slipped inside, purposely ignoring several curious heads turning, even when they lingered with recognition. Tamping down the urge to hide in one of the back pews and wait out the rest of the service, she hurried halfway up the aisle and shuffled toward an empty seat in the middle of the row. Avoidance wouldn't win her any points with her mother.

As she sat down, she chanced a quick look to her left, only to find her mother's disapproving expression. She should have made an excuse not to be here. But she hadn't. For her mother, even public humiliation wasn't reason enough to skip church. Failing to attend would only have compounded her sins. Incurring Katherine Dennis's wrath wasn't on today's to-do list.

She crossed her arms over her chest and slouched in the pew. Defiantly, she ignored the tension radiating from her mother—the straight back and stiffness in her shoulders that always reminded Olivia that posture matters. Usually, she subscribed to the same theory. She'd been fresh out of the State Law Enforcement Academy when she'd first learned that the way she carried herself could aid in altering perceptions. But, lately, she didn't have the energy for appearances.

She forced her attention back to Pastor Dan. He strode out from behind the podium, relying on the tiny microphone looping over his ear and hovering in front of his mouth to broadcast his voice. Today, as always, his suit appeared perfectly pressed, light gray in contrast to his dark-blue dress shirt. She had often wondered if he thought his signature garishly patterned tie made him seem more approachable—like when he insisted that everyone call him "Pastor Dan." But it all felt a bit too scripted for Olivia.

She wasn't into his message, but right now she preferred it to reminiscing about her early days as a sheriff's deputy or examining her current problems. At least the pastor had laid off some of the hellfire and brimstone for today's sermon. With the country's changing legal climate, he made it his mission, at least once a month, to remind the congregation that the church was, in fact, against homosexuality and gay marriage. On those Sundays, Olivia fidgeted in the pew, hoping no one could detect the guilt that burned deep in her stomach. She was sweating through her church clothes by the end of those sermons. Today, she had a different reason for plotting a quick escape.

As soon as Pastor Dan offered his final words, she stood and surged forward, searching for a way to slip around the elderly woman shuffling in front of her. But just before she made it into the aisle, her mother grasped her elbow tightly.

"Since you missed the first half of the service, I trust you'll be joining us for dinner at home. I've invited Pastor Dan and his wife."

Olivia pressed her lips together against her refusal and nodded. As she wove her way through the loitering parishioners toward the parking lot, she returned several polite greetings, but no one engaged her. By now, the news of her most recent trouble had spread, but no one was brave enough to broach a question. She also caught a few nervous glances at her father. She hadn't looked at him yet, but she could feel him there, looming large behind her mother.

"Olivia, how lovely to see you."

She jerked to a stop at the top of the steps at the saccharine voice and tried not to stare too longingly at her car in the parking lot. Instead, she focused on the woman who tottered toward her on impossibly high heels. The only thing higher and more tenuous than those shoes was the cotton-candy-like swirl of her ash-blond hair, swaying in the light breeze.

Olivia forced a smile and returned the greeting. She'd never called this woman by her given name, often didn't even remember it, simply referring to her as "Mrs. Pastor Dan" in her head.

"I'm so glad you could join us this morning." Her tone indicated she was aware of Olivia's tardiness.

"I wouldn't miss it. I apologize for being late. I, uh—" She fought the urge to shove back the unruly curls she hadn't bothered to restrain this morning. She hadn't slept much, but she didn't want to explain why, so she settled on saying, "I'm sorry."

Mrs. Pastor Dan gave her a sympathetic smile, and Olivia shifted her eyes to the floor. Of course, she'd heard about Olivia's most recent trials. Collins County, Tennessee was just big enough for you to get into trouble but small enough that everyone knew about it when you did.

Olivia ducked away from the pastor's wife and had made it to the bottom of the stairs when an arm thrown around her shoulders stopped her.

"Hey, there, big sister." Andrew Dennis, Jr. spoke with a gentleness that belied his large build. Two years her junior, her brother had outweighed her since the third grade. By high school he'd amassed a solid layer of muscle and become their school's star linebacker.

"Knock it off, Andy." She shoved her hand against his ribs but he didn't budge.

"Hey, I heard what happened." The concern in Andy's voice contradicted his expression. He kept his thick hair, the same jet-black hue as hers, respectably short and tamed in a style the church ladies would approve of.

"Who hasn't?" she grumbled. "Please don't look at me like that. I can't handle judgment from you."

"I'm not judging."

"Sure you are. You're just like him." After an injury in college had sidelined his football career, he'd followed her and their father into law enforcement. Honestly, he would most likely have been on that path anyway. Football was never taking him to the NFL.

"Have you talked to him?"

"Not yet. But since Mama is making me come back to the house, I'm sure we'll have it out there."

"He's pissed."

"No shit." She shifted and tugged at the waist of her dress. The black wrap-dress was fashionable but bordered on too short for church, and she'd chosen it just to offend her mother's sensibilities.

Andy narrowed his eyes. "You're thinking about ditching. Don't. You'll hurt Mama's feelings, and you'll have to face him eventually anyway."

She nodded. He was right.

"Besides, I want a front-row seat."

She shoved him again and he walked away laughing. His joking tone aside, his words had a level of seriousness. They'd always been competitive, and when he thought she might come up short, he took a measure of pleasure in her failures.

Before she could make another move toward the parking lot, her best friend, Frankie, pulled her into a quick hug.

"Go easy on him." Since she'd married Andy, Frankie had deliberately split her loyalty between the two of them.

"Uh-uh, Frankie. You can be his wife or you can be my friend. But sometimes you can't be both." She and Frankie had been friends since junior high. During their senior year, when Frankie started dating Andy, their friendship had undergone a rough patch, but they'd come out of it closer than ever.

"I'm determined to try." Frankie's blue eyes sparkled with humor, and her smile was quick and broad. She'd always been easy-going and apparently was the perfect complement to Olivia's high-strung brother. She was as thin and fair as he was hulking and dark.

"Yeah, well, just remember, I saw you first."

"And here I thought I wasn't your type," Frankie said with a wink.

"Frankie." Olivia whipped her head around to check for anyone within earshot.

"Relax, no one heard."

"It's fine to play around when it's not your life we're talking about, huh?" She'd first started questioning her sexuality in junior high and had confided in Frankie, but no one else since. Frankie had even kept her secret from Andy, although she hadn't really had much to tell. Olivia's forays into lesbianism consisted of sneaking off to a dingy gay bar three hours away. She hadn't even been in a real relationship with a woman, unless you counted stilted conversation, awkward kisses, and a handful of clumsy hookups.

"I'm sorry." Frankie squeezed Olivia's shoulder. "I just hate seeing you lonely. I wish you could find someone and—"

"And what? Be as deliriously happy as you and my brother?" She'd given up on that dream when she'd stopped pretending to date men. But she just couldn't bring herself to take the next step and come out to her very strict, very religious parents. She had no doubt about what their reaction would be.

"You could have a worse fate. I'm not saying having *your* family as in-laws is easy, but you're kind of worth the trouble." Frankie gave an exaggerated shrug, and then her teasing melted away as something across the room clearly caught her attention. "Your father doesn't seem happy."

"He's not." She didn't look and didn't need to in order to imagine his expression.

"Has he said anything yet?"

"No. But he will."

Frankie leaned close and whispered in her ear, cloaking her words in a supportive hug. "Maybe now's the time to come out to him. Distract him, and he won't know which he's madder about."

She couldn't help but laugh. What a mess that conversation would be. *Daddy, I know you're pissed that I'm being investigated and could lose my job, but by the way, I'm a dyke.* His face would turn purple, and he might just have a coronary right there in front of her. Actually, more than likely she'd end up with the imprint of his hand emblazoned on her cheek.

Her father was a tough guy who believed in old-fashioned discipline. She'd cut her own switch more than once during her childhood. But now that she was too grown for him to turn over his knee, she figured he'd settle for a well-placed slap if she dared to be so disrespectful to him.

Some of those early lessons were still on her mind thirty minutes later when she pulled her old Jeep to the curb in front of her parents' house. She killed the engine but didn't get out right away. Though she'd barely waited until her first paycheck as a deputy had cleared before moving into her own apartment, this house still felt like home. But today, when she looked at the wrap-around porch where she and her brother had played on the tire swing on the tree in the front yard, or the window to her second-floor childhood bedroom, she only felt a knot of dread in her stomach. She forced herself out of the car but, with every step, felt like she was walking to her execution.

As she pulled open the screen door, the predictable squeak grated on her ears. As she passed through the foyer and into the kitchen, she tried to blend in among her extended family and friends. In addition to their own Sunday family dinners, once every couple of months, her mother took a turn hosting her church family. She would have spent yesterday afternoon dredging chicken in preparation for frying and loading side dishes into disposable aluminum pans that she could stick in the oven today.

Olivia slipped through the crowd, trying to reach the living room, where she knew Frankie and Andy would be. She was almost there when she heard the creak of a board behind her, and she froze. She knew its exact placement, as it had gotten her in trouble in the tenth grade when she tried to sneak in through the back door after curfew.

"Olivia." She could barely handle the disappointment in her father's voice.

"Sir." She turned and inclined her head in what she hoped was a sufficient show of respect, though it wouldn't help her plight.

"A word." It wasn't a request.

She clenched her teeth and followed him down the hall. They stepped through the French doors onto the back porch, effectively shutting out the rest of the family. But no one in there would be coming to her rescue anyway.

The screened porch stretched across the entire back side of the house and was her mother's favorite place to sit in the mornings. Olivia pulled in a deep breath of fresh air, glad he hadn't taken her to his office. She didn't think she could stand to be surrounded by the photographs she'd studied since she was a toddler and he'd had to lift her up to see. Over the years, he'd posed with most of the local power players. He'd served as county sheriff through four mayors and three district attorneys, one of whom was Olivia's godfather. His carefully crafted expression remained eerily similar in each picture, just enough smile to appear trustworthy, but stoic enough to be feared. Only the added gray at the temples of his full head of hair indicated the more recent shots.

The porch felt restrictive enough, and she quickly crossed to the other end, wishing a little distance would ease the knot in her stomach. Today, she couldn't mistake the controlled anger and embarrassment in his expression.

"Sit." He waved toward the outdoor sofa as if they were about to chat about the weather. "Would you like to tell me what happened?"

"I imagine the version you've already heard is accurate enough." Though he'd retired as sheriff a year ago, he still had contacts in high places, and he'd certainly already read the complaint against her, as well as the statement she'd given to her captain. She sat, because refusing required too much effort.

He took the chair beside her. "I'd like to hear it from you."

For just a moment, she wished she could find some softness— some compassion in his voice. She longed for the gentle father who once supported her unconditionally, but she couldn't remember the last time she'd seen that man. She stared at her hands, tamping down rebellion before she responded.

"It should have been a simple domestic disturbance. I got there first and went to the door." She paused, expecting him to berate her for not waiting for her backup. But when he stared silently, she continued, her mind replaying the scene in vivid detail.

The wife had answered the door and allowed her inside. She'd just started questioning her when her intoxicated husband barreled around the corner, nearly knocking Olivia down. In the scuffle, he'd grabbed for her gun but couldn't get it out of the holster. Olivia slammed the heel of her hand under his chin—fast and hard. He reared back, howling in pain, and she took him down quickly.

Before his sluggish senses could catch up, she had him laid out prone with her knee in the center of his back. She'd clicked handcuffs on him, leaned over, and growled in his ear, "Assault. Add that to your charges."

She'd stuffed him into the back of her car, adrenaline still singing through her body. She'd been challenged before, by men bigger than this guy, and had a reputation for holding her own.

The next day, she found out she wouldn't escape unscathed either. Her captain informed her that he'd filed a brutality complaint and restricted her to desk duty pending an investigation.

"Where?" her father asked, though she suspected he knew and only wanted to hear her humiliate herself by saying it.

"Security detail. Five-C." She'd be watching security monitors at the front desk of the Collins County Communications and Command Center, commonly referred to as Five-C. The building housed the dispatch, headquarters, and administrative offices for the County Sheriff's Department and the Reinsville Fire Department. Her new post at the reception desk, though hopefully temporary, would leave her front and center while the investigation went on. She already dreaded it. "Second shift."

He nodded stiffly, but she wasn't sure if that meant he agreed with the punishment or was simply acknowledging her.

"I report there tomorrow. I wish they'd suspended me."

"Buck wanted to. I called in a favor."

"You called—this is supposed to be a favor?"

"Yes. So show some gratitude."

"I'm so sorry, Daddy. Of course I'm grateful that you and Buck Martin decided to put me on display."

"That's Sheriff Martin to you." Though her father referred to his long-time hunting buddy by his first name, he wouldn't abide Olivia doing the same.

"Don't kid yourself. He's not doing this for you. He wants to show he can be some kind of hard-ass and not just your right-hand man."

"Watch your mouth, young lady." His voice was sharp and loud. "I've given you leeway because I know you're upset. But I will not excuse your attitude. You'll report to your assignment and serve as required until the investigation is complete."

"Yes, sir." She wanted to argue—to yell at him that if he really wanted to help her, he would at least try to act like he believed she'd be exonerated. But she clamped her mouth shut, because if she asked for what she needed, it would come out too much like a plea. And admitting that fact only made her angry at herself.

"One-forty." The gruff voice of one of the on-duty sergeants crackled over the radio and into dispatcher Hillary O'Neal's headset.

She stepped on the pedal at her right foot, keying her microphone. "Go ahead."

"This is a confirmed code four. Send me a crime-scene tech and notify the medical examiner, please."

"Ten-four." She quickly typed the updates into the computer and began notifying the requested resources. Less than ten minutes ago, she'd dispatched the sergeant and two deputies to an apparent overdose behind one of the larger apartment complexes in the county. They'd had three overdoses in two weeks, but this was the first person who'd died as a result. Now, having confirmed the victim's death, the deputies would be on the scene for quite a while longer.

She spun in her chair, made eye contact with her supervisor across the room, and turned her thumb down. She twisted back to the three computer monitors on her console and settled in for a long, hectic shift. Having that many deputies tied up on a major incident meant the others would have to work harder to keep up with the busy evening workload.

Hillary wouldn't have any problem keeping up, though. After nine years, she'd grown accustomed to the steady hum of activity. She'd mastered the ability to simultaneously absorb and tune out her surroundings. At the far end of the room, three other dispatchers answered the 9-1-1 lines, as well as several administrative numbers. When law enforcement, fire department, or medical assistance was needed, they entered an incident in the computer for dispatch. The dispatchers for each discipline opened the call and assigned the appropriate responders. Tonight, Hillary handled the distribution of law-enforcement resources. Next to her, another dispatcher manned the frequency for the fire and ambulance services, while a third dispersed the requests for animal control, codes enforcement, public works, and other various resources.

"One-forty. Get me an ETA on crime scene. We need to get this scene documented before the rain starts."

Hillary acknowledged the sergeant's transmission, already reaching for the telephone receiver next to her.

For the next thirty minutes, she worked steadily to stay on top of both the ongoing incident as well as the new calls coming in. As the changeover from day shift to evening shift approached, the call volume would increase. Sometimes, it seemed people carried their work stress home only to take it out on their families and neighbors. Hillary was assigned to evenings, or second shift, but today she'd come in early to pick up some overtime on days.

"Hey, Hill."

She didn't have to turn to recognize the deep voice of her closest friend. Everything about Jake was big, from his voice to the thick muscles that clung to his six-foot-five frame. His boisterous personality made him popular with the other dispatchers and, when it carried over the radio, the officers as well.

She glanced at him, craning her neck briefly before looking back at her computer screens. "You're early." Their regular shift didn't start for another hour.

"So are you."

"Day shift needed help."

"You work too much overtime."

She shrugged. "What else am I going to do?"

Even in a small town where jobs were scarce, the turnover rate for dispatchers was higher than in most professions. If a dispatcher made it past the first few years, the odds they stayed went up, but a large number washed out in those early days of busy shifts, stress, and working every holiday. After someone left, hiring and training a new employee took several months. Citizens didn't stop calling 9-1-1 because they were short-staffed. Subsequently, Collins County dispatchers could pull as much overtime as they desired.

Without volunteers, command staff filled shifts with mandatory overtime. If Hillary didn't work, they would just call in someone else. Since she didn't have a spouse or kids to go home to, she tried to help out those who did. Besides, it never hurt to pad the savings account, in case she ever decided to take that vacation she'd been putting off for years.

"What's your excuse?"

"I went to the gym, but I wasn't feeling it so I bailed early," Jake said.

She scanned his face for signs of illness. He rarely cut his daily workouts short. She suspected the regular physical exertion was the only way he could handle such a sedentary job. "Something wrong?"

"Nah." He shrugged. "The gym was crowded. I couldn't get the weights I wanted. You would have thought it was January instead of June and all the resolution patrons had showed up."

"That's not very nice. You should encourage those who want to make a positive change."

"It's a proven fact. You've done it yourself. Except you don't even pretend during January anymore."

She swatted at his shoulder, but since she didn't take her eyes off her computers, she didn't get close to making contact. "It's too damn hard to get out of those gym contracts once you sign up, so I end up paying them every month for nothing."

He laughed. "At least you try to eat healthy."

"Yeah. I'm committed to being lazy, so it's the only way I can control my weight." Theirs was an unlikely friendship—one she wouldn't have predicted when Jake had started working with them a year ago. At nineteen, he'd hired on at the same age as Hillary did. Despite very different lifestyles and an eight-year age gap, they'd quickly developed a sibling-like bond. As a dispatcher, Hillary had taken young Jake under her wing, but socially, Jake often led her into new situations.

"Okay, on to gossip."

She keyed her microphone and answered an officer, then dispatched another one to a theft report. Then she turned back to him. "All right, hit me."

"You hear about Dennis?" he asked as he rested his butt on the edge of her desk.

"Which one?"

"Olivia. Her one-oh-eight from the other night filed a complaint on her." He used the code for the paperwork that deputies filled out after any use-of-force incident.

Hillary forced her expression to remain neutral and waved a dismissive hand. "I'm sure it's a formality. She's a Dennis. What are they going to do to her?"

She'd gone to high school with Olivia Dennis. More accurately, they'd gone there at the same time. But they'd never traveled in the same circles. Even if super-feminine cheerleader Olivia hadn't been a year ahead of her, she wouldn't have socialized with awkward, teenaged Hillary. Olivia had been the object of Hillary's first girl-crush. She'd worked out her sexuality with PG-rated fantasies of Olivia Dennis's shiny, blue-black curls, trim waist, and firm legs. After all, even though she was a lesbian, she hadn't gone to the football games for the sports.

Years after she'd let go of childhood emotions, Hillary had been surprised to find that Olivia had followed in her father's law-enforcement footsteps. The Olivia she remembered wouldn't have chanced breaking a nail. But even as a rookie, Olivia had quickly earned a reputation as a hothead and more than a bit reckless, making traffic stops and looking for trouble even when she didn't have many calls from citizens requesting assistance to keep her busy.

"I don't know. I heard Sheriff Martin is trying to prove he's not running a good-old-boy department like Senior did." He paused for dramatic effect, then looked annoyed when she kept working instead of giving him her full attention. "She's manning our security desk until she gets cleared."

"Wow. Well, that will prove his point. They only put officers on the desk when they're really in trouble."

"Right? But at least we'll have some decent scenery around here."

She wrinkled her nose. "That's in poor taste, buddy. Her career could be on the line." She'd never told him about her adolescent crush.

"Hey, I didn't say I wanted it to be permanent." He shrugged, then gave her a wide grin. "But if she's being punished anyway, it might as well be here."

CHAPTER TWO

Olivia waited for the security gate to open, granting her entrance to Five-C. Though she was five minutes late reporting to her assignment, she wasn't in a hurry to get inside. She'd parked as far from the building as she could and took her time walking through the lot. Halfway there she regretted passing up the closer spots. Sure, she needed the time to settle her head, and since she'd be sedentary at work for who knew how long, the exercise wouldn't hurt either. But Mother Nature seemed intent on unleashing the hottest, most humid summer in years, and it was only mid-June. She pulled the front of her shirt away from her stomach, already feeling the fabric sticking to her back under her suit jacket where she couldn't reach.

She picked up the pace, eager for the air-conditioning. The door slid open as she approached. She flashed her identification to the deputy at the door and passed through the metal detector. The building was old and had obviously undergone at least one renovation over the years, but a coat of paint could only hide so much. And she'd bet her salary those ceiling tiles contained asbestos. The place smelled like someone had drenched old library books in pine-scented cleanser. She hoped, probably in vain, that her time here was short.

She slowed as she approached the reception desk. When she caught sight of the man behind the desk, she wished she'd been assigned to the metal detector instead. But since she'd handed over her gun when she'd been suspended, she was forced to act as a glorified receptionist. And her new coworker didn't seem to be giving even that role a good name. Wrinkles so deep they could be razor-sharp creases bisected his Oxford button-down. He clearly hadn't had a haircut lately and apparently couldn't even be bothered to find a comb this morning.

"Can I help you?" He barely glanced up.

"Olivia Dennis. I'm on second shift here."

"Oh, right. Sarge told me you'd be in today." He scrubbed his hand over what had to be three days of stubble, and not the kind that had been trimmed to look purposely scruffy. "I'm Holt. Crime Suppression."

She gave him a slow nod strictly out of politeness. Was she supposed to be impressed that he worked in the unit responsible for undercover enforcement? And if so, was that still notable, since he'd clearly been suspended from the unit for the time being?

"Come on around and I'll give you the tour."

As she rounded the desk, he balled up a handful of fast-food wrappers from the desk and dropped them in the waste can underneath. The smell of greasy cheeseburgers and grilled onion assaulted her already queasy stomach. Several splotches of mustard dotted the desk.

She hoped to God one of them got reinstated before too long. And she really wanted to be the one.

"We've got a pretty basic camera set up here." Twenty cameras covered the building, depicting everything from the dispatch center to the hallways outside the administrative offices of the sheriff's department and fire department. Though they all recorded on the virtual servers and could be reviewed later, they had only six monitors at the front desk. He showed her how to cycle through them as well as how to research the archives to call up old footage.

He pointed to a hallway to the left and indicated the administrative offices, and the door to the right that led to the dispatch center. She bit her lip to keep from reminding him this wasn't her first time inside headquarters, just her first time behind the desk. He showed her the phone-number list for the building's occupants and explained how to sign in visitors in great detail. She suffered his explanations with as much patience as she could.

"What are you in for?" He leaned close.

"What?" She'd always hated the stale smoke odor that wafted from smokers.

"DUI." He jerked his thumb at his own chest. "But my lawyer says he'll get it dropped."

She nodded, not quite sure how she was supposed to respond. She didn't think a sheriff's deputy should take so much pride in skirting the law. "I heard yours was brutality. That true?"

"Allegedly." She didn't mind if this guy was a little afraid of her.

"Want my attorney's name?" He patted his pockets. "I have a card here somewhere."

"No. I got it covered."

"He's real good."

"Thanks anyway." She was becoming more and more certain she'd be gone before he was.

"Suit yourself. Usually, we overlap by a couple of hours before my shift is through. But since you're here, I think I'll cut out early. It's been a long day."

She wasn't sure he had the authority to alter his shift. But she wasn't about to stop him.

"Think you can handle this?"

"It's not brain surgery." She didn't care that she was being rude. She resented being here with him, as if their shared placement somehow put them on the same plane. She might stretch the limits of policy at times while dealing with criminals, but she'd never put innocent lives in danger by getting behind the wheel after drinking.

"Okay. I'm out. Have a good one."

After he'd gone, she grabbed a couple of napkins from the stack he'd left on the desk and went to work cleaning up the mustard, hoping she wouldn't be adding housekeeping to her daily duties. She glanced toward the hallway leading to Sheriff Martin's office. She imagined the look on his face if she burst through the door and insisted he reinstate her or fire her. She smiled at her melodramatic thoughts, then pressed her lips tightly into a grimace. Her father would lose his shit for sure.

She settled into her chair and trained her eyes on the monitors in front of her. She wouldn't be staging her rebellion today. So she'd just have to figure out if she could find *anything* interesting to watch in this building.

❖

"Time for lunch," Hillary's relief dispatcher stood at her left elbow.

Hillary nodded. She unplugged her headset from the radio console and stepped out of the way. She stretched her back. She'd taken two steps toward the kitchen to heat a boring frozen meal when Jake appeared by her side.

"Come on. Let's go by the front desk and cruise Deputy Dennis." Without waiting for a reply, he grabbed her arm and pulled her toward the hallway.

"Jake, I'm hungry and I don't want to cruise any—" As they stepped through the door from the dispatch center into the lobby, whatever she was about to say was suddenly not important. Olivia Dennis sat behind the reception desk with a cell phone to her ear.

Hillary had expected her to be in uniform but now remembered that decommissioned officers had to wear civilian clothes. She wore a black suit jacket over a white button-down shirt, open at the neck. Her dark hair cascaded to her shoulders—there was no other way to describe the fall of full, luxurious curls that made Hillary's hands twitch with the urge to bury her fingers in them. Olivia's dark eyes shifted from screen to screen intently, though Hillary doubted she would find much of interest going on in the building.

"See something you like?" Jake laughed.

"What?" Despite the flush Hillary felt warming her face at being caught staring, she didn't look away.

"Honey, you're staring."

She shook her head and forced her attention back to Jake's face, then scowled at his smug expression.

"I don't blame you, she's gorgeous. Hell, you've probably got as much chance as anyone. She's shot down most of the guys in dispatch, and on the force, too, I hear."

Gorgeous? Yes, she always had been. But that didn't seem like the right word. Elegant, slightly aloof, and altogether stunning. Maybe Hillary hadn't quite left that adolescent attraction behind.

"She shot you down?"

He gave a quick, self-deprecating grin. "Cold and fast."

"Wow." She'd never seen any woman resist Jake's soulful eyes, purposely shaggy hair, and lazy smile, and she'd watched him work his game on plenty of them.

"Ever met her?"

She nodded. "Kind of. She was a year ahead of me in school."

He lifted a brow. "Let's go say hi."

"Jake, she's on the phone." Just as Hillary offered the excuse, Olivia set her phone down on the desk. Hillary wiped her hands against her hips, hoping her nervous motion was more discreet than it felt.

"Come on. Hey, if you're the one that finally bags her, you'll be legendary."

"I don't think I'll be *bagging* anyone."

She'd been out at work from her first day and had even had a couple of short-lived relationships, with a deputy sergeant and with one of her coworkers. Of course, she'd had some regrets about the latter since Ann had been promoted to second-shift supervisor not long after they broke up. They'd had several months of uncomfortable working conditions and only recently settled into a professional relationship that included as much distance as was possible.

"Hey, Dennis," Jake called out as he took Hillary's arm and dragged her toward the desk. "How's it going?" He flashed his trademark grin.

Her answering smile was polite but tight. "Not bad, Jake."

"You know Hillary O'Neal, don't you? She's a dispatcher, too."

"Deputy Dennis," Hillary said with a nod.

"Reinsville High. I remember." She gave Hillary a polite smile. "Call me Olivia." Something in her tone made Hillary think she wasn't just being friendly—that she felt uncomfortable with her title. When Olivia's brown eyes shifted to hers, an ache pierced Hillary's chest at their intensity. Not aloof? Careful, maybe.

"We were just going out to grab some lunch. Can we bring you back something?" She latched onto something to talk to Olivia about.

Before Olivia could answer, another dispatcher called out as he walked by, "Hey, Dennis, welcome to Five-C. Make yourself comfortable. It could be awhile."

"That's funny." Olivia glared at him, then shifted her gaze back to Hillary. "Desk duty. Until this investigation is over."

"I heard."

Olivia tightened her lips and nodded. "I'm sure you did."

"I mean, I don't know the details. But I—we—someone said you'd be here." She didn't want Olivia to think she'd been gossiping about her. "So—um—food?"

"Oh, no, thanks."

Was that nausea that passed over Olivia's expression? "Did you bring your lunch?"

"No."

"I hope you're not planning to rely on the vending machines here. Because they're surprisingly poorly stocked considering we're a twenty-four-hour operation."

"I'm not really—"

"Not eating?"

"I was going to say, not hungry."

"But my way was more accurate, huh?"

Olivia's brows drew together, then smoothed as if she'd decided to be honest. "Yes, I suppose it is."

"So? What kind of sandwich do you want?"

"You don't have to do that."

Hillary adopted her sternest expression, the one that matched the assertive tone she injected into her voice when dealing with a difficult caller.

Olivia bit her lip, then rolled her eyes. "Ham and cheese."

"Mayo?"

"Spicy mustard."

"Bold choice."

"Thank you." Olivia's smile was wide and genuine, and Hillary nearly forgot what they were talking about. She'd never before understood the expression "her eyes lit up," but now—well, Olivia's irises practically glowed golden brown, and Hillary swore she could feel the warmth.

"Hill?" Laughter laced Jake's voice.

"Yeah?" She turned to him, unable to put together the expectation on his face.

"Let's go." He steered her toward the door.

"Hey, wait. Let me give you some money." Olivia grabbed her purse from under the desk. Her head down, she dug her hand into the bag as she circled the reception desk and came toward them.

"Shit," Jake hissed.

When Hillary followed his stare, she barely managed to hold back an echoing exclamation. She'd assumed Olivia wore a pantsuit, but her slim skirt stopped above her knees, leaving an impressive length of bare, muscular legs.

"Hillary?"

She jerked her eyes up to Olivia's and saw curiosity and a bit of humor there. Olivia raised her outstretched hand a little higher to get Hillary's attention. The bills folded in her hand penetrated the fog that Olivia's ridiculously sculpted calves caused in Hillary's brain. She'd never even realized she had such a weakness for calves.

"No. It's okay. I've got it." She waved off the money.

"Yeah. We've got it." Jake pulled on Hillary's arm. "But we only have an hour."

He waited until they'd cleared the door before he spoke more quietly. "Not that I wouldn't mind looking at her for the next hour."

"Sure. If you hadn't already been rejected."

"Ouch. You're mean."

"No. I'm hungry."

Chapter Three

Hey, I'm glad you made it." Frankie grabbed Olivia's hand. "Let's get you a drink."

Olivia could practically feel everyone looking at her as she followed Frankie through the people packed into the modest two-story house. She recognized a bunch of deputies and purposely avoided several gazes, knowing that the one thing she didn't want to discuss was all anyone wanted to talk to her about.

"This was a bad idea," she muttered, pulling up short, and she considering leaving. After five minutes, she was already sorry she'd let Frankie persuade her to attend the fortieth birthday party for one of the other deputies. He'd apparently invited the whole department. When her father was sheriff she'd avoided these parties because, even though she could give a shit what people did with their personal lives, having the sheriff's kid around made people uncomfortable. She would never have reported back to him, but some of the guys had never fully accepted her. Since her father retired, she still hadn't gone, mostly out of habit and partly because she didn't want to explain why she never accepted an invitation when one of the guys got tipsy and brave enough to ask her out. But tonight she'd been in a funk and grabbed an opportunity to escape her own lonely company.

"Stay a little longer. Andy made me come with him and I don't know anyone else here."

"You know plenty of people." Though he'd been on the force two years less than her, Andy had been accepted from day one. He had the kind of personality that made people forget about anyone but him. He shared a name with the sheriff, for God's sake, and they still liked and trusted him more than they did Olivia. She tried not to be bitter.

"Okay. I don't like anyone else here."

Olivia laughed. "I didn't come out here just to hear you complain about the other wives."

"So why did you come?"

"Apparently because I'm a better friend than you are."

Frankie passed her a plastic cup of beer. "Drink."

She shrugged and turned up the cup. A little alcohol couldn't make her feel worse.

"You're overreacting to this whole situation, you know? Andy says a lot of the guys think you're getting a raw deal. You were doing your job and they know it. You've got more support than you realize."

"Yeah, I know." She was the story of the week, and it would all die down, most likely before those assholes in Professional Accountability finally cleared her to go back to patrol.

She glanced around, taking in the faces around her. Judging by the turnout, either everyone liked the birthday boy or wanted an excuse to drink and let off steam. In addition to a bunch of other deputies and their spouses, she'd seen some of the civilian administrative staff, and even a few dispatchers. As she swept the room, her gaze stopped on two dispatchers in particular.

Hillary and Jake had just walked through the front door. She'd met Jake about a year ago, when he'd first started working at dispatch. He'd come to the station to ride along with one of his buddies for a shift and had barely waited for their pre-shift briefing to conclude before he'd hit on her. She could definitely see why women fell for his charm, but she'd had no problem politely rebuffing him.

He leaned close and spoke to Hillary. When she smiled at whatever he said, Olivia's jealousy surprised her. Aside from their shared alma mater, they barely knew each other. In the past week, she'd seen Hillary only a handful of times. That first day, she and Jake had returned in time to drop Olivia's sandwich off and go back to work. Two other days, Hillary had delivered what appeared to be a homemade lunch to the front desk, ignoring Olivia's insistence that she didn't need to be fed.

In high school, Hillary had hung out with the emo kids. They seemed to cherish their individuality, but as a teenager, Olivia had thought they were covering for the fact that they weren't very cool. She figured they just pretended they didn't care about popularity. Back then, being liked had mattered a great deal to Olivia.

Over the years, she'd heard mention of Hillary, mostly the kind of updates one overhears at the grocery store or from gossiping family friends or acquaintances. After Olivia joined the force she'd heard the usual rumors through the department grapevine. She'd been a little surprised to learn that Hillary was an out lesbian. She wouldn't have equated that kind of confidence with the timid girl she remembered.

Hillary had changed physically since high school, as well—maybe even more than Olivia had. She'd always had a couple of inches on Olivia's five-foot-four frame. Hillary's light-brown hair had just looked mousy back then, but now it appeared silky and shot through with blond highlights. The angled cut that followed her jawline was far more fashionable than the way she'd worn it before. Either she'd grown into her curves, or she was just dressing better for her body now. Her light-blue scoop-neck shirt appeared to be the same shade as her eyes. Olivia couldn't make them out from across the room, but she remembered being struck by their pale shade when they'd reconnected at Five-C earlier in the week. The shirt tapered at her waist, and Olivia let her eyes wander over the gentle swells of her denim-encased hips. Was it possible that Hillary had looked like this back then and Olivia had been repressing her attraction to the female form that much?

"Someone you know?" Frankie pressed her face close to Olivia's to follow her line of sight.

"Yes—no. Not really."

"That clears it right up." Frankie bumped her shoulder against Olivia's. "Do you know her or not?"

"Remember Hillary O'Neal? She was a year back in school. She's a dispatcher."

Andy draped an arm around Frankie's shoulders. "Word is she's a dyke."

"Andy." Frankie elbowed him in the ribs.

Olivia stared at her feet, trying to will away the flush crawling up her neck.

"What? I can't warn my sister about the chick she's hanging out with."

"Who—who said *hanging out*?" Did Andy notice the tremor in her voice? And how in the hell did a couple of lunches at the security desk turn into "hanging out"?

"You know how rumors fly around the department."

"Just rumors," Olivia said with a defensive sniff, rebuilding her protective shell. "And nobody's business."

"Whatever you say. Just be careful. You don't want to be labeled by association. I'm going to get another beer." Andy patted her shoulder as he moved away.

Olivia glanced around to see if anyone appeared to have overheard them, but everyone nearby seemed engaged in their own conversations. Her face flamed and she'd started to sweat. She needed to get out of this crowd.

"Hey, hold on." Frankie grabbed her hand. Olivia jerked free, hypersensitive to touch after her brother's ribbing. But Frankie recaptured her hand and squeezed hard. "Okay, don't freak out. You'll only call more attention to yourself. Just stand here with me and breathe."

Olivia took a couple of deep breaths and her panic began to ease.

"So, you've been hanging out with her? You can't make a new friend without telling me, you know."

"It's nothing. She brought me lunch at the front desk a couple of times. We've barely talked without her friend over there with us, too." She jerked her chin toward the door, but Jake had disappeared and Hillary stood alone. Before Olivia could look away, Hillary glanced at her. She smiled, and Olivia couldn't keep from returning the gesture. Hillary must have taken her smile as an invitation, because she moved into the crowd and picked her way across the room.

"Hey, Hillary," Olivia said when she got close enough to hear.

"How are you, Deputy Dennis?"

"I keep asking you to call me Olivia. You've brought me lunch three days this week. I know that doesn't make us friends, but it counts for something, doesn't it?"

"I suppose it does." She lifted a brow. "Olivia."

"Do you remember Frankie?" She grabbed Frankie's arm, searching for a distraction from the nervous flutter in her stomach at the sound of Hillary saying her name.

"Sure. Frankie Turner."

"It's Dennis now."

Hillary glanced at Olivia's hand still clutching Frankie's arm.

"I married her brother, Andy."

"That's right. I think I'd heard that somewhere."

"No doubt. News travels fast in this town. It was good to see you again, Hillary. I'd better go check on my husband." She slipped around Hillary and gave Olivia a wink behind her back.

"You can stop with the lunches, you know."

"You don't like them?"

"Of course I do." She almost said she could get used to Hillary cooking for her, but she somehow managed to keep that thought in. "But you're not responsible for making sure I eat."

"Maybe somebody needs to be," Hillary mumbled.

"What?" Olivia leaned in to hear her better and immediately caught the scent of citrus and something woodsy.

"Nothing." Hillary took a step back.

"Okay." Should she take offense that Hillary clearly wanted to put space between them? She should be thanking her. Given Andy's comment earlier, distance was her friend. "Well, thanks again for the lunches. But I've already got a mother."

Hillary pressed her lips together and nodded stiffly. "Message received."

When she started to turn away, Olivia grabbed her upper arm, not wanting to let her go on a sour note.

"Wait, I didn't mean—"

"Hey, Dennis, did somebody let you out of the time-out corner for the night?" The snide comment jerked her attention to a deputy she recognized from the traffic division. She released Hillary's arm quickly.

"I'll think about you out working wrecks in the rain while I'm kicked back in an office chair with my feet on the desk." She waited until he'd continued out of earshot before she muttered, "Prick."

She turned back to Hillary and found sympathy and confusion in her expression. Great, they'd moved from awkwardness to pity. "Sorry about that."

"Aren't these guys supposed to be your brothers?"

Olivia shrugged, not in the mood to explain that sometimes "sisters" weren't treated exactly the same. She had plenty of loyal friends on the force, but as for the rest—a shared uniform didn't necessarily make a man into an evolved being.

"How can you take this so lightly?"

She tightened her jaw against the protests raging to spew out. She inhaled slowly, attempting to control the temper she'd been trying to smother since she walked into this stupid party. "I'm not taking it lightly. But apparently I can't do anything about it."

"I just—I'd be a wreck if I'd been accused—I'm sorry. It's none of my business."

"You're damn right it's not. How do you know I'm not—where do you get off—" Anger and distrust were becoming familiar emotions these days. But the compassion simmering in Hillary's eyes diffused some of her rage. She sighed. "Come with me." She grabbed Hillary's wrist and pulled her toward the back of the house, releasing her as soon as she was sure Hillary had followed her. In the backyard, she found a couple of chairs far enough away from the crowd for some privacy.

"Have you ever heard of a level-three retention holster?" she asked after they'd both sat down.

"You don't have to tell me—"

"I want to." And, surprisingly, she did. She wanted to have this conversation with Hillary—the same one she'd been avoiding with everyone else. "So, the holster?"

"Sure. It has to do with how you draw your gun, right?"

"Exactly. The holster requires three distinct motions before it will release the handgun." She dropped her hand to her empty hip as if demonstrating. "You have to flip the top thumb strap, press a button on the side, and rock the gun backward before it'll come free." As a rookie, she'd spent countless hours perfecting the smooth motion. The movement needed to be fluid and second nature in order to minimize the chance of the weapon hanging up in an emergency. By the time she'd graduated from the Tennessee State Training Academy, she had the quickest draw in her class. "The idea is to decrease the likelihood that a suspect can use our own weapon against us. That thing saved my life that day. The guy was trying to get my gun." She flashed back to the instant of fear when she'd thought he might gain control of her firearm. A tremor raced through her already-tense muscles.

"I can't imagine what must have been going through your mind."

"Nothing. It's pure instinct. He wanted my gun. I couldn't let that happen. He got a little roughed up in the process. But honestly, it could have been a lot worse."

"That's it, huh? It's that easy." Hillary tilted her head, her tone light, but something in her eyes indicated the conversation bothered her more than she let on.

"I did my job." Despite wanting to open up to Hillary, she just couldn't seem to stop spouting macho shit. She wanted to tell her that of course she was scared—then, that he would have shot her without a second's hesitation—and, now, that she might have fucked up her entire career. She wanted to tell her that sitting here talking with her was the first time she hadn't felt angry and nervous about the whole situation. Instead, she simply shrugged and stared at Hillary's hand, wishing she had the guts to take it in hers.

"Did you go home with Olivia last night?"

"What? No!" Hillary glared at Jake. Several of their coworkers turned at her sharp denial. How many of them had heard Jake's question? She definitely wouldn't have rejected Olivia if she'd asked her to take her home. Each day the previous week, she'd seen her as she passed the security desk and tried hard not to stare at whatever slick little suit Olivia had worn that day. Some days, she paired a jacket with a skirt or over a fitted dress, and on one disappointing day, she'd worn slacks. Hillary might have missed her amazing legs if she hadn't been distracted by the way her sleeveless shirt revealed her toned arms. Thank God that day's jacket hung on the back of the chair.

"You'd know if you hadn't abandoned me there."

"Hey, you know the rules—when one of us has a shot at an eight or higher, no loyalty applies." He leaned back in his chair and rested his hands behind his head. He clicked the button on the cord attached to his headset to key up his microphone, then answered an officer's transmission.

"Don't kid yourself. She was a six, at best." She'd seen him leave with a deputy from the neighboring county. She was actually a pretty girl, but Hillary wouldn't let him off the hook for bailing early. Hillary responded on her radio to one of her officers as well, then typed his update into her computer. They carried on between working, each waiting until the other finished and then picking up the conversation where they'd left off.

"Whatever. What happened with Dennis? I saw you two talking in the corner for a while."

"Just talk." They'd sat together for almost an hour until Olivia had excused herself to get another drink. She'd been friendly enough, but not overtly flirtatious or suggestive. In fact, except for when she'd opened up about the incident that got her assigned to Five-C, she'd been distant. "I don't even think she's gay."

"I've never seen her talk to any of the guys for that long."

"Maybe she's just picky." Hillary had lingered outside for a few minutes after Olivia headed for the kitchen, but she didn't return. She'd talked to her brother and Frankie, then left much earlier than anyone else.

"When you look like she does, you can be as picky as you want."

Hillary smiled. "Yeah, she's definitely better than a six."

He nodded. "Solid eight-and-a-half." He grinned when her expression changed. "You don't agree?"

"She's every bit a nine."

He raised a brow. "So you *are* interested?"

"Interested in what? I barely know her. If she's gay, she's clearly not out. And I'm not looking for another closet case." She'd spent too much time hiding her relationship with Ann, which, given the fact that they worked together, had been extremely difficult. Jake knew about it, but he was one of only a few. She shook her head. "No. We might become friends, but beyond that, she's only good for eye candy."

Jake opened his mouth to respond, the smart-ass comment shining in his eyes. But before he could speak, another voice broke in.

"Who's eye candy?"

Hillary managed to contain a grimace. "Hello, Ann." Apparently, just talking about her closeted ex had conjured her.

"Hill. Jake." Ann smiled stiffly. "Jake, have you found yourself a new trophy?"

Before Hillary could stop him, he grinned and shook his head. "Not me."

His implication sunk in immediately and Ann's expression changed. At one time Hillary would have done anything to see emotion in Ann's cool blue eyes. But her obvious jealousy came too late.

She'd had a long road getting over their breakup, partly because she'd been forced to continue seeing her every shift. For a while, even catching sight of her auburn waves was enough to send a jolt of pain through Hillary. But she'd finally reached a place of closure and acceptance, where hearing Ann's laugh or seeing her smile didn't touch her. These moments of weakness in Ann still brought a measure of satisfaction. She suspected anyone would take some pleasure in knowing they weren't quite as easy to get over as Ann had made it look.

"Hillary, do tell. I didn't know any new prospects were in town."

"You're right. No one new has come to the monthly meetings in ages." Hearing the edge to her voice, Hillary forced a lighter tone and a casual laugh. "We don't all know each other, Ann."

"Well, you don't do anything but work. And we haven't hired any lesbians lately. So where did you find this eye candy?"

Jake grinned, seeming ready to jump out of his chair at the idea of letting Ann know Hillary was interested in someone hotter than her. "Actually, she's—"

"Never mind. It's just me letting my imagination get away with me." Hillary squashed her own pettiness in the interest of privacy.

Ann didn't appear convinced. She glanced at Jake as if she couldn't speak freely in front of him. But Hillary had told her long ago that Jake knew about them. "We were friends. We can talk about this stuff, right?"

"Yeah, sure." She managed not to scoff in Ann's face. *Sure, let me tell you about the chick I've had a thing for since we were teenagers. And, oh, by the way, she's sitting in the lobby. That won't be awkward at all.*

Ann looked at her expectantly.

Hillary sighed. "There's nothing to tell." It was mostly true. Anything that had happened between them was all in her head. If Olivia was gay she would have heard about it through the rumor mill. She wasn't about to embarrass herself further by opening up to Ann about her crush.

CHAPTER FOUR

Olivia leaned back in her chair and rubbed her hand over her face as she stared at the security monitors in front of her. Could she actually go crazy from boredom? She avoided looking at the clock for what would be the fourth time in the hour and a half since she'd arrived. The remaining six hours on her shift before she left for the weekend were sure to drag by just as slowly.

Only her pride kept her from calling the investigator on her case to see how much longer she'd be confined here. Hell, his office was just down the hall. Maybe she should drop in on him, just to remind him that she was still waiting to be cleared.

She'd called Frankie to bitch about it but hung up when she heard Andy in the background reminding her she'd been here only a week and government never moved that fast. If she'd wanted to answer phones and kiss the command staff's ass every morning, she'd have applied to be one of their administrative assistants. She needed space and fresh air—or as fresh as it could get inside an overused patrol car shared by three shifts. She wanted out of this building, and most of all, she wanted her control back.

Beside her, Holt was tearing through a bag of potato chips. She clenched her jaw against the sound of the rustling bag, open-mouthed crunching, and him slurping the same greasy fingers he'd used to adjust the camera settings only moments ago.

"What's with the bouncing?" Several crumbs flew off his hand as he pointed at her jittering knee. "It's kind of annoying."

She stared at him.

"What?" He finally caught on and grabbed a napkin from the desk. "What's going on? Are you nervous about your case?"

"No."

"Then what?"

She debated blowing him off, but since he was apparently the only company she'd have for a while, she might as well talk to him. "Just a little stir-crazy."

"That'll pass." As if proving a point he leaned back in his chair. Though he wasn't that bold, Olivia thought that, in his mind, he'd just kicked his feet up on the desk. "This isn't that bad a gig. No one's shooting at me and I'm still getting paid."

She didn't bother replying, instead slumped silently in her own chair. She checked the monitors and leaned forward when she caught sight of Hillary. Today, she'd been assigned to answer the phone, so she'd fielded 9-1-1 calls, the various administrative lines, and made calls for the dispatchers. Olivia settled back into her chair but didn't take her eyes from the screen, telling herself it was her job to monitor the cameras. In fact, she'd spent the past three days since the party convincing herself that she was watching the dispatch center, not stalking Hillary—which was increasingly hard to do when Hillary offered only a courteous greeting whenever she passed the front desk. Despite their impersonal exchanges, Olivia didn't stop looking at her.

When Hillary stood and another employee took her place, Olivia followed her to the next camera, in the hallway, then to the one in the dispatchers' lounge.

Olivia stood. "I'm going to grab something to eat. You want anything?" She asked out of politeness.

"No, thanks." Holt waved a hand at the fast-food bag currently leaving greasy stains on the paperwork in front of him. "I've still got leftovers. Take your time. I've got this covered." He waved at the row of monitors in front of him.

She nodded and started down the hallway. While on limited duty, they were allowed a meal break and one fifteen-minute break. Holt managed his schedule much more loosely and often encouraged her to step away from the desk as often as he did. But after years in patrol, she'd grown accustomed to squeezing lunch in between calls and accounting for the time down to the minute. If she regularly took as much time as Holt did, her patrol sergeant would've had her ass.

Because the dispatch center operated twenty-four hours a day, the employee lounge contained a full kitchen in addition to a couple of vending machines. Olivia entered and stopped in front of the snack machine. Hillary leaned against the counter near the microwave, absently watching the timer.

"Hey." Olivia stuck her hand into her pocket for her money.

"Deputy Dennis."

"If you're not going to call me Olivia, at least drop the title. It's just Dennis." She fed a dollar into the machine.

Hillary crossed to stand next to her. "Let's make a deal. I'll call you Dennis, and you don't make me watch you try to subsist on whatever junk you were about to buy." Without waiting for an answer she pushed the coin return, then moved back to the microwave and popped open the door. "I can't believe you eat the way you do and still look like that."

Olivia let a slow smile spread across her face when Hillary immediately seemed embarrassed by her words. "Look like what?"

"Never mind. Come over here. I have enough to share."

Olivia retrieved her money and slid into the chair across from Hillary. "Despite my protests about you feeding me, I can't bring myself to turn down home cooking." She let Hillary's comment slide but noted the flush that colored her cheeks.

"Don't get much of it at home?" Hillary passed a fork and napkin to her. "I don't have an extra plate. Hope you don't mind sharing." She pushed a Rubbermaid dish full of delicious-smelling food closer to Olivia.

"I don't mind." She sunk her fork into the bow-tie pasta dish and took a bite. The bright taste of sun-dried tomatoes cut the rich Alfredo sauce and spicy sausage.

"So, are you shattering my illusions of Sheriff Dennis and his family gathered around the table for dinner every night?"

"Not really. My mother used to make dinner every night. That part's right. But my father often didn't make it to the table. And these days—" She'd revealed too much.

"What?" Hillary set her own fork down and gave Olivia her full attention.

"These days dinner with my family—well, let's just say, sometimes I'd rather microwave frozen meals in my apartment. With my folks, it's never a simple dinner anymore."

"Ah, family drama."

"Yeah. You know it?"

"Not really. My family is pretty cool. I mean, even when I came out to my parents they didn't love the idea, but they accepted me all the same."

The urge to withdraw while Hillary spoke so openly about being gay was strong and instinctual. Had Hillary somehow figured out she was gay? The thought sent a momentarily debilitating panic through her. Her stomach rebelled, and she struggled to keep down the few bites she'd consumed. She tightened her jaw and forced her eyes back to Hillary's.

"Guess I just outed myself there, huh? Does that bother you?" Her expression held no apology. In fact, she seemed to be projecting a challenge of sorts.

"No. I—I don't judge how anyone lives their life." Olivia forced the words out through a tight throat. She took a slow breath, trying to calm her racing heart. Maybe Hillary's concern really was about her own disclosure. She could show Hillary that she accepted her without revealing her hidden sexuality.

"Okay. Good." Hillary leaned over, moving into the space between them. Olivia held her breath, but Hillary just took a bite and then sat back.

"Yep." Olivia nodded, uncertain what else to say.

"Hey, I didn't mean to make things awkward."

"No. Of course not. Actually, you saved us. Continuing to talk about my family dynamic, now that would have been awkward." Olivia smiled. "Didn't your parents move away?"

"Yes, about five years ago, to Texas, where my dad's family is from."

"Do you see them often?"

"I try to go out there once a year, and they come back here a couple of times a year as well. Mom's sisters still live here." Just when Olivia had started to relax, Hillary steered the conversation back to the one topic Olivia wanted to avoid. "So, I divulged my secret. You should tell me one."

"Was that a secret?"

"Ah, so you heard it before." Hillary raised her brow.

"Rumors. I try not to pay attention, but people do talk around here."

"I get it. But all the same, I shared mine. So, if you tell me about your family stuff, we'll be even."

"I'm not sure we have time." Olivia glanced pointedly at her watch. Hillary's soft laugh warmed Olivia and she couldn't hold back a smile. "My father—well, he is who he is. He's strong and stubborn, and he's certain he's always right. And here I am, decommissioned— temporarily, I hope, but all the same, they took my badge and gun. Needless to say, I'm a bit of a disappointment."

"Maybe you're being too hard on yourself. I'm sure he loves you."

"Oh, believe me, I'm not nearly as hard on myself as he is. His displeasure is evident." Olivia took a bite of pasta, stalling. She glanced around, reminding herself that someone could come in any time. Not to mention that she needed to get back to the desk soon. Those were just two of the many reasons she shouldn't be rehashing her family issues. "How about a different confession?"

"Shoot."

"I know you. I mean, I know your voice. From the radio."

"You do? I recognize officers' voices, but all I do is sit and listen to you guys. I figured you have too much else going on to pay much attention to who we are."

"We can tell as soon as we get on shift what kind of night it's going to be by who we hear on the radio."

"It really makes a difference?"

"Sure. Everyone likes you. You're a good dispatcher. We're confident that you'll know what's going on and where we are, not jerk us all over the county." Though each deputy had an assigned area, or zone, when a call came up in another zone that required more than one officer, or when that zone officer was already on an incident, they could be pulled to cover for them. With the wrong dispatcher, they could spend most of the shift meandering through small towns, just trying to get to the next call.

"That's nice to hear."

"It's true." Olivia gathered her trash and stood. "I really do have to get back. Thank you for lunch. It was amazing. But you—"

"Please don't tell me again that I don't have to feed you." Hillary held up her hand. "I enjoy it."

Olivia returned her smile, trying not to think too much about the flutter in her stomach at the thought of sharing more meals with Hillary. Maybe they could go out somewhere together and Olivia could pay; at least then she wouldn't feel like a freeloader. She shook the idea out of her head as she headed back down the hallway to her post. She could fantasize all she wanted about an intimate dinner out with Hillary. But if anyone saw them together, that juicy bit of gossip wouldn't take long to get back to her family.

❖

An hour later, while watching Hillary work on the dispatch console, Olivia was still imagining how that dinner might go. The conversation would flow easily between them, as it had so far. Maybe she'd even figure out how to work some flirting in.

"She'd probably laugh in my face," Olivia mumbled to herself, grateful that Holt had left already. As an out lesbian, Hillary was probably used to women with experience, not awkward closet cases. Wishing things could be different only left Olivia frustrated, and it would continue to until she got some balls and made some changes. She had no problem being fearless in every other area of her life, but the thought of coming out to her parents left her paralyzed with anxiety.

Movement on the video screen caught Olivia's eyes. Hillary sat up straight, her posture suddenly tense. Olivia leaned closer, her stomach twisting as she studied the tight mask of Hillary's expression.

She grabbed the handheld radio off the desk and switched from the security frequency to the patrol channel.

"—send me an ambulance. Signal ten."

The code for the medics to come as quickly as possible, along with the rising panic in the officer's voice, sent adrenaline coursing through Olivia's body. She shoved out of her chair, driven by an ingrained need to back up her fellow officer. Instead, she could only pace behind the desk and listen to the excited chatter as others rushed to the scene.

Between the trembling voice of the deputy on scene and the frantic demands of those rushing to their aid, she was able to piece together the details. Two deputies had closed the road down to work a vehicle accident when a reckless driver in a large delivery truck had barreled through their scene, striking one of them.

"Shit." She wished she'd been paying closer attention to the radio. Where was Andy? She closed her eyes and whispered a prayer that he hadn't been on that scene. She felt guilty for her momentary lack of concern about who else it might be. "Just not Andy, please."

"Give me an injury code." The responding sergeant raised his voice to be heard over the wail of his siren in the background.

"Jesus, get that ambulance down here. He's pinned under this truck."

Olivia jerked back, realizing she'd leaned ever closer to the radio as the details emerged. Her stomach clenched as she imagined the officer trapped under the large vehicle, and for a moment she feared she might throw up.

"Don't say anything else until I get there," the sergeant barked.

Olivia could already visualize the scene and suspected he didn't want anything more graphic going out over the radio. Judging from the panic in the deputy's voice, he wasn't holding it together very well. The tightness in her chest eased slightly when she heard Andy check on the scene of the accident. He was safe.

The ambulance arrived, along with several pieces of fire apparatus. Olivia forced herself into her chair as phrases such as "extended extrication" and "devastating injuries" crackled across the air. She turned to the security monitor, seeking solace in watching Hillary work.

Through it all, Hillary's voice remained calm and steady as her fingers flew over the keyboard. Her eyes shifted from one to another of the three computer screens in front of her, and her clipped, efficient tone seemed to be the only calm one in the jumble crowding the radio frequency. She managed the notification of crime-scene techs, investigators, and command staff.

Several coworkers approached, presumably to offer assistance, but Hillary waved them off, her focus glued to her computers. One of the women Olivia recognized as a supervisor approached and stood behind her. She put her hand on Hillary's shoulder and leaned over to speak to her. Hillary shook her head in response to whatever the woman said. The supervisor straightened but left her hand resting on Hillary in a gesture far too familiar to be professional. Irrational jealousy streaked through Olivia, but she couldn't pull her eyes from Hillary's stiff posture. Whoever this woman was, Hillary didn't seem to take any solace in her nearness.

For the next hour, Olivia split her attention among the screen in front of her, the radio, and the increasing flow of command staff that entered the building. The shift commander, two under-sheriffs, and eventually even Sheriff Martin passed through the lobby. None of them stopped to acknowledge Olivia. The conference room, which had been set up as a temporary command center, soon filled with officials from law enforcement and the fire department.

Eventually, Hillary pushed back from the console, rolling her neck and shoulders as she stood. Another dispatcher slipped quickly into her place. She walked stiffly across the room, as if holding herself back from fleeing altogether. Olivia followed her on the cameras until she reached the back exit. Hillary managed to clear the door and step onto the deck employees used for smoking during their breaks before sinking down against the wall. She crouched there and covered her face with her hands. Her shoulders shook.

Olivia curled her hands into fists and stared at the screen. She felt a little guilty for witnessing what Hillary no doubt thought was a private moment. But she couldn't look away. Only her duty to man this desk while the bigwigs filtered in kept her from making her way out there to offer—what? Comfort? Hillary probably didn't want comfort from her right now.

Onscreen, Hillary stood and swiped her hands against her face, rubbing her fingers under her eyes. Her shoulders rose, then fell in fits, and Olivia could practically feel her breath shaking out of her body. Hillary opened the door and walked back down the hall. Her face showed no sign of weakness as she resumed her place at the console.

CHAPTER FIVE

"Do you need a light?"

Hillary jerked her head up, relieved to find Olivia standing in front of her. After her shift ended, she'd fled to the far end of the parking lot trying to avoid both Ann and the peer counselors that had been called in to offer support to the dispatchers who knew and had worked with the officer who died. Hillary didn't know him personally, and, though she thought it might hit her later, right now, she was simply numb. But once she reached her car, she wasn't ready to drive home, yet. At least not until she stopped feeling so shaky.

Olivia nodded toward the cigarette tucked between Hillary's fingers.

Hillary shook her head. "I don't smoke."

"All evidence to the contrary."

"I quit. Four years ago." She flipped the cigarette between her fingers. "Do you even have a lighter?"

"Of course not. I don't smoke." Olivia grinned when her comment earned a small smile.

"When I'm stressed, I like to hold a cigarette. It's familiar—calming."

"You carry them around with you, just in case?"

"I bummed one. Yeah, I don't know—I'm crazy."

"No. You're not." Olivia took a step closer and lifted her hand as if to touch Hillary's shoulder, but then she dropped it back to her side. "Are you okay?"

"I'm fine."

"You don't look fine."

Hillary tensed her jaw, steeling herself against the memories that threatened to rush back. "Rough night."

"I heard—er, rather, I listened." She held up her handheld radio. "You handled yourself very well."

"Yeah. Well, I've been doing this for a while."

Olivia nodded. "I've been doing that a lot too lately."

"What?"

"Deflecting."

"I wasn't—"

"I've seen some guys get in trouble and been in a couple scrapes myself, but I've never experienced anything like what I was hearing in there."

"It was a first for me, too." Hillary tucked the cigarette in her pocket, then because she needed something to do with her hands, she took out her cell phone and pretended to check for text messages. She didn't want to talk about this. Maybe she'd calmed down enough to drive. She moved toward her car. "I should—"

"Do you want to go for a drink or something?"

She did. She wanted to go somewhere with Olivia. Maybe she'd get drunk, maybe do something stupid—like give in to her long-time urge to grab Olivia and kiss her. She almost chuckled to herself. How much would that freak Olivia out? She'd never ask her out for drinks again, that's for sure.

"Can I take a rain check on that?"

"Yeah. Sure." Olivia looked hurt at her rejection, and suddenly Hillary wanted to make her feel better.

"Drinking is probably not a good idea tonight."

"Of course. Are you okay to drive home? I could give you a lift."

"I'm good. Thank you, though."

"Okay." When Olivia reached over and took Hillary's cell from her, their fingers brushed and Hillary's skin tingled. Did that happen in real life? Apparently oblivious to the crackle between them, Olivia typed in a series of numbers, then handed the phone back. "But please, call me if I can help in any way, or if you just need someone to talk to."

Hillary saved the number under a new contact, then met Olivia's eyes. The genuine concern she found there surprised her. The cheerleader she'd known so many years ago had never been this sincere.

"Thanks." She slid into her car. Though the offer eased a bit of the sick knot in her stomach, she didn't think she'd be making that phone call. She'd enjoyed the time they'd spent together, but she just wasn't one for pouring her heart out about work.

❖

Hillary walked through the door to her apartment and dropped her keys on the raised counter that separated the kitchen from the living area. She went down the short hallway to the only bedroom and changed into pajama pants and a worn T-shirt. She glanced at the bed, debating whether to climb in and force herself to try to sleep. Though the events of the past several hours should have exhausted her, waning adrenaline left her restless and jittery.

Over the years, she'd become accustomed to handling even the most stressful types of calls and usually had no problem leaving work behind when she exited the building. Even early in her career, she had been able to compartmentalize the most high-intensity emergencies. But tonight, she couldn't stop the sound of that officer's calls for help from playing in her head.

Jake would suggest she go to the gym and sweat it out. Some people meditated. Others spent time with family or took up a hobby. Occasionally, Hillary indulged in a glass—or a bottle—of wine and some mindless television after a long day, but often, she took extra shifts to help deal with work. Yes, the requisite stress-management training had taught her that she didn't have healthy coping mechanisms. But they had sustained her so far. Until tonight.

Now the walls of her usually cozy apartment felt much too close. She threw open the French doors to the patio and inhaled the humid night air. As she dropped into the chair nearest the doors, the edge of her cell phone poked her thigh. She dug it out of her pocket and unlocked the screen. She opened her contacts and scrolled until she reached Olivia's name. With one touch she could hear Olivia's voice—maybe she still wanted to get that drink. She hadn't even asked where Olivia might suggest they go. Would she have taken her to that bar on Dakota Avenue that the cops frequented?

If today had been any other semi-stressful shift, she might have called Jake and asked him to meet her, either there or at their favorite place near her apartment. But she'd never seen Olivia out. So if she didn't hang out with the other cops, where did Olivia go to unwind? Hillary didn't want to meet Olivia in a bar. She'd much rather invite her over and pour her a glass of wine and—she needed to stop this line of thought. Yes, the sympathy in Olivia's eyes had tempted her to give in, to let Olivia comfort her. But while she didn't doubt Olivia's offer was sincere, Hillary suspected she had extended it out of politeness or some sense of professional courtesy because they both worked in public safety. She'd said she and the other officers liked and respected her as a dispatcher.

"You're an idiot, O'Neal," she mumbled as she wandered into the bathroom. Her tub was too small for a decent bath, so she settled for a hot shower. She willingly admitted to a teenage crush, but she didn't need to turn a fledgling friendship into an embarrassing obsession. "Just be cool."

Ten minutes later, wrapped in a fleece robe, she left the steamy room and immediately felt the chill of the artificially cooled air. She raised the setting on the central air on her way to the living room. The unit had been working overtime to fight the outside temperatures during the day, so she might as well give it a break.

She settled on the sofa and picked up her phone, again contemplating calling Olivia. But what would she say? She couldn't admit that being alone with her thoughts right now was damn near driving her crazy—that her apartment was so quiet she could hear the echo of hours' old radio transmissions.

She could call her family. If her father answered, he would listen patiently. And when she'd exhausted herself with conversation, he would offer a few valuable words. His wisdom would be spot-on, but more than what he said, the calm, steady sound of his voice would comfort her.

In the end, she put her phone on the coffee table while she curled up on the sofa. Talking about the wreck meant reliving her end of it, and she wasn't ready to do that. Her parents would see the news coverage about the deputy's death and ask her about it eventually, but she didn't need to provide them with details beyond the media-approved story. She often sheltered them from anything more than a sterilized version of her day. She pulled a throw over her lap, turned on the television, and began searching for something inane to watch.

Hillary jerked awake, a choking cry dying in her throat. Her heart pounded high in her chest, in the hollow between her collarbones. She swept a hand against the hair plastered to her forehead, and her fingers came away damp and clammy. She braced her hand against the sofa cushion and levered herself into a sitting position. She'd spent a restless night trying to sleep on the couch, in front of the flickering glow of the television. When she'd finally been able to drift off, the voices coming from the speakers didn't drown out the ghosts in her dreams.

Her overactive imagination had placed her at the accident scene instead of on the other end of the radio. She'd seen the deputies arrive at the original vehicle accident and step out of their cars. They'd casually gone about their work as they had dozens of times before, angling one patrol car to block traffic. One deputy pulled the involved drivers aside and began interviewing them while the other directed the slowing traffic flow around the two damaged cars. She saw the delivery truck before the deputy did and tried to scream, but neither the deputy nor the distracted truck driver heard her. She turned her head at the moment of impact, but she couldn't block out that sound— the concussion of solid machinery hitting a human body, louder than she'd thought it would be. She'd come awake to the deputy's cries, dreaming of her own voice screaming for help over the radio.

She'd tried to go back to sleep after a while, but more than once, she'd awakened sweating and stirred up. All told, she'd be lucky if she'd pieced together a couple hours of sleep.

She rubbed grit out of her eyes and leaned forward, turning the volume down on the too-cheerful morning-show hostess. Good God, who could be so happy to be up this early? Morning was one reason she worked second shift. She dragged herself to her Keurig, wondering how bad this day would be since she was already cursing the fastest coffeemaker in the world.

Her cell phone rang, piercing the silence and boring directly into her already aching head. She retrieved it and glanced at the screen, but didn't answer. Seconds later, she ignored the predictable chime of her voice-mail notification.

"And follow-up text," she said as she picked up her coffee and returned to the couch. A few seconds later, the text came through. She read it but didn't respond.

Just checking on you. Call if you need to talk.

Of course Ann would reach out. At work, she'd be professionally distant, but behind closed doors, or in this case a text, she acted like they actually meant something to each other. Some things didn't change. *Call if you need to talk.* Fat chance. She'd be more likely to call Olivia, and she barely knew her.

She would probably see both of them later at work, and right now she didn't want to talk to anyone until she had to. Instead she turned on a *Frasier* rerun and pretended it distracted her from the knot in her gut that even her nearly black coffee couldn't burn through.

Four hours later, her stomach still empty and churning, she stood in the parking lot of Five-C staring at the building. She'd received one more text from Ann telling her that she could take a couple of days off if she needed them. She didn't. Work would get her through this. She hoped.

"We have to stop meeting in parking lots like this." Olivia smiled as she approached.

"I can think of worse places." Hillary glanced at her, then turned back toward the building.

Olivia stood next to Hillary, their shoulders almost touching. She'd seen Hillary getting out of her car as she pulled in the lot and hoped she could catch her before she went inside. She didn't expect to find her still at the far end of the lot, apparently stalling. Hillary's eyes carried the fatigue of a sleepless night. Olivia had seen that look in the mirror before.

Should she close the gap between them and offer comfort? She wasn't experienced at reading Hillary but thought she picked up on apprehension, at best, possibly bordering on downright fear. Instead, she tried to reach her with words.

"I didn't think I'd see you today." When Hillary didn't respond, she continued. "Wouldn't they let you take some time before jumping back in?"

"I didn't ask."

"You good, then?" Olivia kept her own tone light in response to something in Hillary's that indicated she didn't want to be told what to do.

Hillary met her eyes, and Olivia thought she saw gratitude. Hillary's arm brushed Olivia's lightly as she shifted away. "I'm good."

"Want me to walk you in?"

"Sure."

As they moved toward the door, Olivia gave in to her urge to touch Hillary, skimming her hand against Hillary's lower back as she waited for her to walk in front of her. Hillary slowed slightly, as though enjoying the touch. Olivia itched to slip her fingers under the hem of her shirt and thanked God it was tucked in. She couldn't lose her tight control in the parking lot of Five-C, of all places. She dropped her hand at the reminder that anyone could see them.

"Do you have lunch plans?" she asked, as if today were any other day.

Hillary held up her cooler bag. "Baked chicken and broccoli. You in?"

Olivia grimaced, then tried to cover up her repulsion.

"Not a fan?"

"Of baked chicken and broccoli?" She let her tone reveal what she thought about potentially the blandest meal she could think of. "Isn't that what they feed you at the hospital when you can't stomach anything else?"

"You've never had mine." Hillary's flirty little look tickled something in Olivia. Men and women hit on her often, probably more than they would have if she didn't spend most of her time in a uniform, but it had been a long time since she'd been tempted to flirt back.

"You know where to find me," she said with a wink as they stopped beside the front desk. Okay, maybe she was rusty. But she didn't want Hillary to take her too seriously when she wasn't prepared to follow through.

"I do," Hillary said quietly, glancing at Holt.

"Have a good day." Olivia angled herself so her back was to Holt, wanting to keep Hillary to herself for a moment longer.

"I'm off to a good start." Hillary smiled warmly.

Olivia watched her head down the hallway to the dispatch center. When she turned back to the desk, Holt looked up.

"She the one who worked the wreck yesterday?"

"Yep."

"That's tough."

Olivia nodded as she dropped into the chair next to him. They sat quietly, each apparently lost in their thoughts about the accident. She could guess the subject matter of his musings because she hadn't been able to stop thinking about how it could happen to any of them. They trained to handle themselves against all kinds of danger, criminals, and guns. But how did they defend against a distracted driver or poor road conditions? She'd stood outside directing traffic a hundred times—defenseless against errant vehicles. And it was only her dumb luck so far that no one had hit her.

She'd tried to stay busy last night so she didn't have to think about it too much. After accomplishing most of her list of household chores, she'd hopped on her bicycle and set out on the road near her condo. But she'd cut her ride short when she caught herself flinching every time she met a car.

Since now she had nothing to do but sit in this chair, her emotions swamped her. When had her life become so limited? During her tenuous time on this earth, she'd chosen to live with secrets and fear instead of being courageous enough to be genuine. But every time she considered coming out to her family, her heart thudded heavily until she thought it might fly right out of her chest. Her father would likely disown her, and her mother would follow his edict. Frankie already knew, and maybe she wouldn't lose Andy. Some days she thought about telling them just so she wouldn't have to attend any more post-church Sunday dinners.

She told herself she'd see a sign and then she'd know she was ready. She would sit them down and take the leap and let the consequences wash over her. But until she could think about that moment without wanting to vomit, she'd chosen to keep her mouth shut.

CHAPTER SIX

S tart us some backup over here."

Olivia glanced at her radio when Hillary didn't acknowledge the officer's hurried request. She'd turned the radio to Hillary's frequency not long after she sat down. If Holt noticed, he didn't say anything.

"Dispatch?"

She flipped the camera selector until Hillary appeared on the monitor. She hadn't been watching Hillary, because her growing obsession with her voice was less creepy if she could control the desire to see her, too. Hillary sat stiffly in her chair, her fingers hovering over the keyboard. She stared at the screen, eyes wide.

Olivia grabbed her handheld radio, shot out of her chair, and strode down the hallway, emotion driving every step. She heard Hillary finally respond as she shoved open the door to the dispatch center.

"Are you okay?" she demanded as she reached Hillary's side. She saw heads turning in her periphery but ignored them. Hillary looked a bit more relaxed than she had on camera.

"I'm fine." Her fingers trembled as she stroked the keys.

"You should get someone to relieve you."

Hillary didn't say anything to Olivia, but she did key up her mic to answer the officer.

"Let her work." One of the dispatch supervisors stepped between Olivia and Hillary's desk. Something hard, and not altogether professional, flashed in the woman's eyes. "She said she's fine."

Olivia narrowed her own eyes and glanced between Hillary and this woman. If they didn't already have something personal between them, it wasn't because this woman didn't want it. "She needs—"

"She needs to finish her shift. And your presence is disruptive. We all have work to do, as, I'm sure, do you." Her tone made it clear what she thought of Olivia's current duties.

Olivia didn't give a shit what she thought, but Hillary's embarrassed expression penetrated her concern. She nodded tightly, and with one more glance at Hillary, she left.

By the time she reached the desk she was fuming. But she was most angry with herself. She'd acted like an idiot, storming in there like she knew what Hillary needed—like she knew her at all. Sure, they'd been friendly, but not more than courteous. She'd given Hillary her cell number, and though she'd obviously had a rough night, she hadn't called. She didn't need Olivia's help. And Olivia didn't need to be seen as chasing an openly lesbian colleague.

"Deputy Dennis, may I have a word?"

She turned to find the supervisor approaching. "I can't leave the desk."

"I've got this," Holt said from behind her, making her want to slap him.

The supervisor raised a brow.

Olivia strode out the front door and took several paces away from the building and out of the way of the entrance.

"You shouldn't question Hillary's abilities in front of her peers."

Olivia took a breath, reminding herself that though this woman wasn't in her chain of command, the brass likely wouldn't back her if she went up against a dispatch supervisor. "I don't question her ability, but I would think anyone who has been through—"

"She's not like the rest of us."

"The rest of us?"

"She doesn't get emotional." Somewhere in those words was a dig against Olivia and her temper.

It wasn't that she thought Hillary was an overly emotional person. But she'd listened to those radio transmissions, too. They'd affected her, and she hadn't even been the one sitting in that chair. "You expect too much from her."

"I don't expect more than she can handle."

"And you think you know what she can handle?" Olivia hated the jealousy driving her irrational behavior.

"I know her better than you do." She wasn't gloating, merely stating a fact. And maybe she wasn't wrong. They clearly had a history, and Olivia was—what? "This job—just because you're a cop doesn't mean you can understand what we do."

"I—"

"She's right." Hillary's voice, soft yet firm, stopped Olivia's response. Hillary looked at the supervisor with contrition in her eyes. Was she apologizing for Olivia's behavior? "May we have a minute?"

The supervisor looked like she wanted to argue, but she nodded and headed back inside.

Hillary waited until she was gone before turning fully toward Olivia. "You can't confront my supervisor like that. It undermines her and diminishes me as well."

"I wasn't trying to—I wanted—" Frustrated, she blew out a long breath. "What's her deal anyway?"

"Ann and I used to be involved."

Ann. Olivia didn't actually like putting such a gentle name to the woman she'd been ready to battle moments ago. "You dated your supervisor? Maybe you're not the good girl I thought you were." Olivia smiled, trying for levity.

"She wasn't my supervisor at the time."

"Bad breakup?"

Hillary tilted her head as if just now considering the demise of their relationship. "Not great, at first. But we're okay now."

"Clearly." She nodded toward the door Ann had just left through.

"That was work."

"Maybe to you."

"What is this, Dennis? Do you have a problem with me? With Ann?"

"I'm concerned about you." More concerned than she had a right to be.

"Don't be."

"Yeah? You've got it all under control, huh?" Suddenly, she wanted to push Hillary a little. She wanted to see even a hint of the confusion that churned inside her reflected in Hillary's expression.

"Yes." Despite the conviction in Hillary's voice, her eyes remained emotionless.

Olivia didn't buy it, and she wouldn't let it slide. Too often, public-safety professionals expected each other to toughen up and get through the things they heard and saw. But eventually that kind of emotional suppression could catch up with them. "You're clearly exhausted. And you're here working way too soon. Did you get any sleep last night?"

"Some."

"Nightmares?"

Hillary stared at her for several seconds, narrowed her eyes, then nodded.

"Panic attacks or flashbacks?"

"Not yet." At least she seemed willing to admit she might eventually experience them.

"One could argue you had the beginnings of one in there just now." She jerked her chin toward the building.

"Because I took a few seconds longer than usual to respond to a deputy?"

"It was more than a few seconds."

Hillary's face got harder with every word. "I know how to do my job."

Olivia touched Hillary's forearm, then told herself not to be offended when she flinched. Instead of pulling back, she pressed more firmly. "I only wanted to help."

"Pissing Ann off isn't helpful."

"Okay." She nodded. "Noted. So what can I do?"

Hillary shook her head once, a quick jerking denial that gave way to an uncertain look. "I don't know." She glanced at her watch. "I have to get back in there. I only got relief to come out here and save you from Ann."

"Who says I'm the one that needed saving?"

Hillary smiled. "I've seen her angry. Trust me, you don't want that. My lunch break is in an hour and fifteen."

"I'll see you then." Olivia readily accepted the olive branch, deciding not to examine why she was so happy at the prospect of lunch with Hillary.

❖

"I know a little something about nightmares and flashbacks," Olivia said as she slid into the chair across the table from Hillary.

Hillary's appetite fled. She handed Olivia a fork and the container of food she'd already heated in the microwave. "Can we talk about something—anything else?"

"Five years ago. I hadn't been out of the academy for long. I went on a domestic. My backup was coming from across county. I thought I was hot shit and tried to cancel them and take it myself, but my sergeant told them to stay in route."

Hillary sighed and set her own fork down.

"It was a routine call. I'd only been released from my training officer for a few months, and I'd already taken three just like it. The wife opened the door, and when she stepped back, I entered." She gave a humorless laugh, but her expression darkened. "This guy—he was on something other than alcohol. Don't get me wrong, he was a big dude, but that night he was practically superhuman. He had me pinned against the wall with his forearm against my throat before I knew what was happening." Olivia rubbed her neck.

Hillary's heart raced and she had trouble catching her breath. Coming back today had been harder than she'd expected. Just sitting down behind the console made her feel like she wanted to vomit. She'd been powering through, because she didn't know what else to do but work. But now, between her own demons and Olivia's soft voice, she felt like she was living the event with her.

"Tequila."

"What?"

"He was drinking tequila. To this day, I can't stand the smell of it." She took a deep breath, as if trying to fill her lungs with fresh air instead of stale memories. "He screamed at me that he would kill me. I passed out from lack of oxygen, thinking he'd surely succeed." Her hand tightened against her throat.

Hillary gently grasped her wrist and eased her hand away. She laced their fingers together on the table between them. The parallels between that incident and Hillary's most recent one might explain the explosive reaction that had landed her at the Five-C desk. "But he didn't."

"Nope. Luckily, my backup got there in time." She pulled her hand free and shoved both of her hands under the table, into her lap.

"How did you deal with it?"

"I made sure I was never that weak again." Olivia seemed surprised by her own words and Hillary thought she understood why. She'd started this conversation to help Hillary, but her past issues were obviously still a sore spot for her.

"Do you still have nightmares?"

"Sometimes. When I'm stressed. But I do what I can to make sure that doesn't happen."

"Like what?"

"Physical exertion helps."

Hillary raised an eyebrow but held back the suggestive comment that flew through her head.

"The gym, usually."

"I don't even have a membership." She wrinkled her nose. Going to the gym usually left her feeling intimidated and bored.

"I can get you a guest pass to mine. I do cardio and weights. Until I'm too exhausted to think."

Imagining Olivia alone in the gym, pushing herself to her physical limit until she had only enough energy to get home and collapse, made Hillary sad. A part of her wanted to agree to go, just so Olivia would have company. But her disinterest must have shown in her expression.

"Maybe something other than the gym. Do you do any cycling?"

"I don't even own a bike."

Olivia laughed softly. "Okay. That's a no, then."

"Sorry. I don't work out much. I tend to rely on diet to control my weight."

"Hey, whoa, I'm not making a comment on your weight." Olivia raised her hands in front of her.

"I know. And I know I should be more physical since I sit at a desk all day, but—"

"I have a spare bike. Meet me for a ride this weekend. It'll be fun, and I guarantee you'll feel at least a little bit better."

"I haven't been on a bike since I was a kid."

Olivia shrugged. "There's nothing to it. It's literally like riding a bike."

"Fine. When?"

"Saturday morning. Meet me at the park at eight."

"In the morning?"

"It'll be too hot later in the day."

Hillary sighed. She must have a bigger crush than even she realized if she was ready to agree to cycling at dawn. She picked up her fork. "Eat your lunch." When Olivia made a face, she said, "If I have to ride a bike, you can eat broccoli."

Hillary took one last sip of her coffee, put her travel mug in the cup holder, and got out of her car. She'd parked near the same red Jeep Wrangler she'd seen in the parking lot at Five-C but didn't see Olivia around.

She leaned against the back of her car. She'd had second thoughts since agreeing to this outing, but she couldn't turn down the chance to spend time with Olivia. She'd considered talking to Jake about the invitation, but he would figure out why she wanted to go. He'd know she wasn't looking for exercise. She'd been getting mixed signals from Olivia for days. In those tiny moments when Olivia might be flirting with her, or reacting to Hillary's subtle attempts, Hillary thought Olivia might be gay. But the high-school wallflower in Hillary thought Olivia was just being nice and trying to help out a coworker going through a rough time.

She spotted a cyclist riding down the path toward her and slumped farther against her car. She'd heard the phrase "weak in the knees" but never actually experienced it before.

Olivia leaned over the handlebars of the sleekest road bike Hillary had ever seen. Her black sports bra and black cycling shorts covered all of the important parts, but left bare expanses of sculpted limbs that seemed impossibly long for her short stature. As she slowed, then braked, Hillary swore she saw every muscle in her arms engage, from the cords of her forearms all the way to her well-rounded shoulders. She'd known Olivia was in shape, but she'd only seen her in street clothes. Olivia, in the flesh, surpassed even her most vivid fantasy.

Suddenly she felt frumpy in her too-long athletic shorts and T-shirt. She did actually own a sports bra, but nothing really appropriate for serious cycling. At this point, she just hoped her lack of endurance didn't embarrass her too badly.

"Hey. I got here early, so I thought I'd warm up." Olivia coasted to a stop while smoothly swinging her leg over the bike. She dismounted near the back of her Jeep.

"So you'll be able to keep up with me?"

"Yeah." She released the straps on the rack secured to the spare tire, then set the second bicycle down in front of Hillary.

"This is your spare bike?" The all-white Trek was nicer than any Hillary had ever owned.

"It used to be mine. Until I saw that one and fell in love." She lifted her chin toward the gorgeous piece of machinery she'd ridden up on.

Hillary nodded and carefully circled Olivia's bike. A lime-green stripe broke up the otherwise flat-black frame. Thin tires, a narrow seat, and all-black handlebars added to the aggressive appearance. Somehow, she knew that if she lifted the frame, it would be impossibly light.

"Specialized Tarmac." Pride laced Olivia's voice. "I went to the cycle shop for some chain lube, fell in love, and came out with that."

"That's one hell of an impulse buy. Are you going to do that every time you need lube?" She lifted her eyebrows suggestively.

Olivia laughed, a full, hearty sound that made Hillary smile.

"So, when you see something you want, you don't hesitate, huh?" She gave Olivia a wink but didn't get the reaction she'd hoped for.

Olivia turned away, poked her head inside her Jeep, and grabbed another helmet. Without making eye contact, she shoved it into

Hillary's hands. "Test out the seat height and see if you need me to raise it for you."

"Okay." She carefully mounted the bicycle. "Seems fine."

Olivia moved around the bike, checking out the fit. She bent and grasped Hillary's ankle firmly, testing her stability on the pedal. "Not bad." She stood. "How are the handlebars? Need them adjusted?"

"I think they're good."

"Okay." She reached back into the Jeep and grabbed a bottle of water, then leaned close and slipped it into the bottle cage attached to Hillary's bike frame. She glanced up and met Hillary's eyes. Sweat shone on her skin, and looking down at her, Hillary had a great view of her chest.

"Do you want to follow me?"

I would follow you anywhere right now.

"Hillary?"

She jerked her eyes to Olivia's and her face got hot. She couldn't tell if Olivia knew what had distracted her.

"Sorry?"

"I said, do you want to follow me?"

"Yes, please. I'll try to keep up."

Olivia smiled and gave her a wink. "Don't worry. I won't leave you behind." She slipped onto her bike and pedaled away.

Hillary followed, though not quite as smoothly. As they approached the trailhead, Olivia slowed so Hillary could pull alongside her.

"This greenway is pretty flat. We're early enough to miss some of the crowds, but if we approach someone I'll call out and we'll pass single file on the left."

As she fell in behind Olivia, she didn't allow her eyes to linger on her ass. She had more class than that. But forcing them upward didn't make her feel any more respectable. The subtle concave of Olivia's lower back glistened with sweat, and the racerback of her sports bra bisected her strong upper back, all of which combined to drive Hillary's heart rate up. If she wasn't getting enough cardio with the bicycling, she probably didn't need to worry about that now.

Soon, though, keeping up with Olivia required all of her energy. Finally, she settled in, taking cues from Olivia on when to pedal and when to coast. Despite finding a comfortable rhythm, by the time they circled back to the parking lot, her backside was screaming for relief.

At the Jeep, Olivia stowed the bikes back on the rack, then pulled two fresh bottles of water from a cooler in the backseat.

"Do you want to find a bench to sit on?" Olivia handed over one of the bottles.

"No, thanks. I don't think I want to sit for a while."

Olivia laughed. "Okay. Maybe we can just lean right here, then." She rested her arms along the side of the Jeep.

Hillary mirrored her pose on the other side of the Jeep and smiled at her across the open air of the backseat. She twisted the lid off her water bottle and took a long drink. "Thank you for today. I enjoyed it."

Olivia nodded. "No problem. I do this every Saturday, weather permitting. You're welcome any time."

"I'll keep that in mind."

"But I probably won't see you next week," Olivia guessed, sounding disappointed.

"I suppose that depends."

"On what?"

"On whether I can walk tomorrow." Hillary smiled. "Actually, the exercise did feel good. I feel much more relaxed than I have in days."

"Good. Let me know if you sleep better tonight."

"Should I call you bright and early tomorrow?"

Olivia shrugged. "I'll be up. My mother gets on my ass when I miss church."

"Do you go every week?"

"Doesn't every good Christian daughter?" Olivia grabbed a T-shirt from the Jeep and pulled it over her head.

Hillary hated to see those abs disappear. "I wouldn't know. My parents are agnostic."

"What about you?"

"It's complicated."

Olivia flicked her brows up, then back down. "Is there an answer that's longer than a Facebook status?"

"Well, I've felt spiritually connected, at times. And I do believe in God. But I grew up in the South. I haven't found many churches around here where I don't face certain judgment just for being who I am."

Olivia nodded. "I get that. But you might find some out there, if you look hard enough." She smiled. "Not my family's. But maybe some other ones."

Hillary searched Olivia's face but found none of the judgment she feared. In fact, the warmth and interest she saw in Olivia's eyes made her feel connected in an entirely different way.

CHAPTER SEVEN

W hat are you thinking about right now?" Olivia watched Hillary's expression change and couldn't contain her curiosity. Olivia guessed their conversation about religion hadn't brought the sudden softness to her eyes or the blush on her cheeks.

Hillary straightened and took a step away from the Jeep. "If I tell you, it's a complete subject change."

"Go for it."

"I was thinking that it's probably a good thing you're not gay?"

Olivia fought to keep her expression nonchalant, despite the panic twisting in her gut. "Why's that?"

"Look at you. There wouldn't be a woman left for the rest of us." Hillary put on a look of obviously exaggerated distress. "Just a trail of broken hearts following your patrol car."

Olivia laughed. "That's an amusing image. But I'm not sure the department would approve."

"I mean, seriously, you have what it takes to be a true player."

"Yeah?" Olivia enjoyed the shot of arousal in response to the way Hillary looked her up and down. Though she couldn't act on it, a part of her preened under Hillary's interest. "That's how you see me?"

"Not me. We're friends. I don't chase straight women."

"Why does it sound like there's an *anymore* on the end of that statement?"

"In this case, I'm talking about the ladies you'd be trying to bed."

"Ladies I'm trying to bed? This is not a Victorian romance." Olivia scowled. "But apparently I give the impression that I'm the careless—what—roguish type?"

"You're making this more complicated than I intended. I'm trying to pay you a compliment."

"*You could be a player?* In what world is that a compliment?"

"I'm saying you're hot."

Olivia grinned and nodded. "Now I'm getting mixed signals."

"For someone else—you're hot—I guess I mean some lucky guy will—" Hillary practically stuttered. Olivia liked seeing her flustered. "Are—are you looking?"

"Look, tell Jake, for the last time, I'm not interested in him." Olivia made a joke, because any other answer would have to be a lie.

"He told me you shot him down. Along with some of the other guys."

"I'm not interested in dating any of the guys I work with." She danced as close to the truth as she dared.

"Okay, I can tell by your expression you want me to drop it."

"What about you? Why are you single?"

"For starters, Reinsville doesn't have a lot of out lesbians. And I've had my fill of the closeted ones. You know about Ann, and in the spirit of privacy, I won't name any other names."

"Have you dated any openly lesbian women?"

"A few. One outside the department who really didn't understand why I let work rule so much of my life. And two in law enforcement."

"In our department?"

Hillary nodded.

"What happened?"

Hillary shrugged. "Sometimes things just don't work out. No drama. We just weren't *it* for each other."

"*It*? So you're no more specific about what you're looking for than I am."

"I want the fairy tale, or at least the real-life version of it. I don't expect a perfect relationship. But I want honesty, warmth, and support, as well as the sparks and all the steamy, flirty goodness."

Olivia chuckled at her description. She met Hillary's eyes and could tell that Hillary knew she wasn't laughing at her. "That actually sounds pretty good."

❖

"Damn, how much are you working these days?" Jake leaned against the desk next to Hillary.

She held up one finger, asking him to wait, and keyed up her radio. "One-thirty-two, that tag comes back on a 2000 Ford Explorer, orange in color, to a Jorge Vargas of 115 State Street."

"NSR?" The officer used the code to verify that the vehicle didn't have a stolen hit.

"NSR." She turned back to Jake. "Day shift needed overtime."

"How are you?"

"I'm good. How are you?"

"No. I mean, how are you really? We didn't get a chance to talk the other day, after—"

"I'm fine."

"If you need—"

"Jake, I'm good. Don't worry." When she leaned over to punch him lightly on the arm, she pulled against the sore muscles in her back and grimaced.

"What's wrong?"

"Nothing."

"I saw your face. What's going on?"

She didn't want to face his concern, so she threw out something she knew he'd latch onto. "It's nothing, really. I went bike riding Saturday and am a little sore."

He laughed. "You don't own a bike."

"Okay. It's not that funny. I went with Olivia."

Telling him was worth seeing the look of shock on his face. "Dennis?" he practically shouted.

She bit her lip to keep from shushing him, as that would only draw more attention to them, but he got the message.

"Sorry," he whispered. "But seriously? You're hanging out with Olivia Dennis now?"

"Yeah. We're—well, I guess we're sort of friends."

He stared, clearly trying hard to process this new information. "Friends?"

"It's no big deal. After that day—um, we talked in the parking lot and she invited me to the park for a bike ride. So, I went."

"And now you're friends?"

"Stop repeating it. You're making it weird."

"It is weird. You and Dennis." He leaned closer. "Does she know you're gay?"

"Yes. She's fine with it."

"Wow. I mean, with her father—well, I just thought she wouldn't be cool. Does she know you have a big crush on her?"

"I do not."

"You do. Don't lie to me. Do you really think I couldn't tell?"

She rolled her eyes. "Okay. Please, please don't gossip about this. I don't want things to be awkward with her. I've had straight crushes before."

"Yeah. I remember how the last one turned out."

She cringed, thinking of how she'd cried on his shoulder over Ann. "This is different."

"I sure as hell hope so. I'm not interested in putting you back together again."

He was exaggerating, but just barely. He'd kept her sane and made working in the same room as Ann, in those early months, almost bearable.

❖

She was reminded of her promise to Jake a couple of hours later when she walked into the employee lounge and found Olivia pacing the room. She held her phone to one ear and gestured sharply with the other hand.

"I understand the need to be thorough, I do. But how long can it take to find out that I was doing my damn job." Olivia's voice sped up and rose at the end of the statement. She skirted the lunch tables and strode to the far end of the room. "Okay. Okay. So do your job and get me cleared to—" She spun around and slammed her hand down on a table. "You know they'll leave me here until next summer if you don't ride their asses."

She glanced up and noticed Hillary in the doorway. Some of the storms cleared from her eyes and she stood a little straighter. She listened to the person on the other end of the line, then took a deep breath. "Just, please, get it done, man." She ended the call and shoved the phone in her pocket while waving Hillary into the room.

"If you need privacy, I can—" She gestured toward the door. Part of her wanted Olivia to ask her to leave, because the part that wanted to stay would win every time. She found Olivia even more attractive when she was a bit riled up. Her small frame practically crackled with energy, and she emanated more power than Hillary would have thought possible. Today she'd paired a patterned blouse with a pair of low-waisted white pants that fit her scandalously well. A wide black-leather belt emphasized her hips. Hillary apparently had become even more fascinated with Olivia's clothes after having seen her in next to nothing at the park two days ago.

"Please, stay," Olivia said. "That was my union rep."

"Ah, clearly not much progress then."

"Nope." Olivia fed a dollar bill into a vending machine and pushed the button for a diet soda. "Do you want to sit?"

"I have a few minutes until I have to get back out there." Hillary groaned as she lowered herself into a chair across from Olivia. "I knew I was out of shape, but this is ridiculous. How do I still hurt this much after two days?"

"I can help you with that."

"Gee, thanks. I might have gone with—there's nothing wrong with your shape."

Olivia raised her brows. "Not such a player now, am I?"

Hillary laughed. "I guess not. Maybe you should help me get in shape, and I can help you work on your game."

"It's a deal." Olivia stuck out her hand, then dropped it when Hillary didn't grasp it.

"I was joking."

"I'm not. At least not about working out with you. I don't have any real need for *game*, so that's kind of out."

"But you want me to work out with you?"

"If you'd like." Olivia rolled her eyes. "There isn't anything wrong with your body. But you said the exercise was exhilarating—"

"I'm not sure I said *exhilarating*."

"It's good for stress relief and helps clear your head. It might be just what you need right now. It would probably beat the double shifts you've been pulling lately."

"I'll think about it. It kind of sounded like you could use some stress relief right now, too." She shifted the focus away from her own poor coping techniques. Exhausting herself at work hadn't succeeded in driving away her nightmares. As much as the cycling had taxed her body, she'd awakened in a sweat both nights since then as well. Each time, she had trouble falling back to sleep, wary of returning to the dreams that haunted her. Some of them were filled with the specific images from that night, some included other situations where responders were injured and she couldn't help, and still others tapped into even more personal fears.

Instead of fighting to find sleep again, she got up and made coffee. She'd figured her body would eventually get accustomed to the lack of sleep and she'd feel less like a zombie.

"What I need is to get back to work." Olivia curled one hand so tightly into a fist that her knuckles popped. "I've never felt so stagnant or useless."

Hillary stared at Olivia's hands, wishing she could reach across the table and cover them with her own. A few seconds later, she was glad she'd resisted the urge when Holt swung open the door.

"Sheriff Martin wants to see you in his office." He gave her a slimy-looking smile.

"Thanks."

He nodded and withdrew.

"What do you think Martin wants?" Hillary asked as they both stood.

Olivia shrugged. "Maybe he's firing me."

"Yeah, he's firing Sheriff Dennis's daughter. Sure."

"My father's not the sheriff anymore."

"Maybe not officially. Good luck in there." Hillary pulled open the door to the dispatch center and nodded toward the hallway leading to the sheriff's office.

Olivia shoved her shoulders back and rolled her head slightly. "Maybe I won't need it."

Hillary tried to give her a reassuring smile, conflicted by the mixture of bravado and vulnerability she sensed in Olivia.

❖

"Sit down, Dennis." Sheriff Martin didn't look up from his computer screen when she entered his office.

"Yes, sir." She crossed to one of the two black leather chairs sitting at 45-degree angles to the opposite side of his desk.

"Professional Accountability has completed their investigation. You've been cleared of the allegations and approved to go back to work."

"That's great." She scooted to the edge of the chair, fighting the urge to jump out of it and flee the office now that she'd gotten what she wanted. So much for the value of a union rep. That idiot was apparently so left out of the communication loop, he hadn't even known this news was imminent. She'd expected the investigation to take longer; a lot of them did. Martin might have pushed it through in deference to her father, but right now she didn't care.

"While you were gone, we made some adjustments to cover the shift. And those changes have worked out for all personnel involved." He finally raised his eyes and seemed to be searching for resistance. She schooled her features carefully, not offering him any ammunition. He folded his hands on the desk and stared at her as if daring her to speak.

Apparently, things have worked out for everyone but me.

"You may return to the field. But you'll report to your new sector." He passed a sheet of paper across the desk. "Check in with Sergeant Gilleland next Monday."

"May Gilleland?" Unless she was mistaken, she'd just been assigned to the same shift and supervisor as her brother.

"We have only one Gilleland." He met her eyes as if challenging her to say anything.

"Thank you, sir. I don't mind starting there earlier if they need—"

"You will complete your commitment to Five-C this week. Take the weekend off, and then report to Sgt. Gilleland on Monday."

She nodded and stood.

He waited until she'd made it to the door with her hand on the knob before he spoke again. "Give your father my regards."

She stiffened but didn't turn. "Yes, sir."

She left and headed directly for the dispatch center. Her first thought was to tell Hillary. She pulled herself up as soon as she realized her intention and altered her course. Instead, she texted Andy and Frankie. Her mother and father would expect more than a text, so she'd deliver the news via a phone call later.

After she settled back in her chair at the front desk, she searched the video screens and found Hillary, entrenched in whatever was happening at her radio console. In just over two weeks at Five-C, she'd grown accustomed to seeing Hillary whenever she wanted to. Given her attraction to Hillary, continuing their friendship when she went back in the field could be dangerous, but she'd take the risk if Hillary seemed willing.

CHAPTER EIGHT

Olivia sat in her family's formal dining room with her hands folded in her lap. She tried to project an air of ease, hiding the tension she'd felt since she'd followed her father's sedan home from church an hour ago. She'd passed along the news of her return to patrol through her mother several days ago, but she'd spoken only briefly to her father. The memorial service for the deputy's line-of-duty death hadn't been the place to talk about her career path. She'd stood silently by her father, brother, and Frankie, trying to keep her eyes off the cluster of dispatchers on the other side of the church. She did, however, indulge in a lingering moment of eye contact and a welcoming smile, which Hillary returned.

"Are you ready to get back to work?" Andy asked between bites of pot roast.

"Absolutely. I'm so tired of sitting on my ass."

"Olivia, language."

"Sorry, Mama."

Her mother smiled, mollified. "I'm glad you'll be working with Andy now. You two can watch out for each other."

"I hope you learned something from your little field trip." Olivia stiffened as her father finally spoke.

"Sir?" She'd never thought she'd been wrong, and she'd been cleared in the investigation. Yet, he still seemed to believe she should adjust her thinking.

"You shouldn't have gone in there alone and let your temper get the best of you."

"My temper had nothing to do with what happened in there."
She'd been cleared. Didn't that mean she didn't have to alter how she
handled these incidents? She hadn't done anything wrong.

"Olivia." Andy tried to intervene, but she ignored him.

"In hindsight, I could have waited for backup, I'll grant you that,
but—"

"You did what you always do, rushed in hotheaded and not
willing to listen to anyone."

She bit her lip against the urge to defend herself. He'd already
made up his mind and wouldn't be swayed by anything she could say
today. Instead, she curled her fingers tighter until her nails bit into her
palms and waited for dinner to be over.

Thirty minutes later, she finally felt relief unwrapping the
tension in her stomach. She and Frankie sat next to each other in the
high-backed white rockers on the front porch that paid homage to her
mother's North Carolina childhood.

"Why do you let him get to you like that?" Frankie shoved her
toes against the floor and the rocker squeaked against it.

Olivia shrugged. "Why can't Andy stand up for me instead of
taking his side?"

"He isn't taking sides."

"If he's not backing *me* up, then he's choosing *him*."

"That's not fair."

"That's the way things are. If he doesn't step up against Daddy,
then he's in agreement with him, and I'm just some emotionally
unstable, temperamental girl."

"Hey." Frankie grabbed Olivia's forearm, but Olivia wrenched it
away. "Okay, let's talk about something else."

"Gladly."

They rocked together for several minutes, the rhythm of their
chairs against the porch covering the faint sound of the television
from inside the house.

"Did you tell Hillary how much you'd miss her when you left?"

Olivia scowled and glanced at the door leading to the house.

"Oh, relax. Andy and your father are smoking cigars on the back
porch, and your mother is engrossed in her program." Frankie made

air quotes around the word. "When did she start watching *American Idol*, anyway?"

"I know. It's crazy, right?"

"So, what did Hillary say when you told her you were leaving?"

"I'm not leaving town. I'm going back to my real job." She'd had lunch with Hillary twice during her last week at Five-C. They'd left the future of their friendship uncertain, but on Saturday she'd loaded the extra bike on her Jeep and headed for the park. She couldn't ignore the lightness in her heart when she arrived to find Hillary already waiting for her. "Why are you so interested in Hillary? Are you jealous that I might have another friend?"

"Maybe. A little." Frankie smiled. "I don't know. She's good for you. I know these last few weeks have been hard. But something tells me they would have been worse if not for—well, whatever you're starting with her."

Olivia leaned back in her chair and sighed in frustration. "I can't be starting anything, can I? She doesn't hide who she is. And she certainly doesn't want to be with a coward like me."

"Have you given any more thought to just telling them?"

"I can't even think about it without getting sick to my stomach."

"I know it scares you. But maybe that just means it's more important that you do it. You shouldn't let fear make you pass on having a complete partner in life."

"And you think Hillary is that person?"

"Couldn't she be?"

Olivia had spent years telling herself she didn't need what everyone else had—Frankie and Andy, and even her parents, they must have done something right for the past thirty-five years. Some days she couldn't imagine how they'd survived, but marriage obviously worked for them. And in her weaker moments, Olivia considered how it might feel to have someone so totally in for her.

She'd been hiding some part of herself since her early teens, so long ago she couldn't recall a time when she'd been completely genuine with her family. She'd soon figured out she was adept at playing straight. She'd joined the cheerleading squad and dated the right guys. But every so often she'd stare a little too long at a crush and worry she'd be found out. Frankie provided some relief from the lies, but even with Frankie, she held something back. She was afraid that after so long she wasn't capable of giving all of herself.

"Don't fret, pal. You know you'll always have me. And I have my ways of making sure Andy doesn't shut you out, too," Frankie said.

"I don't want to hear about your methods."

❖

"Sergeant Gilleland?" Olivia tapped her knuckles against the open door of the shift supervisor's office.

"Come in. Sit down." The intense green hue as well as the sharp appraisal in Sergeant Gilleland's eyes impressed Olivia.

She wasn't pleased about how much time she'd spent sitting across the desk from supervisors lately. But she lowered herself stiffly into the chair, hoping to avoid any show of disrespect. Maybe she could view this as a fresh start.

"Deputy Dennis, in the interest of honesty, I've been warned to keep an eye on you."

So much for a clean slate. Whatever information Sergeant Gilleland had received had almost certainly come from Sheriff Martin. Despite all the arguments clamoring in her head, Olivia kept her mouth shut. She wouldn't denigrate the sheriff in front of her new superior.

"I'm not a fan of letting others dictate how I run my shift. But I can't afford any foolish risks right now. So, you're on probation."

"Sheriff Martin didn't mention—"

"Not with him. With me." She smoothed a hand over her already flawlessly restrained hair. Olivia appreciated the work that went into her look, from the polished up-do to the makeup that flattered her caramel complexion and verdant eyes.

"Yes, ma'am." Olivia didn't hesitate to show the respect the sergeant deserved. She had a reputation for being tough and fair. If they didn't end up on opposite sides, when all was said and done, Olivia suspected she would actually like Gilleland a great deal.

"That said, I'm not hard to get along with. I'm not a fan of traffic-stop quotas, but that goes over my head. So try to meet the minimum numbers the brass puts out. Beyond that, answer the dispatch calls, be polite and courteous, and don't cause any trouble."

All but that last part seemed standard. As the sergeant tacked on the last sentence, she gave Olivia a hard look. Olivia nodded silently. Gilleland had probably seen her personnel file, and Olivia had no explanations to offer. But at least she hadn't said she hoped she worked as hard as her brother.

❖

"One-thirty-seven."

"Go ahead." Hillary smiled as she acknowledged Olivia's unit number.

"Send me that vehicle break-in. I'll go take the report."

With a few keystrokes, she assigned Olivia to the incident and transmitted the information to the computer in Olivia's car. She pulled out her cell phone and shot off a quick text.

Good to have you back on the radio.

She dispatched several more calls and tried not to glance at her phone, knowing Olivia wouldn't text her while she was driving to her call. Olivia had been back in the field for two days, but today was Hillary's first day manning the police frequency. Hillary had texted her Monday night to ask how her first day on duty had gone, and they'd ended up texting late into the night—or rather early morning. Since Hillary hadn't been sleeping well anyway, getting to know Olivia was certainly a better way to spend her time.

She could tell by the tone of her texts how happy Olivia was to be in a patrol car again, even after only one day. And today, she could hear the same contentment in her voice. While she appreciated the change in Olivia's demeanor, she also felt apprehensive. She had plenty of acquaintances on the other side of the radio and had even hung out with some of the deputies outside of work. She never worried about them. But with Olivia—she couldn't explain the nervousness twisting inside her right now. Olivia was a good cop—tough, strong, and well trained. But she also had a reputation for being hotheaded and brave to the point of recklessness. Hillary had seen those traits before while dispatching to her, and today, they were in the forefront of her mind.

Her phone vibrated against her desk just seconds after Olivia changed her status on the computer screen to indicate she was on scene.

Hearing your voice makes my night.

❖

Hearing your voice makes my night.

Olivia stared at the text she'd just sent and wished she could get it back. She meant it—of course, she did. Every time her phone signaled another text, her heart leapt with anticipation, and with each abbreviated message or silly emoticon, her feelings for Hillary grew. And though she knew things between them couldn't go anywhere, she hoped their communications helped Hillary in some way as well. Despite the front Hillary tried to put on, Olivia knew she'd been struggling. But every time Olivia tried to steer the conversation toward the events of that day and how she was coping, Hillary changed the subject or abruptly had something pressing to do.

Glad I could make someone's night. Now go knock out that report, hotshot. I have other calls holding.

Olivia shoved open the door of her patrol car. She tucked her phone in her pocket, still smiling as she walked to the front door of her complainant's house.

❖

Hillary reached the park before Olivia on Saturday. She wasn't in the mood for working out, but Olivia would say that was why she needed to. Seeing Olivia had motivated her to drag herself out of bed that morning more than exercise had. She got out of the car, too restless to sit still. She sipped from the travel mug containing her second cup of coffee for the day and paced a dozen or so steps away, then back to her car.

Olivia's Jeep rounded the corner at the far end of the parking lot, and Hillary couldn't help staring as Olivia steered into a spot nearby. With her hair pulled through the back of a baseball cap, dark sunglasses hiding her eyes, and the fitted tank top clinging to her torso, she was every lesbian's fantasy in a topless Jeep.

"Probably every straight man's, too," she mumbled, needing the reminder to keep it clean as Olivia jumped out. Olivia tugged the hem of her shorts back into place, drawing Hillary's eyes to her thighs, which of course led to those beautiful calves.

"Hey, sorry I'm late. Are you ready to go?" Oblivious to the carnal images her calves evoked, Olivia grabbed her bike and began lifting it off the rack.

"Do you mind if we just take a walk today?" Suddenly, Hillary wanted more intimacy than a bike ride provided.

Olivia paused and looked at her, then nodded and secured the bike back on the rack. "Sure. Everything okay?"

"Yes. I—I just thought we could talk, and me struggling to keep up with you on the bike doesn't lend itself to that." While she couldn't complain about the view on their rides, she needed more than just a nice ass to stare at today.

"Okay." When Olivia pulled a T-shirt back over her tank top Hillary began to rethink the suggestion. She had to trade looking at those shoulders for some conversation? "Let's do the shorter trail."

Olivia was apparently content to wait her out as they walked in silence for several minutes. They met a couple pushing a stroller, then an older man walking a dog. Aware that Olivia was also letting her set the pace, she didn't rush her strides, content with a leisurely stroll. She felt only a little guilty for hijacking Olivia's typically strenuous workout.

She took a deep breath and forged ahead with the reason she'd asked for this walk. "Sheriff Martin wants to give me a commendation."

"For your work on the radio during—"

"Yes." She'd avoided thinking the deputy's name and didn't want to hear Olivia say it either.

"Congratulations."

"He's just doing it for the publicity."

"Still—"

"I'm going to decline."

"What? Why?" Olivia stopped, and Hillary did too, turning toward her. "You did well that day."

"I did my job."

"And what's wrong with honoring that?"

"I don't want it," she snapped, her voice echoing through the trees around them. She began walking again. Maybe she shouldn't have brought this up.

"Hillary." Olivia touched her arm and Hillary jerked around quickly, coming face to face with her.

"I didn't *do* anything." Her voice sounded shaky and rough. "I can't change that. I can't fix it. And I sure as hell don't need you to make me feel better about that."

"I just want to—"

"He's dead, Olivia." Tears filled her eyes quickly and spilled down her cheeks before she could stop them. "He's dead. And I don't want a commendation for that."

"Oh, honey." Olivia stepped close and wrapped her arms around Hillary.

Hillary stood there and let Olivia hold her, because she couldn't do anything else. Pain spread up her chest and into her throat, as if trying to find a route out of her body. She melted into Olivia, letting her absorb the agony, unable to hold back a sob.

"Okay." Olivia rubbed Hillary's back. She squeezed her tighter, then eased back. She brushed a thumb over her cheek. "Let's find a place to sit." Olivia took her hand and led her farther along the path until they came to a bench. As they settled next to each other, Olivia kept hold of her hand.

Hillary said, "Sometimes I feel like I can't breathe. And I need to. I need to breathe or I think I'm going to die."

"Hillary—"

"You being this close—it doesn't help. I mean it does, I knew it would, but it kinda doesn't." She angled toward Olivia and found confusion in her beautiful eyes. Hillary's face flamed as she realized what she'd revealed, so she surged forward before Olivia could decipher her words. "I've been working insane hours and keeping myself busy—so busy, because then I won't have time to think. But it doesn't help, because even though I'm exhausted, my brain won't stop—it won't stop playing that day over and over. And I mean the whole day. And I just cannot second-guess whether I should have had that bagel for breakfast one more time. Do you know what I mean?"

"Um, not really. Listen, I want to—"

"But now I'm keeping myself so busy that I feel like I don't have time to breathe. And I don't know how to stop—to just slow down and—" She let out a long, deep sigh. "I'm going to suffocate."

"What you're feeling is normal."

"I don't feel normal. And I can't keep freaking out every time an officer asks for an ambulance on my air."

"You should talk to someone about this. A counselor."

Hillary started shaking her head even before Olivia stopped talking. "I should. Maybe. I don't know. But the thought of sitting in a chair—which I know sounds crazy because I sit in a chair all day at work. Yet when I'm doing three things at once, I don't have time to think. And if I have to sit there staring at a therapist and just talk—"

"You'll suffocate?"

"Exactly."

"Okay." Olivia laced their fingers firmly together. "Well, we're sitting here now. So let's breathe together."

Hillary stared at their joined hands and wondered if she'd ever felt more grounded in her life. When she heard Olivia pull in a slow, deep breath, she automatically synced her own inhalation. They sat quietly, just breathing together, and her panic started to ease.

"Bagel notwithstanding, what else are you questioning about that day?" Olivia asked quietly after some time.

"It all happened so fast and—"

"I was listening. You did everything you should have. You weren't out there, Hillary. You couldn't have done anything to save his life. You got an ambulance there as quickly as you could. There was nothing anyone could do."

"Maybe I should have sent another car to the initial wreck."

"You assigned two units to it. That's standard. If you won't seek counseling, maybe you should reach out to some other officers who were on the air that day. I'm sure you're not the only one feeling this way."

Hillary shrugged. "They probably don't want to talk about it any more than I do." Right now, she felt like she didn't need anyone except Olivia. She knew it wasn't true—that getting through this would take more than just sitting on a bench with her. But in this moment, she couldn't think of anywhere she'd rather be. She squeezed Olivia's hand and closed her eyes when Olivia squeezed back.

"Come with me to my parents' house tomorrow."

Hillary snapped her eyes back open at Olivia's almost blurted invitation.

"I—I have to go to church. But you don't have to do that. You could meet me afterward and go to their house for Sunday dinner."

Dinner at the Dennis home didn't sound like a relaxing affair. But curiosity and a desire to spend more time with Olivia had her agreeing before she had time to consider the invitation further.

CHAPTER NINE

Olivia sat in one of the rockers on her parents' front porch, intent on intercepting Hillary before she reached the door. She'd been nervous since she'd issued the invitation. She didn't typically ask anyone to join her family on Sunday, friends or otherwise. She'd spoken to her father on the phone last night and explained that Hillary was having a difficult time with the aftermath of the crash. She'd tried to make it seem like that's why she'd asked her to dinner.

But in reality, she didn't know why she'd done it. Hillary was upset. Olivia had been bothered by the idea of parting ways at the park and not knowing when she would see her again. She'd already committed to dinner and wouldn't dare call her mother to back out. So having Hillary there was the next logical step.

When Hillary's car pulled into the long driveway, Olivia stood. By the time Hillary had parked and gotten out, Olivia waited on the top step, leaning against the porch.

"Your folks' property is amazing." Hillary waved at the open space around the house. The closest neighbor was just visible through the tree line. "You grew up here, didn't you?"

"Yes."

Hillary raised her brows. "Does that mean there's a childhood bedroom around here that will give me insight into who you were when you were younger?"

"Hardly. My mother turned my room into a guest room a month after I moved out." Katherine Dennis wasn't the sentimental type.

The flower patterns and lace now adorning her old room wouldn't give any hints about who Olivia had been. "Besides, you knew me when I was younger."

"No. I knew *of you* when you were younger. We never traveled in the same circles."

Olivia nodded.

"And I certainly would never have been invited to your bedroom." Hillary reached the top of the steps and stopped with only a foot or so between them.

Olivia laughed to cover up the bolt of arousal that weakened her knees. *If I knew then what I know now.* What would her life have been like if she'd been braver in school? Could she and Hillary have been kindred spirits, or at least friends? Her laughter died when she met Hillary's eyes and saw the same tentative heat that stirred within her.

"Hi." Hillary's soft voice across the small space between them hit Olivia low in her stomach.

"Hey." Olivia glanced at her Jeep, parked in front of the barn, and wished they could get in it and take off. She wanted to be alone with Hillary—wanted, almost desperately, to explore the growing attraction between them. "How are you feeling?"

"I'm okay. Thanks."

"No suffocating today?"

"Nope." Hillary sucked in an exaggerated breath. "See?"

"Well, just in case, I brushed up on my CPR."

Hillary tilted her head. "Wow. That's the worst pickup line I've ever heard."

"Oh, I'm not—I didn't—"

Hillary raised her eyebrows, and Olivia stopped stuttering and smiled. "And, you're teasing me."

"It's just so fun."

"Okay. Smart-ass. But you still have to go inside with my family, so I'll have the last laugh."

"So, you only invited me here to watch me squirm?"

"You'll be okay. They don't bite—much."

Hillary held up a wine bottle. "I hope red is okay. I didn't know what we were having for dinner."

"My parents don't drink."

Hillary crinkled her nose and gave the bottle an accusatory look. "Guess I'll be making a stellar first impression today. What's worse, bringing booze or putting it back in my car and showing up empty-handed?"

Olivia chuckled. "It's okay. You'll probably need a couple glasses to get through this."

Hillary smiled. "Great."

"Come on. Andy, Frankie, and I will drink with you." Olivia pulled open the door and ushered her inside. She led her through the foyer and into the kitchen, where her mother had just removed the pot roast from the oven and Frankie was loading a serving bowl full of dinner rolls.

"Mama, this is Hillary. She's one of our dispatchers."

"Your favorite dispatcher, actually," Hillary teased her. "It's very nice to meet you, Mrs. Dennis."

"Please, call me Katherine."

"Yes, ma'am."

Olivia smiled at her stilted response and doubted Hillary would ever address her mother by her first name. "You remember Frankie, right?"

"Of course. It's good to see you again."

"You too." Frankie sent her a warm smile.

Olivia took the bottle from Hillary, rounded the island, and opened a drawer in search of a corkscrew. "Hillary brought a nice red. Frankie, would you like a glass?"

"Sure, thank you."

Olivia ignored the look her mother gave her as she popped the cork and poured three glasses. She caught Hillary looking away in embarrassment and guessed she'd seen Katherine's disapproval as well.

Katherine carried the roast into the dining room, as if she didn't even want to be in the room while they imbibed. Olivia grinned and handed Frankie a glass.

"Ah, devil's juice," Frankie joked before taking a sip.

"She can't get mad. She's the one with the wineglasses and corkscrew in the house. It's a little bit like being anti-drugs yet carrying a crack pipe in your purse." Olivia turned to Hillary and held out a glass.

Hillary dropped her eyes to the floor as she took it. "I'm so sorry."

Olivia gently grasped her wrist and waited until she met her eyes. "Don't worry about it. She's seen us drink wine before. You're not corrupting her little girl." Hillary stared at her, and Olivia wondered what she might be holding back right now. Instead of asking, she turned away and picked up her own drink. "Let's take this out back. That's where she banishes my father with his cigars. It's where all of the debauchery happens."

"You two go ahead. I'm going to take Andy a glass," Frankie said mid-pour.

Hillary followed Olivia through the house to the screened patio and closed the door behind them.

Olivia slipped out of her suit jacket and draped it over the back of a chair. "I didn't have time to go by my place and change out of my church clothes."

"You look very nice." Olivia looked amazing in the charcoal suit and pale-blue blouse, and Hillary didn't think she succeeded in keeping the appreciation out of her tone or off her face. She was certain of it when Olivia turned quickly. Was that lust in Olivia's expression? They were standing so close, Hillary would barely have to move in order to kiss her. God, she wanted to kiss her. She started to turn away, but Olivia grasped her forearm and she froze as heat sizzled up her arm.

"Hillary?"

"I'm sorry about the wine." She latched onto something to say, anything but an answer to the question in Olivia's eyes.

"Please don't apologize for that again."

"Well, then what should I apologize for?" Should she be sorry for the desire coursing through her for her straight friend? For the urges that would surely ruin the friendship she wanted only minutely more than she wanted to know what Olivia's mouth tasted like.

"Absolutely nothing," Olivia whispered as she closed the small space between them.

Her kiss was gentle, tentative at first, but then she slid her hands around Hillary's waist and drew her closer. Hillary quickly got over the shock of finding Olivia Dennis's lips against hers and responded with her very best effort. She touched Olivia's neck, then took Olivia's face between her hands, intent on memorizing the taste and texture of her mouth. She held herself back, letting Olivia lead—letting her be the first to introduce a tender bit of tongue. When she did, Hillary fought even harder for a bit of restraint.

When Olivia jerked back with panic in her eyes, Hillary's heart told her she might have just had her one and only chance to kiss Olivia. She guessed Olivia was realizing not only that she'd just kissed a woman, but that they could have been discovered at any time.

Olivia bit her lower lip, and even though Hillary knew she was freaking out, she couldn't help but find it incredibly sexy. When Olivia stumbled back, Hillary started to follow, but Olivia's expression stopped her. Remorse? Did she regret what had just happened?

"I should get back."

Hillary nodded. "I'll be right there." She needed a minute to compose herself before she could face Olivia's family. Olivia didn't wait. The click of the door closing between them went a long way toward icing Hillary's arousal.

❖

"Do you think maybe she wants to corrupt you?" Frankie whispered over Olivia's shoulder. Olivia didn't turn, knowing she'd been caught watching Hillary help her mother clear the table.

"Frankie." Olivia growled a warning.

"I'm proud of you. This is a brave new step."

"There's no new step. I invited a friend to dinner. That's all."

"Does she know that?"

"Yes."

"Because I saw her sneaking glances at you during dinner and—"

"Drop it." What she'd intended as a demand sounded more like a plea.

Her parents had been pleasant during the meal. Her father had engaged Hillary with questions about the dispatch center. He'd spent some time there early in his career during the days when sworn personnel supervised the dispatchers. He'd often said being sent back to the field when they put civilian supervisors in charge of dispatch had been the best thing to happen to him. His tenure there had led to a promotion to captain and eventually to his election as sheriff.

Olivia knew she'd been quieter than usual and she'd felt Hillary's eyes on her, but she couldn't organize her brain enough to fake her way through dinner, so she mostly remained silent. Their shared kiss had shaken her. Somehow she'd known it would, yet she hadn't been able to stop from taking Hillary in her arms.

"If you truly hope to keep everyone in the dark, you need to get a better grip on it. Because if you two keep looking at each other like that, your family will figure it out in no time." Frankie got in one last comment.

Olivia nodded, unable to summon the energy to deny it. She'd struggled through dinner and was now torn between the desire to spend more time with Hillary and wishing she would leave soon. Her only hope of keeping her secrets would be if Hillary believed their kiss had been an impulsive one-off for Olivia and that she'd never done that before.

However, she didn't want it to be a one-time thing. She felt like she'd been practicing her whole life for this moment—like every girl she'd kissed was only a prelude to what she'd been waiting for all along. She already wanted to kiss Hillary again. She wanted much more. But she couldn't have it, at least not until she got the guts to come clean with her parents. Anything else wouldn't be fair to Hillary. Not only that, but, in a town as small as Reinsville, covert relationships didn't stay that way for long. She couldn't let her parents find out through the rumor mill. So for now, she and Hillary could only be friends. Hopefully, she hadn't ruined even that.

Intent on finding out, she crossed the room. Disappointment flooded her heart at the change in Hillary's expression when she saw her approaching.

"I should go," Hillary said before Olivia could speak. She turned to Olivia's mother. "Thank you so much for dinner. It was delicious."

"I'll walk you out," Olivia said.

"No need."

Olivia followed her anyway. She waited until they were well clear of the house and had almost reached Hillary's car before she spoke. "I'm sorry if I've confused you."

"*If* you've confused me? One minute we're kissing on the patio and the next, I'm a dispatcher you know from work. Look, I don't understand exactly what that kiss meant. And I'd planned to ask you, but given the fact that you can just turn whatever this is off at the drop of—"

"It's not like that. Can we please talk about this?"

Hillary glanced back at the Dennis house. "I don't think this is the time or the place."

"I'll call you later?"

Hillary nodded, but Olivia wasn't convinced she'd answer the phone.

Hillary glanced in her rearview mirror as she drove away. Olivia still stood next to the driveway, though she was too far away to see her face clearly.

"Shit," she muttered. "You really screwed that one up."

At least Olivia wasn't working at Five-C anymore. She wouldn't have to face her until she was ready. She didn't even know what she would say. *Hey, I'm sorry I threw myself at you in your parents' house.* In the former sheriff's house. Shit. But had she initiated the kiss? Maybe she'd leaned in, but Olivia had covered the remaining distance. She touched her fingers to her lips as she replayed that moment in her mind. Olivia hadn't kissed her like a woman who kissed men. Hillary hadn't registered the variance at the time, but now she recognized the subtle difference in the tender yet confident way Olivia had caressed her lips.

"Oh my God. She's kissed a woman before." The more she considered the idea, the angrier she got. She'd been beating herself up for her attraction to a woman she'd assumed was straight. But even when she'd outed herself, and then again when they talked about her dating history, Olivia had continued to let her think she wasn't gay.

She'd heard that Olivia didn't date any of the male officers that hit on her; that made sense now. But she'd never heard a rumor of her dating any females, either. If she was gay, it could be the best-kept secret in the Reinsville Sheriff's Department.

CHAPTER TEN

By the following Saturday, Hillary still hadn't heard from Olivia. She'd waited until Tuesday, telling herself the next move belonged to Olivia. But she wasn't accustomed to kissing a woman, then not speaking to her for days. And, as much as she didn't want to admit it, she missed her. So she called her cell and, when she didn't answer, left a voice mail. After another day passed with no callback, she texted her. She woke early on Saturday morning with no messages on her phone, so she dressed and headed for the park.

She didn't want to give Olivia up and was convinced they could get past the kiss. But that first conversation would only become more awkward as time passed, so they might as well get it out of the way.

She was still giving herself that pep talk as she climbed out of her car in the parking lot. Olivia's Jeep was there, but the bike rack held only one bike. Olivia's prized ride was gone. Hillary decided to take heart from the fact that Olivia had brought the second bike. She thought about taking it down and heading after her, but she didn't know how much of a head start Olivia had. So, instead, she climbed into the passenger side of the Jeep, reclined the seat, and closed her eyes. She'd never understand the almost fanatical appeal Jeep Wranglers seemed to have, but she could imagine that the humid air rushing against her sun-heated skin might be exhilarating. And Olivia certainly looked hot in it. Speaking of hot, she hoped Olivia returned soon. Spending an hour or so in the thick summer air would feel positively stifling.

"I guess it's not a vehicle burglary if I don't have a top or windows, huh?"

Hillary jumped at how close Olivia's voice was. She opened her eyes, then slammed them shut again, unprepared for Olivia's sexy, sweaty appearance. She'd leaned into the cockpit of the vehicle, her face only a foot or so from Hillary's.

"I haven't stolen anything, yet," Hillary said as she pushed back against the seat, hoping for a couple inches of sanity.

"That's a matter of opinion."

"What?"

"Nothing." Olivia went to the back of the Jeep and loaded her bike.

Hillary jumped out and followed. "Were you planning to avoid me forever?"

"Probably not. If I do, are you going to keep stalking me?"

"This is not stalking." Hillary retrieved a paper bag and two cardboard coffee cups from her car. "I brought breakfast."

Olivia lifted her chin toward a picnic table a few feet away. "Over there."

After they'd settled at the table, Hillary unpacked a couple of breakfast sandwiches from Pacey's Diner. While she'd waited for Olivia to return, the grease had soaked into the paper, making it nearly transparent. "Bacon or sausage?"

"Bacon. Always bacon."

Hillary handed it over and passed her a coffee cup. "Sorry if it's not hot anymore. Sugar and creamer are in the bag."

Neither spoke while they worked on their sandwiches. When they were through, Olivia put their balled-up wrappers back in the bag and carried it to a trash can. On her way back to the table she took a deep breath and smoothed her hands down her hips, wishing she knew what to do next. With almost any other woman, she'd walk away if things got complicated, but now she wanted to salvage something. She couldn't let Hillary go, but she didn't know if she could be friends without wanting her.

"So, I guess you want to talk about it, huh?" She met Hillary's eyes, searching for a way to avoid this conversation. But Hillary nodded, her expression wary. Olivia searched for some possible explanation for her behavior after their kiss but came up completely blank. "I—uh, my parents don't—I haven't—" She rubbed a hand against her jaw.

"Olivia, whatever's going on, you can tell me."

"You don't understand."

Hillary stared at her for an uncomfortable length of time.

"I'm gay," Olivia blurted. "Fuck." She searched for anger, or disappointment, but Hillary's expression was closed. "I'm gay."

"Why do you seem so upset by saying it?"

"Don't you get it? That's not an option for me." Olivia pinched the bridge of her nose. Hillary seemed calmer than she'd expected after she'd practically kissed-and-ran, but that didn't alleviate Olivia's stress level.

"Clearly it is. I didn't get the impression that was your first time kissing a girl."

"No, it wasn't. But I'm not out. You can't tell anyone."

"No one knows?"

She shook her head. "Just Frankie."

"Wow. That is a well-kept secret. Especially considering where we work."

"And I'd like it to stay that way." A moment of panic flooded her. *Had she just ruined her carefully constructed life?*

"My lips are sealed." Hillary swiped her fingers across her lips and mimed throwing away a key. "But why didn't you say something earlier? You let me embarrass myself talking about what a threat you'd be *if you were gay.*"

"Habit, I guess."

"You don't trust me?"

"I do." She thought she did. Was that crazy, given they'd known each other only a month? "I want to. I guess I don't have a choice now."

"You can." Hillary covered Olivia's hand and stroked her thumb over her wrist. "I won't tell anyone. Maybe I don't get it because I've never had to hide, but—you're not the first closeted person I've known."

She nodded. Hillary had said she didn't want to date someone in the closet, and that thought disappointed Olivia more than she'd like to admit. "Do I need to apologize for the kiss?"

"No. But maybe we should talk about it."

"Okay."

"Do you regret it?"

"No."

Hillary pulled her hand back and furrowed her brows. "This will go a lot easier if you give me more than one-word answers."

"I don't regret it." She wanted to take Hillary's hand but didn't want to confuse things. They couldn't date, but she didn't want to give Hillary up. So she'd settle for being friends and hope that no one saw through to her attraction to her. "But I've enjoyed getting to know you, and I don't want to mess that up."

"I don't, either."

"So, I guess we should chalk it up to a moment and a bad decision on my part?" Olivia resumed her place across the table from Hillary.

"You weren't alone—"

"But I initiated it. I take the blame."

"Blame? Wow."

"What?"

"Nothing." Hillary seemed to be studying her, and she fought not to look away. She didn't know what Hillary was looking for, but she suspected she'd be found lacking at the end of her inspection. "Can I ask you a question?"

"Sure."

"Are you hoping to find some acceptable guy to marry and please your family?"

"No." Olivia answered with hesitation. "That wouldn't be fair to anyone, especially the poor guy."

"Then I don't get it."

"What?"

"Aren't you going to have to come out to them eventually?" Rising panic seemed Olivia's natural reaction to that question, and it must have shown in her face because Hillary went on. "Long term— what do you want?"

She hadn't let herself want anything in so long. "Sometimes, I want what you're talking about—honesty with my family, openness in my relationships. Hell, I've never even had a real relationship with a woman."

"What about love?"

Olivia laughed. "You're going straight to the corny shit, huh?"

"Make fun if you want to. But don't you think it would be a little freeing to tell them?"

Olivia hated the bit of hope she saw jump into Hillary's eyes. "It's not that easy. My family—I get hives just thinking about telling my father. There's a better than fifty-fifty chance he'll disown me."

"You're willing to spend your life alone to make them happy? Your dad may be a bit hard to read, but he clearly loves your mom and she him. Don't you think they would want you to have a partner in life?"

"Not if it's a woman."

"You're pretty young to condemn yourself to a life alone."

Olivia shrugged, not knowing what else to say. Her family wouldn't change, and they'd think her selfish for expecting them to. Maybe they were closed-minded, but they were the only family she had. If she threw them away for a chance at something with a woman and the relationship didn't last, she'd be alone.

"Still just friends?" Doubt colored Jake's tone. As much as Hillary had wanted to confide in him, she'd managed to keep their one kiss under wraps, and she wouldn't disclose it today either. It had been just over two weeks since she'd confronted Olivia about her avoidance, and she hadn't seen her outside of their Saturday mornings at the park. But they had been getting to know each other better through texting and a handful of phone calls.

Hillary nodded while she keyed up and answered an officer on her radio.

"How does that work? Because I've never successfully been *just friends* with a woman."

"Hey." Hillary acted offended and indicated herself with her thumb.

"With a straight woman, then. I've had acquaintances. But never good-enough friends to hang out with. Someone always wants more and gets their feelings hurt."

Hillary shrugged. There was a pretty good chance she would get hurt. But when she thought about not seeing Olivia again, she decided she had to risk the heartache.

"But I might take a chance at being friends with Olivia Dennis. She could definitely be worth it."

Hillary bit her lip to keep from telling him that he still wouldn't have a straight friend. She was saved from any further comment when Jake turned his attention to his computer screen and increased the cadence of his voice. Today, he'd been assigned to the fire-department frequency. With a few keystrokes, she checked his calls. He had a full response headed to a reported structure fire at an apartment complex. He'd be too busy to think about her friendship with Olivia for a while at least.

❖

Two fire trucks and an ambulance with screaming sirens flew by the Walmart parking lot. Olivia had just finished taking a report on a shoplifter. She'd issued the suspect a misdemeanor citation and given her a court date to attend later. She wouldn't complain about the paperwork, though. At least she wasn't sitting behind a desk at Five-C.

In the four weeks since she'd been reassigned, she'd kept her head down and answered every call she could while squeezing traffic stops in between them. She didn't want to give Sergeant Gilleland a reason to watch her too closely. Though Gilleland ran a tight shift, the five men and one other woman assigned under her clearly respected her. The other six deputies, including Andy, seemed to rely on each other a bit more than Olivia was used to. She tended to be more of a lone wolf of sorts, never depending on someone else to back her up.

She still didn't like the circumstances that had led to this assignment, but the outcome could have been worse. She'd been exonerated, and the allegations would be forgotten when the next scandal came along.

She touched the screen on her laptop, hitting the button that would indicate she was available for the next call. She smiled when Hillary immediately stated her call sign.

"Go ahead." She liked to think that Hillary had been watching for her to check in-service, though she knew that was silly. Hillary's job was to dispatch the next incident, so she noticed every deputy who checked in.

Hillary gave the address and the type code for her next call, which concerned a missing person one town over. Collins County covered a large area and encompassed several small municipalities. Olivia's new area included a business park, a low-income apartment complex, a subdivision full of moderately sized houses, and two strip malls.

"Ten-four." She acknowledged the transmission, fighting the urge to send Hillary a text. Instead, she put the car in gear and pulled out onto the street.

After their conversation in the park, she'd planned to keep things between them distant and platonic for a while. She didn't want to send mixed signals. But she couldn't ignore Hillary's texts. And every time, she ended up getting drawn quite willingly into a conversation. What was worse, the more she talked to her, the more she liked her. She could see them becoming lifelong friends, like only Frankie had been before—that is until she thought ahead to the day Hillary told her she'd started dating someone. The mere idea stirred jealousy like she'd never felt before. Worse, even, than when Frankie and Andy had started dating.

She'd covered about half the distance to her assigned location when Hillary put out a higher-priority call. The gas station in Reinsville had just been robbed. Officially, she'd dispatched Andy, another deputy, and Sergeant Gilleland. But several other deputies had volunteered to go aid in the search for the suspect. Olivia decided to go, too. She didn't advise Hillary, though, leaving the air clear for the closer responders in case they had emergency traffic. She flipped on her lights, activated her siren, and did a U-turn in the middle of the road.

The suspect had fled on foot and was described as wearing a bright-orange T-shirt and matching baseball cap. Not the wisest choice if one hoped to disappear after committing a crime. As other deputies gave their locations, she soon realized she'd be one of the last ones into the area. She didn't rush to the scene. She would be more helpful as part of the perimeter that would hopefully contain him until they caught him.

❖

"I need an ETA on K-9," Andy Dennis said over the radio.

With only two K-9 units to cover the whole county, sometimes they were too far away to do much good. A successful apprehension depended not only on the suspect's head start, but also on the other deputies' ability to set up a perimeter around the area to contain him, as well as their ability to keep bystanders from contaminating the scent.

After checking on their location, Hillary keyed her microphone. "K-9 is about five minutes out." He would be flying across the country roads to get there in time. And the other K-9 deputy had most likely started that way as well. A dog could track for only so long, especially in the summer heat, before he needed relief. Often, another dog could pick up the track and continue the search.

Hillary monitored the radio transmissions and added the appropriate updates to her computer. When the dog arrived and started the track, Hillary made the notation as well. Later, the K-9 deputy would ask for the time they'd started as well as when they terminated, whether they successfully caught the guy or not.

"We're on the railroad tracks, headed your way." She recognized the voice of the dog handler.

"I've got the other end sealed off." She was surprised to hear Olivia's voice. She glanced at her status screen, though she knew it still showed Olivia on the missing-person call.

"Hold what you have." Other than a few updates, the other deputies let K-9 have the air. As he gave his location, they adjusted accordingly so as not to confuse the dog by potentially crossing their scents with the trail.

"We've got eyes on him. He's running southbound on the tracks," the K-9 officer called out.

Hillary glanced again at Olivia's unit number on her screen, as if she could see Olivia herself. She checked the map, trying to visualize where Olivia was in relation to the suspect. He was headed straight toward her.

"Everyone, stay on your toes. Unless he's ditched the gun, he's still carrying," Sergeant Gilleland said.

Hillary clenched her jaw against a rush of anxiety. She tried to shut out thoughts of Olivia confronting a gun-toting criminal. She shook her head, forcing her focus back to her work.

"He just jumped off the bridge. He's in the river. Send us an ambulance, code three."

If the code for emergency didn't spur her into the action, the urgency in Andy's voice should have. But the anxiety that laced his tone vibrated through her body, freezing her at the console. She couldn't shut out the memories of the last time she'd heard panic come across the air. Her fingers hovered over the keys, refusing to obey the commands she'd been trained to execute. She slammed her eyes shut, trying to reset her brain, but that only made the images more stark. Her stomach protested the violent image of the deputy being hit, dragged, and then trapped—to die beneath a large-box truck. She swallowed hard, trying to contain the bile that rose in her throat—the acidity making her mouth water.

Raised voices continued spewing information over the radio, and though she couldn't discern their words from the buzzing in her head, somehow she knew they required—no, demanded—a response.

"Dispatch, did you copy my last?"

"Dispatch?"

"Hillary?" Olivia's voice, soft and filled with worry, came over her headset and broke through the haze.

Hillary blinked. Then she spun in her chair and called out to the fire-department dispatcher to send an ambulance and water-rescue units to her scene. She turned the other way and met Ann's eyes. As if reading the panic in them, Ann popped out of her chair and crossed quickly to her.

"What do you have?"

"K-9 was chasing a suspect, and he jumped off the railroad trestle rather than face the dog." The brief summary didn't explain why her hands trembled and a cold sweat coated her skin.

Ann dropped a hand on her shoulder, and Hillary hoped she couldn't feel her trembling. "Are you good?"

Swallowing again against the nausea that threatened to overtake her adrenaline, she shook her head. "I don't think so." She might not have admitted that to anyone else, but a part of her still trusted Ann to take care of her.

"Okay. I'll relieve you."

"I—" She couldn't get up—couldn't let everyone else in the room see her give up.

"Just give me your headset and step out. Come back when you're composed."

"Thanks, Ann." She pulled off the headset and handed it over, moving quickly out of the way. As she crossed the room, she stared at the floor, not wanting to see either pity or judgment in her coworkers' eyes.

She sat outside on the bench in front of the building and stared at her hands until they stopped shaking. As her fear subsided, anger moved in. She prided herself on her ability and professionalism, and she'd failed in both this evening. All said, the delay in response for the ambulance had probably been only seconds, but it had felt like a lifetime to her.

By the time she'd calmed down enough to return, Ann had swapped another dispatcher in on her radio.

"Thanks. I'm good," she said as she picked up her headset from the desk where Ann had left it.

Her coworker glanced behind her as if asking for permission. She didn't have to look to know he was checking with Ann.

"She told me to stay up here."

"Until I got back."

"For the rest of the shift." Apology graced his features, but he didn't move from behind the computer.

She nodded and headed for Ann's desk. Maybe Ann just needed reassurance that she was okay.

Ann held up a hand as Hillary approached. "I don't want to hear it. He's there for the remainder of the night."

"I need to work." Hillary appealed to the part of Ann that used to know her intimately. She had to know that Hillary's brain would torture her less if she kept it busy.

"Then go answer the phones. You're not working a radio anymore this shift. And I'm only letting you do that much because I know you. I should be sending you home."

Hillary resisted the urge to stomp across the room and fling herself into a chair. But she did drop into it a little heavily and had to steady herself with her feet so the wheels didn't send it out from under her.

Two hours later, she'd fought through a dozen or so legitimate phone calls and a handful of curious inquiries about the pursuit from earlier in the evening, spurred by the news coverage it garnered. She gave out the number for the sheriff's department representative and shared only what wasn't considered confidential—that the suspect was no longer at large and thus there was no cause for concern about public safety.

When the operator for the next shift arrived, Hillary passed along all pertinent information and gladly surrendered her post.

As she stepped out the front door, she stopped. Olivia was on her way up the sidewalk, her head down. Olivia cut a striking figure in her uniform, and the memory of their kiss, still fresh in her mind, made the vision even more potent. Her hair had been semi-restrained in a high ponytail that swung from side to side as she walked. Her navy-blue pants contrasted nicely with the lighter-blue shirt, but it was her broad shoulders and compact body inside the clothes that drew Hillary's eyes. Her usually trim torso and waist looked bulkier with the Kevlar vest and various pieces of equipment attached to her gun belt.

When Olivia looked up and saw her, she stopped too, only a few feet away. "Hey."

"You didn't have to come." Hillary's voice sounded unusually breathy, and she wanted to attribute it to her rough day rather than Olivia's appearance.

Olivia closed the distance between them and pulled her close. Hillary melted into her, but the firm planes of the thick vest under Olivia's shirt kept the embrace from feeling intimate.

"I'm sorry I couldn't get here sooner." Olivia stroked her hands down Hillary's back.

"I'm sure you have better things to do on the scene."

"I was on the perimeter. Once the robber went for a swim, they didn't need me anymore. I grabbed a couple of the pending calls, then dropped my car at the station for the next shift and came straight here."

"You weren't where I sent you." Accusing Olivia almost took her mind off what really bothered her. She pulled back and glared at her.

Olivia gave her a small smile and a shrug. She'd heard Hillary's relief dispatcher send someone else on the missing person, so she wasn't concerned with that call.

"What if something had happened to you? I wouldn't have known where you were."

"Andy and the other guys knew. And you could have located my car." Their patrol cars were equipped with locators that tracked their vehicles and driving speeds. "Besides, nothing happened to me. Are you okay?"

"I froze," she whispered.

"Oh, honey." Olivia cupped the back of her head and eased her close again. "Please, tell me you'll go talk to someone now."

She started to shake her head, but Ann spoke from behind her.

"She no longer has a choice."

"What?" Hillary moved out of Olivia's arms but kept hold of her hand.

"I'm mandating you to counseling." When Ann's eyes flicked down to their joined hands, Olivia released her and took a step away.

"Ann—"

"That wasn't a request."

"You can't—I trusted—"

"I'm sorry, Hill. I have a duty to this agency."

Hillary bristled at the familiar shortening of her name. She wanted to shout at Ann—to tell her she couldn't talk to her like a friend and threaten her with duty in the same sentence. But some part of her responded to the shift in their relationship, and she stayed silent.

"Call Advocacy Services tomorrow and make an appointment."

"Okay." At this point, Ann would treat resistance as insubordination.

Ann glanced once more at Olivia, then nodded and walked past them toward her car.

Hillary waited until Ann slid inside and closed the door before cursing under her breath.

"Let me take you home," Olivia said.

Hillary nodded, too tired to pretend she didn't want to be with Olivia right now. She'd retrieve her car later. Olivia lifted Hillary's bag from her shoulder and slung it over her own before guiding her toward her Jeep.

CHAPTER ELEVEN

"Forgive the mess." Hillary dropped her keys on the counter and led Olivia inside. She'd cleaned over the weekend, so the place wasn't dirty, but she would have straightened up for guests.

"Not a problem. You should see my place."

Was it odd that they hadn't yet visited each other's home? She'd been to Jake's house at least a handful of times in the first month she'd known him, picking him up for various mutual outings. Had they avoided the intimacy of being alone in one of their apartments together?

"Do you want me to stay for a bit?" Olivia still stood close behind her.

"Would you mind?"

"Sure. Okay if I get out of some of this gear?"

"Yes."

She watched Olivia take off her gun belt and restrained herself from helping. She wanted to undress Olivia in the worst way. Instead, she took the belt from Olivia and hung it on a hook by the door. Olivia untucked, then opened the front of her uniform shirt. She slipped it off her shoulders, then released the Velcro securing her Kevlar vest. Soon, she was left in only her uniform pants and a white T-shirt, which had wrinkled and clung to her under the weight of the heavy vest.

When she reached back and released her hair, it fell to her shoulders and Hillary barely contained a groan. Though she'd thought Olivia was sexy in her uniform, she was positively devastating half out of it. She laid the rest of Olivia's gear on the floor by the door. As she turned back to her they stood so close that Hillary's hands came up automatically to rest on Olivia's waist. Olivia grasped her shoulders, and for a moment Hillary thought she might push her away, but she just held her there.

Hillary met her eyes, searching for some clue as to what she wanted in this moment. The naked desire she found there mirrored her own feelings. But she didn't want the awkward conversation that was sure to follow another kiss, so she took a step back.

"Thank you for driving me." She crossed to the sofa. "Want to sit down?"

Olivia settled on the other end of the couch. Hillary squashed the desire to ask her to move closer. She missed the circle of her arms. The space between them seemed tangible, and she'd felt closer to her in the very public front of her workplace than here alone.

A knock at the door offered momentary salvation from the awkwardness. But since she suspected Ann stood on the other side, her relief wouldn't last long.

She glanced through the peephole. "It's Ann."

Olivia stood. "It would be less complicated if she didn't see me here."

By all means, let's not complicate things. Hillary stifled the sarcastic remark and nodded toward the hallway. "Bedroom's on the left." Olivia nodded and headed that way. "No snooping." Hillary hoped that teasing her would dispel some of the tension that suddenly flared between them.

"Why? Do you have something in the drawer of your nightstand I shouldn't see?"

"Doesn't everybody?"

Olivia laughed as she stepped inside the bedroom and closed the door behind her. Hiding in the bedroom was a coward's move, but she didn't feel like facing Ann's protective nature or the jealousy she felt whenever she saw the two of them interact. She'd battled it earlier when Ann had found them embracing outside. Her words and actions spoke of a professional relationship, but the way her eyes had lingered on Hillary and the intimacy of her tone indicated deeper feelings.

She eased the door open so she could hear the exchange from the other room, ignoring a twinge of guilt.

"What are you doing here?" The chill in Hillary's voice comforted Olivia.

"I wanted to check on you."

"I'm fine." The voices weren't getting any closer, so Olivia guessed Hillary hadn't let Ann come too far into the apartment.

"Your girlfriend really tried to ride to your rescue today, huh?"

"She's not—she's a friend."

"That's not how it looked. People are talking."

"I don't give a damn what people say. I never have."

"I'm trying to be your friend here." Ann's injured tone indicated Hillary's dig had hit home.

"My friend who mandated me to counseling?"

"Okay, yeah, that was me being your boss. It's complicated. You know that. But your boss wouldn't be here now." The shuffling sound that accompanied Ann's pause made Olivia picture her moving closer to Hillary. Did she reach out to her? If so, how did Hillary react? "She's here, isn't she?"

Hillary didn't say anything.

"Her Jeep is sitting in front of your apartment building. You two aren't exactly being stealthy about this thing."

"There's no *thing*."

"Then why are her gun belt and half of her uniform lying on your floor? What are you doing, Hill? I thought you didn't want to hide in your relationships anymore. You can't really believe Sheriff Dennis's little girl will come out as the poster-child for cop-dykes and you'll live happily ever after."

The truth in Ann's venomous words sent a jolt of pain through Olivia's chest. She could picture the injured expression on Hillary's face and wished she could rush out there and say something to erase it. But she had nothing to offer, so she stayed hidden behind the door.

"I'm not looking for a relationship," Hillary said. Olivia strained to hear the nuance behind her words. Was she not looking for a relationship at all? Or didn't she want one with Olivia?

"If you're looking for casual sex—you can find it in a lot of less complicated places than Olivia Dennis."

"You should go."

"Fine. I'm leaving. But as your boss I have to tell you not to come back to work until you've seen a counselor."

Olivia waited until she heard the front door close. By the time she reached the living room, Hillary had settled back on the couch. She'd leaned over, shoulders slumped, and rested her elbows on her thighs.

"Are you okay?" Olivia lingered in the doorway.

Hillary sighed. "Not really."

"Hey." Olivia moved to her side. "Don't let her get to you."

"It's not just her. I mean, I'm not thrilled about being mandated to counseling. But it's all just catching up with me, I guess."

"She's right, you know. I have nothing to offer you."

"And I assume you also overheard me tell her I'm not expecting anything from you."

Olivia nodded, trying and failing to ignore the flood of disappointment. She should be relieved that Hillary didn't want more than friendship. "I wish I could—"

"Can we table that discussion for now? It's been a long day and I want to go to bed."

"Absolutely." Olivia stood. "I'll leave you to it."

"Would you stay?" Hillary grabbed her hand before she could step away. "Isn't that something a friend would do after a tough day?"

Olivia fought the urge to stroke Hillary's cheek in an effort to ease the uncertain vulnerability in her expression. "Yes. A friend would." She took Hillary's hand and guided her toward the bedroom.

❖

Olivia jerked awake, disoriented. When Hillary kicked her calf, she realized what must have woken her. Behind her, Hillary moaned and thrashed her legs. Olivia rolled over and gently touched Hillary's shoulder, not wanting to startle her.

"Hillary," she whispered.

Hillary nuzzled against her, murmuring something Olivia couldn't understand. Though she knew it wasn't smart, Olivia let Hillary snuggle closer. Hillary draped her arm across her waist and pushed her hand under Olivia's T-shirt. When her fingers touched skin, Olivia cursed herself for giving in when Hillary insisted she sleep in the bed instead of on the couch. She'd told herself she could do so platonically. But the thrill of Hillary's hand against her bare stomach proved her a liar. She forced herself to lie still as Hillary settled again, not wanting to wake her.

She'd successfully endured several more minutes of torture when Hillary cried out and twitched. She caressed Hillary's forehead and murmured what she hoped was soothing nonsense. Hillary grabbed a handful of Olivia's shirt as she stirred. Olivia fought not to cover a groan. Hillary was clearly in distress, so Olivia shouldn't find the firm tug of fabric so sexy. But her rebellious brain conjured up images of Hillary yanking the shirt over her head.

As sleep and confusion cleared out of Hillary's eyes, she flushed and tried to pull back quickly. "I'm sorry." Clearly she wasn't as pleased as Olivia to find herself in her arms.

"Nightmare?" Olivia kept her arm around her, not letting her get too far away.

She nodded. "Damn it."

"Worse than the others?"

"Not particularly." She shifted against Olivia, obviously trying once more to put some distance between them.

"Be still, woman."

"Woman?" Hillary chuckled.

"Yeah." Olivia pressed her hand to Hillary's head and guided her back to her shoulder. "Stop squirming and tell me what's going on."

"I just thought maybe I wouldn't have a nightmare tonight."

"Why not?"

"Because, I—you—"

Comprehension dawned. "Oh. I think that whole 'I don't have bad dreams when I lie next to you' thing only happens in those sappy romance novels you like."

"Then why—" She stuttered to a stop and lowered her eyes.

Olivia smiled. "Go ahead and finish that question."

"I—it's just, if I'm going to have them anyway, I should tough it out on my own, I guess. Instead of making you stay here and disturbing you, too."

"If that's what you want, I'll go." But she didn't make a move to leave. "I may not be able to stop the dreams, but I can be here to hold you after you wake. Maybe that's what matters."

Hillary nodded against Olivia's chest and rested her hand back on her stomach, over her T-shirt this time.

"Does that help at all?"

"Yes."

"Still want me to leave?"

"No."

"Try to go back to sleep."

"How did you know I read romance novels?"

"I'm not sure I can answer that question without sounding creepy."

Hillary waited.

Olivia sighed. "You read during your downtime at work."

Hillary lifted her head and looked at her. "You're right. That's a little creepy."

"There's not much else to do at that desk than watch the monitors." She pressed Hillary's head back to her chest. "Now close your eyes and go back to sleep."

A few minutes later, as Hillary's breathing evened out, Olivia admitted to herself that she'd watched those monitors much more than was necessary.

❖

Hillary rolled over, shifting unimpeded to the empty pillow beside her. She laid her cheek against the linens that still smelled faintly of Olivia. Before she could wonder if Olivia had left, she heard the sound of pans banging in the kitchen. She slid out of bed and, after raking her tongue over her teeth, detoured to the bathroom for a quick brush and a swig of mouthwash.

She found Olivia in the kitchen, keeping watch over two frying pans on the stove. She leaned over her shoulder to check out the contents. Shredded hash browns filled the pan on the left, and on the right, bacon shared space with four eggs.

"How do you like your eggs?" Olivia asked.

"Over well. I can't stand that runny stuff." She jumped when the toaster popped up.

"Grab that, will you?"

She added the two slices to a stack already on a plate and surveyed the spread. "You really like breakfast."

"You must, too. You had all the provisions here, already." Olivia slid two eggs onto a plate, added a pile of hash browns and three strips of bacon, and handed it over.

"Turn all of that off and join me." Hillary settled on one of the chairs at the bistro table on the other side of the counter and took a bite of hash browns. "Very good. Thank you. You didn't have to do all this."

"Like you said, I like breakfast. Coffee?" Olivia pulled the carafe from the machine.

"God bless you. Yes, please."

After pouring them each a cup, Olivia sat down across from her. "Are you going to call for an appointment?"

"Yes."

"When?"

Hillary dropped her fork, oddly pleased when it clattered loudly. "I already have one supervisor."

Olivia didn't say anything. She slowly set her own fork down, took her napkin from her lap, and laid it on the table beside her plate.

Hillary sighed. "I'm sorry. You're concerned, and I'm being a bitch."

"I understand—"

"Please, don't be so nice. You stayed last night, then cooked for me this morning, and I jumped down your throat for being concerned. I just—I know I have to do it. Ann mandated it. I need space to handle it myself." Hillary took a deep breath and let it out slowly. When had she lost control of her life as well as her temper?

Olivia pushed through the door of Pacey's and, after a quick scan of the nearly full dining room, headed for the back booth. She slid into the seat opposite Frankie just in time to hear her order.

"I'll have two eggs over easy, wheat toast, and turkey bacon."

"Coffee, please," Olivia said when the server turned to her expectantly.

Frankie stared at her until the waiter walked away. "Just coffee?"

"Yep."

"But you love breakfast. I've seen you order the steak and eggs fresh off a workout."

Olivia shrugged. "I've already eaten."

"You already—why would you have breakfast when you knew we were meeting today?"

"I cooked for Hillary." She sat back and waited for the inevitable inquisition. She didn't feel guilty in the least at how much she enjoyed Frankie's obvious shock.

Frankie leaned closer. "Explain."

"She had a rough night at work last night so I took her home." Olivia went on to briefly outline the details of the call and Hillary's reaction.

"Her boss is her ex?"

Olivia laughed. "It's good to know you're focusing on the important parts of the story."

"I heard the rest of it. But that's the interesting part. Well, that and the fact that you spent the night with her. But I know nothing happened there."

"How do you know?"

"Because you're too guilt-ridden to just be with her and enjoy it."

"It's not about guilt. Okay. Not only that. How long do you think I could do that before my family found out?"

"Not long. Maybe that wouldn't be a bad thing. You've been trying to come up with a way to tell them."

"That's not fair to them or to Hillary." The thought of reducing her relationship with Hillary to a mere physical encounter bothered her. "I like her. And I respect her."

Frankie shrugged. "I've had sex with guys I respected."

"And now you're married to my brother. So let's not talk about *your* sex life."

Frankie grinned and Olivia couldn't help but join her. Frankie's infectious happiness had always drawn Olivia to her.

"In fact, let's not talk about sex at all." She glanced around, and though they'd kept their voices down, she didn't want to tempt fate.

"Okay. Then tell me how it feels to be back in the field. How's the new sergeant?"

"Gilleland? I like her. She's smart and fair. The others definitely respect her. And that says something for a female sergeant."

"Andy likes her. He's told me before how the guys will rag on a woman or spread rumors about her if they don't like her. They don't do that to her, so I guess she must be doing okay."

"And they say women are catty." Olivia waited while the server delivered Frankie's breakfast. "Much as I hated going to Five-C, I guess it wasn't so bad."

"Yeah. You met Hillary." Before Olivia could protest, Frankie said, "*Made a new friend.* Got a new boss that you like. And you get to work with your brother."

"As long as that investigation doesn't follow me much longer, I'll be okay." She added creamer to her coffee.

"Did Gilleland say anything about it?"

Olivia shrugged. "I don't think she's forgotten it, but she seems to be giving me a fair shot."

"It'll all work out."

"I don't know about all of it. But things are definitely looking up from a couple of months ago." She leaned back in the booth and considered where she'd been. She'd faced her father, scared yet defiant, as she told him she'd been put on administrative leave. She'd gotten through that, exonerated and possibly stronger for it. So why didn't she think she could survive coming out? The very idea still made her heart race and panic sing through her blood. "Chickenshit," she muttered.

"What?" Frankie paused, a pile of eggs clinging precariously to the tines of her fork and dangling over her plate.

"Nothing." She sipped her now-lukewarm coffee and wished it didn't feel like a reflection on her own tepid courage.

CHAPTER TWELVE

Hillary flipped the page of a magazine whose breaking news had happened six months ago. She tried not to glance at the screen of her phone again. She guessed five minutes had elapsed since her last time check, but they'd been five very long ones. Now twenty minutes past her appointment time, she debated leaving. But she couldn't go back to work without a signed mandate slip. After breakfast with Olivia, she'd called the agency-mandated counselor to set up an appointment. Luckily, they'd had a cancellation and could get her in that afternoon. She wasn't in a hurry for this session, but the sooner she got it over with the sooner she could get back to work.

She'd just reached the end of the magazine and tossed it aside in frustration when the door to the inner office opened. The man who filled the doorway wasn't at all what she'd expected. His broad shoulders seemed to nearly touch each side of the threshold, and his shaved head was only inches from contacting the top.

"Hello, Hillary. I'm Roderick Stein."

"Doctor Stein—"

"Not a doctor. Mr. Stein or, preferably, Roderick." He extended his hand and she let his engulf hers, surprised by the rasp of his callused palm. He stepped aside and held the door for her as she went inside.

"Come in. Make yourself comfortable."

The small room felt homier than she'd expected. Instead of overhead lights, the only illumination came from floor lamps in opposite corners and one on an end table. Two leather chairs formed a triangle with a cream-colored sofa.

"On the sofa?" she asked.

"Wherever you're comfortable."

She sat in one of the chairs, wondering what meaning the therapist would glean from her choice.

"Before we start, I'll tell you a bit about my background. I finished my degree in clinical psychology while serving in the army. I spent ten years at Fort Campbell counseling returning veterans before taking this job. I've worked with police and firefighters all across the state following stress incidents large and small."

He glanced at her, seemingly waiting for a response, so she forced a tight smile. He flipped through the papers she'd filled out in his waiting room, then set them aside.

"Even though you're a mandate, what you say to me stays between us. I report back only your attendance or lack thereof and whether you're fit to return to duty. Understand?"

"Yes."

"Good. Why don't you tell me about why you're here."

"You said it, I'm a mandate."

"Yes, but what led you to that point?"

She took a moment to let her urge to be difficult pass, reminding herself that she had to jump this hurdle. She grasped the arms of the chair, focusing on the cool leather under her palms, then swallowed her panic and began to talk about the day of the accident.

He interjected questions occasionally, and she soon realized he was pacing her through the event, assessing her reactions, and steering her toward the emotions beneath the story. He was uncomfortably good at maintaining eye contact. At certain points in her tale, she preferred to look at the lamp in the corner. She skipped over her nightmares, mood swings, and moments of panic since that day. But she couldn't get around telling him about the search for the robbery suspects that had led to the mandate. Finally, she reached the point where she'd shamefully surrendered her radio to Ann, admitting she'd frozen when she should have acted.

"How are you sleeping?"

She stared at him, surprised by the shift in topic. She'd expected some reaction to her last revelation. "Um, intermittently."

"I can prescribe something—"

"No."

"There's no shame in—"

"No. Thank you."

"Working will be easier if you're well rested."

"Are you going to let me go back to work?" She leaned forward, resting her elbows on the arms of the chair.

"Not just yet."

"Then I need to try it my way first."

"How has your way been working for you?"

She didn't respond.

"If you want to hold off on drugs for now, that's fine. But this will go a lot more smoothly if you speak openly and honestly with me."

She wondered how many of his clients fell for that line. She'd been forced here, and now she was supposed to believe she had the control in this situation. She didn't think she'd been in control of anything since the day she'd heard the panicked cries of the officer in her headset. But for now, she didn't have any choice but to play along.

"Neighbor reports strange smells and people coming and going at all hours of the night."

Olivia acknowledged the dispatcher's transmission and turned left on the nearest street. She arrived on scene just behind Andy, who'd been dispatched with her.

The exterior of the house needed some love but wasn't in horrible shape. Pressure-washing the siding and slapping a coat of paint on the porch would make a world of difference. Based on the neighbor's description, Olivia was already thinking meth. Especially considering the rise in overdoses in the county in recent months.

As the drug made its way into small towns, law enforcement had found labs in houses ranging from low to middle income, even occasionally in the trunk of a car. As unemployment rose in small towns, people who might not normally consider drugs as a source of income were turning to meth to survive and provide for their families. Unfortunately, due to the volatile chemicals involved, they couldn't choose a more dangerous alternative.

She followed Andy to the door, letting him take the lead. She glanced around while he both knocked and rang the bell. At this point they didn't have enough to enter the house without an invite, but at the very least they could fill out a field interview sheet and pass the information on to the drug task force. If they found credence in the neighbor's suspicions they would open an investigation that could eventually lead to a search warrant.

The door swung open and a skinny boy she'd put somewhere around seven years old stared back at them. His disheveled hair didn't look like it had been washed in days. The front of his shirt wore the remnants of more than one meal.

The inside of the house obviously hadn't received any more attention than the boy's appearance. Fast-food wrappers covered the coffee table, and a visible layer of thick dust blanketed every surface.

"Hey, buddy. Are your parents home?" Andy asked, taking a step forward, but the boy still held the door and he inched it closed, as if pulling it to him for safety.

"No strangers inside." The boy continued looking at them calmly, seeming almost curious.

"That's good. It's important to know that. But we're not strangers. We're the police and we're here to help."

"No strangers." Now his brown eyes looked sad.

"Hey, what's your name, guy?" Olivia squatted down to look him in the eye.

"Manuel."

"Okay, Manuel. We don't have to come inside. We can talk right here. Are your parents here?"

He nodded.

"Can you go get them so we can talk to them?"

He shook his head.

"Why not?"

"They're working."

"What do they do?"

"They cook for people."

Olivia glanced at Andy and lowered her voice. "Probable cause?"

"Unless they're bakers."

"I don't hear any noise from the kitchen. Are they in there now?"

"Nope. Downstairs."

"They cook in the basement?"

He nodded.

She looked at Andy again, sensing he was as ready as she was to rush inside. How much more did they need? Andy gave a subtle head shake.

"Listen, Manuel, I really need to talk to your daddy about something. Maybe we could just wait in the foyer while you go get him." Persuading a seven-year-old to let them inside was iffy, but she'd try anything right now. Everything about this situation made her Spidey-sense tingle, and she wasn't leaving until she found out what was going on in that house.

Before Manuel had a chance to answer, footsteps sounded behind a door at the far end of the entryway. As the door opened, Olivia caught sight of a man shoving something down the front of his pants. She registered the bundle of plastic baggies inside a larger clear bag in the same instant he spotted them.

She didn't look to Andy for permission again before she flew into the room, touching her hand to Manuel's head on her way by to reassure herself of his safety. The man took off, presumably toward a back door, but she had a head start on him. She tackled him as he reached the kitchen, landing on his back and riding him across the dirty linoleum like a sled.

She cuffed him and hauled him to his feet as Andy called for backup. Olivia took her prisoner and Manuel outside while Andy watched the door to the basement. She pushed her guy against her car and searched him. She threw the bag of drugs, a pocketknife, a roll of money, and a revolver into the trunk of her car and shoved him into the backseat. Then she sat on the curb with Manuel and waited while Andy, another deputy, and Sergeant Gilleland cleared the house.

"That was cool," Manuel said quietly.

"What?"

"You looked like a cop on television."

She chuckled. "You liked that, huh?"

He nodded.

"How old are you, Manuel?"

"Ten."

She stared at him, wondering if he owed his small stature to genetics or neglect.

"What's going to happen to me now?" His voice shook and his chin trembled.

"We'll call someone to help you figure that out."

"Children's Services," he said with a solemn nod.

"They've been here before?"

"Yes. I stayed at a foster home for almost a year until Mama got better. Do you think they'll let me take some of my stuff this time?"

"Maybe. I can ask." Her heart broke for him. She'd never in her life felt as if she didn't own anything that truly belonged to her.

They were still sitting there when Gilleland and Andy led two men and a woman out of the house in cuffs.

"Mama." Manuel jumped up and would have raced across the lawn if Olivia hadn't quickly grabbed him around the waist and held him back. As the suspects passed them, Manuel sobbed quietly. But when Olivia put her hand on his shoulder, he pulled away defiantly.

An hour later, she'd taken him inside to pack a bag and introduced him to the DCS case worker. Long after they drove away in the nondescript government sedan, she could still see the clean trails of his tears down his grungy face. She sat in the driver's seat of her patrol car with her laptop turned toward her, filling out her report.

"Make sure you add a one-oh-eight to that paperwork." Sergeant Gilleland leaned against the open door of her car.

Olivia's fingers twitched, and the word she'd been about to type became a jumble of letters. She bit her lower lip and tapped the backspace key. She'd hoped she could get by without the use-of-force form. After all, she'd barely touched the guy. Gravity did most of the work.

"Please, don't send me back to Five-C." She met Gilleland's eyes, hoping her expression conveyed how badly she did not want to be in trouble again. Gilleland stared back, unflinching, as if assessing something about Olivia.

"This isn't that kind of offense. I talked to Andy. You acted in accordance with department policy and with regard for that boy's safety. I'll sign off on it. But we still need to do the paperwork."

Olivia nodded, still tense with worry.

"Relax. If I thought you'd done anything questionable, I wouldn't let you off that easy. You only tackled the guy. You're not even getting the rest of the shift off for that."

She glanced over her shoulder at the guy still sulking in the backseat of her car. She'd spend most of her shift doing paperwork on the whole incident and booking this guy in. But at least he wouldn't cost her more time off the job. As glad as she was to get him off the street, she looked forward even more to seeing the other deputies book Manuel's parents. Their charges for manufacturing and distributing carried the added enhancement of committing their crimes in the presence of a child. Even if the DA gave them a plea deal, endangering Manuel's welfare would cost them a significant number of years added onto their sentences.

"You're not riding calls while playing on the phone, are you?" Hillary asked as she answered the phone.

"Of course not." Olivia acted like she was insulted at the suggestion.

"It's not like it doesn't happen."

Sometimes during a heavy workload, a deputy would delay checking in from a call because they knew the dispatcher was waiting to send them on the next one right away. If they wanted to get something to eat, use the restroom, or make a phone call, they would just stay assigned to the previous call, or "ride the call," a little longer and go do other things. The dispatchers knew it happened, but during periods of high call volume, they hated it when deputies did it excessively.

"I'm at booking, but I just missed the commissioner going on his dinner break so I'm stuck here waiting for him to come back."

Prior to entry into the county jail system, every detainee appeared before a judicial commissioner, endowed with the authority of a judge, who conducted a probable-cause hearing and set bail. Olivia's drug dealer and Manuel's parents all sat in holding cells awaiting their turn before the commissioner. She hated to even think about them bonding out, but at least they wouldn't be getting Manuel back anytime soon.

No matter how bad the backup, the commissioner wouldn't miss a meal break. So even though two other detainees were ahead of hers, he'd just notified them that he would be unavailable for thirty minutes. Andy and the other deputy had gone outside for some air, but Olivia sneaked away to one of the officer workrooms. The rooms, just big enough for a couple of computer workstations and uncomfortable chairs, had been set up for deputies to complete paperwork prior to booking.

"How's your shift going?"

"Okay. Considering I'm without my favorite dispatcher."

Hillary's soft laugh through the phone felt amazingly intimate. "Well, I'm working on getting back. When I called for an appointment they had an opening earlier today."

"Yeah? How did that go?"

"It was fine. I'd rather not talk about it right now."

"Sure." She shouldn't be hurt that Hillary didn't want to confide in her. She was struggling for what to say next when she saw Andy coming down the hall toward her room. "I hate to cut this short, but I should go see if we're getting close."

"Oh, of course." Did Hillary sound disappointed?

"I'll call or text you later." Olivia left things noncommittal, though she knew she'd be fighting the urge to send a text or make a call all night.

"Would you like to stop by after shift?"

"Your apartment?"

Hillary chuckled. "Where else?"

"Yes—um, sure. If it won't be too late."

"I'll still be awake."

"See you then." She hung up the phone just as Andy walked in.

"What are you smiling about?" He dropped into the chair next to her.

"Nothing." She shoved her phone in her pocket and spun back toward the computer.

"The commissioner just got back, and there's one more ahead of us. You did good with that kid."

"Thanks."

"You ever think about kids of your own someday?"

"Andy—"

"We never talk about this. I do—Frankie and I, we want to have kids. But we're young, right? We've got time."

"Sure. You guys will be great parents." Frankie's sister had three kids, and Olivia had seen her with them enough to know she'd be an awesome mother.

"So what about you? You ever going to give a guy the time of day and settle down?"

"Come on, man. I get enough of this from Mama." She stood and paced across the room. For obvious reasons, she hadn't considered kids a real alternative for her in a long time. She didn't want to lie to him, so her only hope was to distract him.

"You're going to be a great aunt. And I can't wait to see you with my kids."

She turned, surprised by the warmth in his voice. She loved Andy and had no doubt he felt the same. And deep down she knew they were loyal and protective of each other against all others. But neither of them made many emotional declarations.

"I'd like them to have some cousins to play with like we did growing up." Between her father's six siblings and her mother's three, they'd never lacked for playmates as children.

"I—I don't know if that's going to happen." She gave him the only truth she could.

"Just think about it. Unless you want to go it alone, which I can totally respect, you should think about relaxing your dating standards a little."

"Dating advice, little brother?" She laughed. "And it's aim lower?"

"Not too low. But how do you know if any of these guys are the one—"

"The one? Frankie's really rubbing off on you, huh?"

"Okay, make fun, but I'm just trying to look out for you."

"Believe me, I want what you have." *A loving wife.* "More than you can know. It just hasn't happened yet. I'll know when I find it. And you can tell that to all your buddies on the force who ask you to fix them up with me." He'd learned long ago not to bring her the names when it happened, but she had no doubt it still did.

"Don't worry. I know the company line on that subject."

"See that you stick to it." She tapped him on the shoulder. "Let's go lock these scumbags up."

CHAPTER THIRTEEN

Hillary opened the door to Olivia and couldn't hide her smile. She stepped back and let Olivia come inside. She'd apparently stopped by her place and changed after shift. Instead of her uniform, she wore khaki shorts and a navy T-shirt.

"I just opened a bottle of red. You want a glass?" She crossed to the kitchen and pulled a new glass from the set hanging under the cabinet. While waiting for Olivia, she'd lit some candles and opened the wine. She figured this might be the closest she came to the meditation Roderick Stein had recommended.

"Sure."

She refilled her glass and poured one for Olivia as well, emptying the bottle.

"You just opened that?"

"I may have a bit of a head start on you." She knew what Stein would say about drinking right now. When she searched Olivia's face she saw caution but no judgment.

"It's been a long day, so you'll forgive me if I don't hurry to catch up." Olivia sipped her wine before turning toward the living room.

"Of course not. If you'd rather go home, I understand." Hillary followed.

"I went home. Changed. Even thought about calling to get a rain check from you." Olivia settled on the sofa, making it clear she wasn't going anywhere.

"But?" Hillary sat next to her, ignoring the adjacent chair, though it was the safer choice.

Olivia set her glass on the coffee table in front of them and leaned toward her. "But I wanted to see you."

"Are we playing with fire?" Hillary didn't mean to angle toward her as well.

"What do you mean?"

"You know what I mean." When she lifted her eyes to Olivia's she couldn't look away. "I thought we were going to be friends."

"We are friends. And I don't have very many of those." Despite her words, the heat in Olivia's gaze didn't cool.

"And I don't live in closets with my friends. Anymore."

"I don't want you to." The agony in Olivia's voice made room for just enough logic to cloud Hillary's arousal. She pressed her hands against her thighs to keep from reaching out for Olivia. "I want to kiss you so bad," Olivia whispered.

"That won't make the reasons go away."

"Would it help us forget them for long enough?"

"It might." Hillary sat back. She'd invited Olivia here tonight intending to ask her to spend the night again. She'd be lying if she didn't admit a part of her had imagined a less platonic sleepover this time. "But unfortunately, I'm not looking for 'long enough.'"

"Then I guess it's time for me to go." Olivia stood.

"You don't have to."

"I think it's best."

Hillary followed her toward the door. When Olivia reached it, she turned and Hillary took a step back. "I wish I was brave enough—"

"Please, don't. I'm not asking anything from you. If you have things to figure out, you need to do it for yourself, not for me. We're friends. That doesn't need to change. I'll see you on Saturday at the park?"

Olivia nodded, pulled the door open, and left. Hillary closed the door behind her, then leaned her forehead against it.

"Idiot," she muttered. How many times in high school had she dreamed of a shot with Olivia Dennis? And now she could have it. All she had to do was abandon the lessons she'd learned in the ten years since then.

❖

"Come on." Hillary grunted as she pushed the dresser in her bedroom back against the wall. She probably should have pulled the drawers full of clothes out before she tried to move it, especially since sorting through the clothes and weeding out what she didn't wear anymore was her next task.

She'd just finished moving and vacuuming under every piece of furniture in her apartment. This afternoon, after her second appointment with Roderick Stein, she would tackle the kitchen cabinets, clean the oven, and mop all the floors.

She opened the top drawer, scooped out the contents, and threw them on the bed. She picked up the first of far too many pairs of sweatpants, examined them, and tossed them aside. They were her oldest pair, and normally she might be reluctant to let them go, but today, she was in the mood for cleaning house. The next pair, she folded and placed back in the drawer. By the time she'd finished sorting the contents, a small stack occupied one side of the drawer. She liked seeing the empty space.

She'd called her parents after she'd been mandated to counseling and filled them in on what had been going on. Her mother sounded like she might start crying, but her father's deep voice on the other extension kept both her and Hillary from getting too emotional. She did her best to assuage their worries and explain to them why she couldn't come for a visit since she was going to be off work anyway. A trip would have been preferable to counseling appointments, but it would only prolong the inevitable. She wasn't on vacation; she had to get back to work as soon as possible.

She hung up the phone with a promise to call if she needed to talk and to keep them updated on her progress. She hadn't realized that she'd let over a year and a half slip by since her last visit, and she had plenty of vacation time built up. So, she silently vowed to find time to get out to Texas soon.

❖

"Come out with us tonight." Frankie crawled onto the bed next to Olivia, somehow managing to look comfortable on the white duvet, even in her little black dress. Of course she didn't lay her head on the down pillow lest she mess up her hair.

"I'm already in my pajamas." Olivia pulled the covers over her head.

"Yes, and I know how hard it is to get you out of those flannel pajama pants."

"Shut up." She rolled over and swung her pillow before Frankie could react, satisfied when Frankie failed to duck in time.

"Hey, don't mess up my makeup."

"You're messing up my sleep."

"You weren't sleeping. In fact, I think you jumped in this bed when you heard me knock on the door."

"I did not." She'd gotten into bed not long after she got home from work. She'd left her cell phone in the living room to combat her desire to text Hillary. She hadn't heard from her since she left her apartment two nights before, and her pride wouldn't let her initiate contact. She held onto Hillary's statement about seeing her at the park on Saturday. But she wasn't sure she'd be able to hold off that long.

"Andy is dragging me to that cop bar."

"You married him."

"You owe me one."

"Ha. I owe you nothing." Olivia sat up in indignation. "I went to that party with you two months ago."

"Oh, you mean the one where you ditched me to talk to Hillary O'Neal for half the night."

"I went."

"Maybe you'll meet someone."

Olivia sighed in frustration. "Who am I going to meet at a cop bar full of my coworkers and people who know my family?"

"Surely you can't be the only closeted lesbian cop. Isn't there some kind of secret handshake you can use to identify yourself?"

She groaned and flopped back down on the bed. "Please, give it up."

"You know I can't."

She rolled over and met Frankie's eyes, hoping to convey the seriousness of her words. "I can't listen to this anymore. I'm not looking for someone to hide with. I would feel like I'm looking over my shoulder, just waiting to be found out. How many times do we have to have this conversation?"

"Okay." Frankie climbed out of the bed and stomped toward the hallway. "I won't bring it up again."

"Frankie—"

"No. You're right. I'll respect your decision."

"Oh, Lord."

"I'm going to go enjoy my night out with my husband," Frankie called out just before the front door slammed.

Olivia sighed, pulled the covers back up to her chin, and closed her eyes. Frankie would get over it.

❖

"So, how many times have you seen the shrink?" Jake asked as he set a beer down in front of each of them. Hillary had nabbed them a table while he went to the bar for drinks.

"He's not a shrink. But I've been three times." When he'd called asking her to join him for drinks at the cop bar, she'd agreed, needing distraction from her solitude. Three appointments with Stein in four days had left her emotionally exhausted.

"And got the all-clear to come back." Jake clinked the neck of his bottle against hers. He'd been the second person she'd texted, after Olivia, when she found out the good news.

"I'll be under the headset again by Friday." She still had to see Stein once a week, but at least he'd decided she could return to work.

"That's great. We miss you."

"You mean, you miss the overtime I was pulling."

"Of course. I had to pick up two extra shifts this week."

"You may not be done with that yet. Stein won't clear me for overtime. He says that's not a healthy way to deal with stress."

"Of course not. But we're dispatchers. By nature, we don't do healthy coping." He lifted his beer as if making his point.

"I guess that's the problem." Stein didn't let her get away with just playing along. He'd really made her consider some lifestyle changes. She'd always thought she could handle infinite shifts. She wasn't prone to burn out like some others she'd seen. And while she maybe didn't burn out in the same way, that didn't mean too much work was good for her either. She told herself she volunteered for extra work and holidays so those who had something to go home to could do so.

She'd admitted it was time for her to really figure out what *she* wanted outside of work. She wanted a relationship—a partner. But acknowledging that also meant accepting that Olivia Dennis would not be that person. How was it fair that she had to get over the same crush twice? Only this time was far worse, because she'd come to know Olivia and feared she might be dealing with something deeper than a crush. She wanted to retain their friendship but had no idea how to accomplish that when she couldn't seem to be in the same room without feeling like she might spontaneously combust if she couldn't touch her.

She shook her head, as if she could rattle Olivia loose from her thoughts, and took a big swig of her beer. But the universe wouldn't let her shake Olivia yet, because just as she looked up, Andy and Frankie Dennis walked through the front door.

"Hey, Hill." Jake waved a hand in front of her face.

"What?"

"I'm trying to point out a fox at the bar."

"Sorry, where?" Though some might find it sexist, she loved it when he called women foxes. He'd said that he picked up the term from his grandfather, who used to refer to Jake's grandmother as his foxy lady.

"Brunette on the far end. Blue sweater."

She glanced surreptitiously at the woman. "Nice."

"What were you so engrossed in?" He looked back toward the door, but the Dennises had already moved well into the room.

"I wasn't *engrossed*. Andy Dennis and his wife just came in and I recognized them, that's all."

Jake turned from one side to the other until he located them on the far side of the room. "Do you know his wife?"

"Sort of. I went to school with her, but she was in Olivia's grade. In fact, she was Olivia's best friend."

"And she married her brother. Scandalous."

"No. That's just small-town living."

"The brother's younger, right?"

"Not by much. I was a grade behind them, and he was in the one after me."

He watched the couple a moment longer. "She was a cheerleader in high school, wasn't she?"

"Yes."

He nodded. "I can spot them a mile away."

She laughed. "Frankie and Olivia both were."

"And you were the nerdy dyke who crushed on them."

"I was not nerdy."

"Too late. You already told me you were a band geek."

"Okay. But I didn't crush on them."

"Band geeks always lust after cheerleaders. It's the way of the world." He narrowed his eyes, then grinned at her. "So maybe what you meant was you weren't interested in both of them, just one. Perhaps one Miss Dennis?"

"You can't just make preposterous generalizations about high-school stereotypes and think you have my adolescent years all figured out."

"Yet your face has turned as red as my shirt."

"Shut up."

"Don't look now, but one of your cheerleaders is on her way over here."

"What?" She did look, because that's what one does when someone says "don't look." Frankie was weaving her way through the crowd, their table clearly her destination.

"Can I talk to you for a minute?" Frankie asked as she reached them.

Hillary glanced at Jake. "Didn't you want to go buy that woman at the bar a drink?"

"Oh, yeah. Yes, I did." He stood and held out his chair for Frankie.

"Thank you."

"No problem." He winked at Hillary before he turned away.

"It's good to see you again," Frankie said.

"You too." She had a pretty good idea who Frankie wanted to talk about, but she wouldn't be the one to broach Olivia's name.

"She told me that she *told* you." Frankie glanced around as if checking to see who might overhear them. But the crowd of guys at the table nearest them probably had trouble hearing each other over their own raucous laughter.

"Yes." Frankie looked disappointed that she didn't say more, as if she knew about Hillary's own misgivings and how tempted she was to ignore them. "How much did she tell you?"

"I believe I'm up to speed."

"Great."

"Don't be mad at her. She doesn't have anyone else to talk to about this stuff. It's a lot to keep in, and she's been doing it for a long time."

"I'm not mad." She was glad Olivia had a confidant, but she didn't plan to employ Frankie for the same purpose. "It is what it is."

"I never understand why people say that, because it so rarely *is*. So often there's room for change. In this case, she wants to change."

"Listen, Frankie, you seem like you have her best interest in mind here. But my position is clear, as is hers, so things have reached a somewhat comfortable point, and maybe that's where they should stay." She was anything but comfortable when she was with Olivia, but Frankie didn't need to know that.

"No," Frankie blurted. "With the right encouragement from you—"

"Whoa, I don't need you to finish that sentence." She sighed, wishing the situation were as simple as Frankie wanted to make it. "I don't know how certain people are going to react." She flicked her eyes across the room toward Andy, hoping Frankie understood she included the entire Dennis clan as well. "But I know how she thinks they will, and if she's right, it'll be messy. If I force that on her, she could very likely have repercussions and resentment down the road."

"She needs to change. Or she'll end up miserable someday."

"Regardless. It's not my place to tell her what she needs. So, for now, I'll try to be a friend."

Frankie looked at her a moment longer, then nodded, clearly having reached a satisfactory conclusion, but about what, Hillary wasn't sure. "Okay. Hey, maybe don't tell her we had this conversation. I'm not asking you to lie if she outright asks, just not to volunteer it."

"I can do that." She wouldn't gain anything by screwing with Olivia and Frankie's friendship. Chances were Olivia already knew Frankie had a tendency to meddle, but she seemed to do so with her happiness in mind. So, as far as Hillary was concerned, that was between them.

Chapter Fourteen

Hillary stood in front of Five-C and breathed in the scent of a light summer rain. Her umbrella protected her, but if she weren't about to go inside for an eight-hour shift, she would have lowered it and let the rain wash over her. Though she'd thought of little besides going back to work for four days, now her stomach knotted as she neared the building. But she forced herself forward.

When she held up her agency identification card at security, her palms felt clammy. As she passed the front desk, she wished for Olivia's familiar face instead of the weird look she received from Holt. She went into the conference room for the pre-shift briefing and managed to hold back a groan when she ran into Ann first thing.

"Welcome back." Ann moved into her personal space, and for a moment Hillary thought she might try to hug her.

"Thanks." Hillary thrust out a sheet of paper between them. "I brought you a copy of my release, just in case you had any concerns."

"I'm really glad you talked to someone."

"You didn't give me a choice." She wasn't ready to admit to Ann that she'd needed help.

"We're glad to have you back, all the same."

Hillary nodded and took a seat. She exchanged pleasantries with a couple of her coworkers, then listened quietly while Ann announced the day's assignments. She'd put Hillary on the busiest radio for the entire shift, and Hillary wasn't certain if that was a reward or a test. She stood along with her coworkers and gathered her things to head to the dispatch floor. Ann smiled as she passed, and Hillary gave her the politest smile she could muster.

She entered the dispatch room and stopped, then stepped aside as the others crowded in around her, hurrying to their assignments. The hum of dispatchers questioning callers and answering responders on the radio had been the most familiar sound she'd heard for nine years. The glow of the monitors, the click of the keys, and the sounds of foot pedals keying the microphones had been her constants. She hadn't felt nervous inside this room since her first week here. Even through her training, she'd been confident and excited. But today, her chest constricted, and she was mortified to find the beginning sting of tears burning her eyes.

She pushed her back against the wall, concentrating on the solid feel of it, and practiced the breathing techniques she'd learned from Stein. Surprisingly, some of her anxiety seemed to ease. She ignored Ann's curious look, pushed off from the wall, and went to her assigned console. After she slipped her headset on, she adjusted it and signaled the dispatcher she was due to relieve.

She sat down and quickly logged into the dispatch console and the program that allowed her to access the phone system. Then she pulled up the software used to run queries on licenses and vehicle registrations.

"One-thirteen." A deputy called for her attention.

"One-thirteen." She acknowledged his transmission. She tugged her headset away from her ear and reseated it.

"Can you run one by name and date of birth?" When a deputy stopped someone who professed to have a valid license but didn't actually have the card with them, the dispatcher could check them in the computer by name and date of birth or by social security number.

"Go ahead."

She typed in the information as he gave it. While waiting for the results, she dispatched another deputy on a report of a vehicle parked illegally on the street in front of city hall. Then she gave one-thirteen back his driver information.

With each task she relaxed a little, settling into her routine. After each transmission that didn't result in panic and turmoil, she felt her confidence returning. But the shadow of fear lingered in the back of her mind. She planned to ignore it and work through it. At least the feeling that she might vomit had passed.

❖

"Hey, Holt," Olivia called as she approached the front desk.

"Dennis," he called, as if they were long-lost friends. "Nobody told me you were coming back."

"Oh, I'm not back. Just visiting."

"You missed me that much?"

"I'm not visiting you." She headed toward the dispatch center. She'd sooner take an unpaid leave than man the desk with that guy again. But as soon as she walked onto the dispatch floor and saw Hillary sitting behind a console, she knew she was a liar. She'd probably sit next to Holt for eight hours a day for the chance to spend her lunch breaks with Hillary.

Hillary saw her and smiled. Olivia stopped and stared at her. She'd do almost anything to have that smile directed at her.

"What are you doing here?" Hillary asked as she approached.

"I came to check on you on your first day back."

"So far, so good." The confidence in her tone sounded forced.

"I also brought you lunch, because I owe you about a dozen." She set the foam take-out container on the desk beside Hillary. "It's not homemade."

Hillary lifted the lid and leaned in to catch the aroma that wafted out. "A burger from Pacey's is better than homemade. Do you have time to sit for a minute?" With a few keystrokes, she checked Olivia's status on her screen.

"I'm on a legit meal break. You don't have to check on me." She pulled a chair up next to Hillary's desk.

"Well, I assumed you knew better than to show up at Five-C in front of your dispatcher while riding a call."

"Yeah, that would be dumb." She nodded toward her own dispatcher, who occupied the next console.

"Want some?" Hillary held out the burger she'd just taken a big bite of.

"I'm good. Do you need me to grab that radio for you while you eat?"

"Would you mind?" She started to pull her headset off, then smiled and settled it back over her ear. Yep, Olivia would do anything for that smile.

"Maybe you've lost a step while you were gone."

"In four days?" Hillary nodded. "That tells me a little more about your opinion of my abilities."

"Oh, I have no doubts about your abilities." Olivia spoke without thinking because she wanted to be carefree and flirtatious with Hillary. In fact, she'd never yearned so badly for something so simple.

Hillary inhaled sharply, and when she said Olivia's name, her voice was low and laced with arousal.

Anger shadowed her own visceral reaction to the heat in Hillary's stare. Why couldn't she just enjoy the teasing? She owned the blame; her cowardice kept her from moments like this.

Desperate for distance and a subject change, Olivia stood, then said, "I brought you something else." She held up a CD. She'd put off mentioning it until she was ready to leave because she was unsure of Hillary's reaction.

"What's that?"

"It's an audio recording of the incident—of the radio traffic from the day of the accident. I asked Ann to pull it."

Hillary gave a harsh laugh. "Did you tell her what it was for?"

Olivia shook her head. Since the recordings were public record, Ann couldn't deny her request regardless of her personal feelings. "But I'm sure she guessed. You don't have to listen to it, if you don't want to. You said you couldn't stop thinking about your bagel and I—I thought this might help."

"With the bagels?"

"Yes." Olivia smiled. "When we have a complicated incident, we reconstruct the scene, for investigation. Sometimes, it helps to look at things objectively and figure out what happened. What you're replaying in your head is skewed, by emotions and by memories and doubts. But I thought maybe if you listened to it, how it really happened, it might give you closure."

Hillary bit her lip and looked up and to the right in that way that Olivia now knew meant she was considering the situation. Olivia placed the CD on Hillary's desk.

"No pressure. If you don't want to listen, don't."

Hillary's eyes filled with tears, and suddenly she stood and pulled Olivia into a hug. "Thank you."

The husk of her quiet words brought an ache to her heart, but the whisper of her breath against Olivia's ear inspired an entirely different ache. At that moment her eyes clashed with those of another dispatcher at an adjacent workstation, and she jerked back, using her hands that had been grasping Hillary's waist to push her away instead.

"I—uh." She fumbled for an explanation for her panic in what could simply have been an embrace of gratitude. Her face flushed and she silently damned her pale complexion.

Hillary pressed her lips into a firm line and nodded stiffly. "I'm sorry."

"Don't worry about it," Olivia mumbled as she backed toward the door. Hillary looked like she wanted to say more, but she didn't.

Olivia made it to the car before her phone signaled a new text message. She didn't have to look. She couldn't stand to, really. She hated that Hillary felt she had to apologize for hugging her— something that so many people did without thought, which anyone should be able to do freely. And the knowledge that she'd made Hillary regret it hurt.

❖

Hours later, the exchange with Hillary still haunted Olivia. Her last call, an assault report at the hospital, had capped off a busy shift, and now she had to wait for a deputy from the next shift to relieve her. After the victim received the necessary treatment, a deputy would have to escort him down to take out a warrant against his assailant. But according to emergency-department staff, since his injuries weren't life-threatening and due to their heavy patient load, he could be waiting hours yet. After consulting Sergeant Gilleland, Olivia received permission to hand him off to the next shift.

When the deputy finally arrived, she hoped it wasn't too late to make the stop she'd been thinking about for hours. Since the officer would also be taking over her patrol car, Sergeant Gilleland had given him a ride to the hospital. Olivia handed him her keys and climbed into Gilleland's car.

"Thanks for the ride." She pulled the seatbelt across her chest.

"No problem." Gilleland steered out of the hospital parking lot. "You're doing good work, Dennis. I wanted to let you know that, in case you thought I still had reservations."

"Thank you, ma'am." She valued the trust Gilleland had in her.

Since she'd started working with her, she'd learned a little bit about Gilleland's career trajectory. She'd joined the force fifteen years before and spent seven years patrolling Collins County before being promoted. Something had stalled Gilleland's career and Olivia wondered if it was personal or professional, because given her reputation, Gilleland should have at least made lieutenant if not captain in the eight years since that first step up.

"We didn't talk much about how you ended up in my sector. I chose not to listen to the gossip, but I did my research. You've been trying to prove yourself since practically the day you came out of the academy."

Olivia rubbed her fingers against her neck as she recalled why she'd been fighting since day one. But the details she'd so readily revealed to Hillary wouldn't spill out in the confines of Gilleland's car.

"You've had a couple of documented incidents. And I'd guess there were more that we don't know about. Some suspects have underestimated you—why? Because of your size? I've been tested most of my career because I'm a woman. In your case, I imagine guys see a shorter, thinner woman and immediately think they can take you." She glanced at Olivia, clearly expecting an answer.

"Sometimes."

"Our challenge is to stifle the urge to cram it back down their throats."

Olivia smiled, liking Gilleland just a little bit more.

"You're a good cop. Smart, passionate. Control yourself and you can go far."

"Did you not control yourself?"

The muscles in Gilleland's jaw twitched, and for a moment Olivia feared she'd stepped too far over a line she'd hadn't been aware of.

"As a matter of fact, I didn't."

Olivia held back her questions.

"Buck Martin—excuse me, Sheriff Martin, was my sergeant at my first assignment. I tried to give him the respect he was owed as my supervisor." She chuckled. "And he made that hard to do."

Olivia scoffed.

"I finally made sergeant, but apparently I was destined to work for him because he got promoted to lieutenant, then captain, and somehow I stayed in his chain of command. What I'm about to tell you stays between us, Dennis."

"Absolutely, ma'am."

"Okay, you can drop the ma'am stuff. It's just us in the car. If you're not comfortable with May, then Sarge is acceptable."

"Okay, ma'am—Sarge."

Gilleland laughed. "One of my guys got into some trouble. While out with his buddies, he drank too much, decided to drive, and had a wreck. When I questioned him, he lied. I couldn't abide it. I recommended termination. I didn't know he was Martin's stepson. At the disciplinary hearing, your father backed me up and fired the guy. But when promotion time came around again, I found out Martin had been poisoning me every chance he had. I was passed up repeatedly. As long as Martin is the sheriff, I'll be content to keep the stripes I have, but I won't be getting any more."

"I don't have my father's aspirations."

"You didn't strike me as the type. Your brother, maybe."

"Yeah. I can see Andy stepping in the old man's shoes. But I don't plan to answer to the voters."

Suddenly, she saw the irony in how she already let others control her. What was worse, she'd given her life over to what she imagined someone else's reaction would be. She'd spent her entire career trying to prove she was tougher than she looked. But, when it really mattered, she couldn't stand up for herself.

❖

"Thanks, again." Olivia leaned back into the passenger side of the car she'd just exited. Her gratitude extended to the conversation as well as the ride back to the station.

"Have a good night, Dennis. I'll see you tomorrow."

Olivia climbed into her Jeep, her mind swinging back to the visit she'd been anticipating all night. Her chat with Gilleland had detoured her thoughts momentarily, but alone again, she wasn't focusing on work.

Throughout the short drive, she became more resolved. When she reached the house, she paused only long enough to take off her gun belt and secure it in the lock box she'd had installed in the Jeep's cargo area. By the time she knocked, the fire of change burned in her gut. She barely waited for the door to swing open before she spoke. "I'm ready."

Frankie grinned. "Ready for what?"

"For things to be different."

Frankie stepped back and waited for her to enter.

"Where's Andy?" Olivia toed off her work boots just inside the door.

"Poker night."

"He's such a cliché."

"I know. But he's our cliché. Now get in here."

Olivia followed Frankie to the living room, where they stretched out on the sofa together, Olivia's legs draped across Frankie's lap, the way they'd been doing since they were kids.

"Do you want to be with her?" Frankie grabbed one of her feet and pulled off her sock.

"I do." Olivia groaned when Frankie's thumb dug into her arch. "But she wants to be with someone who's out."

"And you're not ready to come out?"

"I want to be."

"So take the first step."

"What's the first step?"

"Tell Andy."

"Will you do it?"

Frankie laughed. "Absolutely not."

"How do I do this, Frankie?" She couldn't imagine how to begin that conversation.

"What if we all go out to dinner together? He can get to know her a little without any pressure. You can feel him out. Then later when you tell him, privately, it's less likely he'll react negatively if he already likes her."

"You think he'll react negatively?"

"I hope not. I'll kick his ass if he does. But you're worried about it. This might ease some of the stress."

Andy was a reasonable man. And hopefully he was more evolved than she feared her father was. If she lost them both, she had very little hope of her mother standing against them. But getting closer to Hillary felt like it was worth the risk.

"Okay. But will you ask him?"

"I'll do better, I'll tell him. Tomorrow night?"

"I'll have to ask her, but that works for me."

"Text me when you know. Then I'll make a reservation."

"Thanks, Frankie." She pulled out her phone and glanced at the time. "Eleven thirty. She's probably still up." She tapped out a quick text.

You still up?

Hillary's response came back quickly.

Yes. What's up?

I need to talk to you.

I can come over. Or you can come here.

I'm not far away. See you in fifteen.

Olivia planted her feet on the floor and turned to Frankie. "I'll go ask her right now."

"You have to do that in person?"

Olivia smiled. "I don't have to. But I'm hoping it'll be more fun."

"Yeah? You think you're going to tell her you're ready for a baby step and she's going to take her clothes off?"

"Not quite like that." Olivia frowned. "But I thought she might be appreciative."

"I don't know what that means, and I don't think I want to." Frankie stood and followed Olivia to the door. "Text me about dinner before she takes your pants off."

"You're crude."

"But now you're hoping she'll take your pants off."

"Try to clean up your mouth before tomorrow night, huh?" Olivia said just before closing the door behind her.

CHAPTER FIFTEEN

Icame to ask if you'd join me for dinner tomorrow night," Olivia blurted when Hillary opened the door to her. She seemed to want to get it out quickly.

"Dinner?" Hillary stepped back and waited for Olivia to enter.

"With me, Andy, and Frankie."

"Dinner with your family?"

"Not all of them."

"What's the agenda?"

"I want to come out to my family. Andy seems like a good place to start. But I want to soften him up with dinner first. Let him get to know you before—"

"Before he rejects us both?"

"I don't know. Yeah, I guess. I'm hoping if he gets to know you and spends time with us together, he won't freak about the idea of us—you know, together."

Hillary smiled and stepped forward, stopping with only inches between their chests. She enjoyed Olivia's reaction to the nearness— the subtle way her breathing changed, feeling the answering tug in herself. "Us together."

"Was that a question?"

"Nope. Just trying it out loud. So, that's what you want?"

"Did you not know that?"

She touched Olivia's lapels, then smoothed her hands down the front of her shirt. "Have I mentioned how much I like you in uniform?"

"Not specifically. But the ladies usually do." Olivia winked. Bravado looked good on her.

"Mmm, but there is one thing missing." Hillary slipped her hands down and grasped the waistband of Olivia's pants. "Duty belt?"

"Are you looking for the handcuffs?"

"Not just yet. Do you think I'm that easy? You come in here talking about taking me out for a fancy dinner with your brother, and I'm supposed to cuff myself to your bedpost?"

"No." Olivia leaned in, her breath feathering over Hillary's lips. "My bedpost is way too far away right now."

"So this dinner—"

"Hillary, I'm about to kiss you. But before I do, let me be very clear. I intend for this dinner to be a beginning—for me and for us. If we're not on the same page, now's when you tell me."

Despite her response to Olivia's words, Hillary wanted to remain cautious. She wanted to remind herself that she'd fallen for broken promises before. Unfortunately, her mouth didn't get the message from her brain. "Kiss me then."

Olivia smiled, then closed the gap between them. Hillary returned the kiss with abandon. She fisted her hands in the sides of Olivia's pants and pulled her even closer, glad now to not have the heavy gun belt between them. As Olivia slid her tongue along Hillary's upper lip, Hillary tugged Olivia's shirt free of her pants and found skin. Olivia's muscles twitched beneath her hands.

"Are you going to invite me farther in?" Olivia asked against her lips.

"Literally or figuratively?"

"Both," Olivia whispered against her jaw, just before pressing a kiss there.

Hillary eased back. "Let's go to the living room."

"Not the bedroom?" Hillary held onto her hand and followed her to the sofa.

"Not tonight, hotshot. I'm going to practice some restraint. Someone has to."

"That's no fun."

"I got the impression from your little speech that you weren't just looking for fun. Or was that just talk to get me in bed?"

"I want you in bed, no doubt." Hillary flushed as Olivia's eyes traced over her. "But it's also true that I want more."

"We don't need to have the most serious conversation right now. As long as we're both headed down the same road, we'll get there eventually."

"Okay. So long as you know that telling Andy and eventually my parents is the endgame for me. This isn't a fling."

Olivia cupped the back of her neck, and Hillary registered an unexpected thrill at the feel of her fingers curved there. *How can I already be this far gone?*

"So, we'll get to the heavy stuff later." Hillary smiled. "Kiss me again?"

"Gladly." Olivia pulled her closer.

Hillary buried her hands in Olivia's hair, freeing it from the loose ponytail that restrained it. "God, I've been wanting to do that since high school," she murmured between kisses.

"Really? Since high school?"

Hillary blushed, teetering on what she was about to reveal. "I may have had a thing—"

"A thing? You had a sexy little baby-dyke crush on me. That's hot."

"I wasn't a baby dyke. Besides, you wouldn't have thought it was hot back then."

"I was too busy denying everything about myself back then. And every day since. God, I'm an idiot." Olivia pinched the bridge of her nose.

"You could look at it like that. I prefer to think it kept you unattached until I could get to you." Hillary took her hand.

"You would. You've been stalking me since high school."

"I never admitted to stalking." She brushed her thumb across Olivia's knuckles. "In the interest of honesty, if we're going to explore anything between us, I need to tell you something."

"Nothing good ever comes after a statement like that."

"It's not that bad. Remember when I said I'd dated someone in the department?"

"Yes."

"Well, May and I—"

"May?"

"Um, Sergeant Gilleland—"

"Are you kidding me?" Olivia pulled her hand free.

Hillary bit her lip and shook her head.

"I can't get away from your exes."

Hillary smiled.

"It's really not funny."

"If it helps, it's an even more civilized situation than with Ann. May and I parted as friends."

"Really?"

"Really. We're totally cool. I even went to her and her wife's commitment ceremony."

"Wife?"

"Last summer. Once the federal government made the change, they decided not to wait for Tennessee to catch up."

Olivia shook her head.

"You don't believe me?"

"It's not that. I'm just—marveling, I guess, at the turns my life has taken in the past couple of months. And it's not over yet. I still have so much change ahead of me."

"Whatever happens, I'm here."

"Don't make promises you can't keep."

Hillary grabbed Olivia's hand, refusing to let her withdraw completely. "Since high school, remember? You're going to have to try pretty hard to get rid of me."

"As long as I come out?"

"I need that to be the long-term goal, yes. If it's not, you should tell me so I can start working on getting over you."

"Don't do that."

"We can still be friends." Hillary smiled. "I'll even invite you to *my* wedding someday."

"I applaud your and Sergeant Gilleland's maturity. But there's no way I could watch you marry someone else."

As panic shadowed Olivia's expression, Hillary kissed her again to distract her from overanalyzing the depth of what she'd revealed.

❖

Hillary stared at her reflection in the mirror over her bathroom sink. She stood on her tiptoes with her back against the wall, trying to see her bottom half. She never remembered that she wanted a full-length mirror until moments like this.

She'd chosen a simple sleeveless black dress that ended just above her knees. Olivia told her they were going to the Italian place on Main, and though it was the most formal place in Reinsville, she would probably still be a tad overdressed. But the dress fit her better than any other she owned and gave her a bit of added confidence, which she might need to spend an evening with Olivia's family. Given the conversation with Frankie at the bar, she seemed to be on their side. But she knew Olivia was nervous about Andy's reaction and, beyond that, facing her parents. She kept telling herself to relax. Olivia wasn't going to tell Andy tonight; she only hoped to soften the eventual blow.

"So, no pressure. Just make a good impression," she mumbled to herself as she turned her attention to the row of shoes in her closet. Though she'd rather wear a low, sensible heel, her eyes gravitated to black pumps. She wasn't into labels and probably couldn't discern the difference in designer shoes. But the higher heels made her legs look longer and leaner, so she slipped her feet into them.

Thirty minutes later, she thought she'd talked herself down, but the way she jumped when the doorbell rang indicated otherwise. After glancing through the peephole, she swung the door open.

"You look beautiful." Olivia traced her eyes over her, while Hillary did the same. Olivia had chosen the first suit Hillary had seen her in, the black one with the skirt. Underneath, her maroon and white pin-striped shirt looked light and silky. The open collar revealed a diamond pendant that rested between her collarbones.

"So do you."

Olivia pulled on the cuffs at her wrists.

"You also look nervous," Hillary said.

"I might be. A little."

Hillary stepped close, took Olivia's face in her hands, and kissed her. "You don't have to do this for me."

"You'd be with me if I didn't come out to my family?"

Hillary hesitated. "I might. Against my better judgment." She smiled and caressed Olivia's face. Now that she'd given herself permission, she didn't know how she'd ever contain the urge to touch her. "Because I can't help myself."

"I don't want you to compromise this for me. And I don't want to hide who I am anymore. I haven't wanted to for a while. It's just—it's a scary thing."

"I know." She took Olivia's hand. "Let's relax and go have a nice dinner."

❖

Dinner was going better than Hillary expected, largely thanks to Frankie's gregarious nature. She interacted expertly with the siblings and even managed to draw Hillary into the conversation as well.

Andy seemed polite, but she sensed tension in the way he watched Olivia. And the stiffness in Olivia's posture indicated that she felt it as well. Hillary wanted to take Olivia's hand under the table, but she decided not to risk Andy noticing.

"So how do you two like working together?" Hillary asked them, determined to fight through any awkwardness. "Do you find it easier to trust each other to back you up?"

"I pretty much trust all of the guys," Andy said.

"That's because you don't have to worry about guys who don't think women can do the job," Olivia stated very matter-of-factly. Hillary worried she might have started something, but Olivia looked at her and gave her a wink that her brother couldn't see. "But I do like working for May Gilleland. What do you dispatchers think of her?"

Hillary narrowed her eyes, but when she answered, she kept her voice neutral. "She seems fair. And she takes calls when it's busy. That's what dispatchers like."

"She's all right." Andy shrugged.

"Do you guys talk about which officers you like best?" Frankie asked.

"We all know which ones are slackers. Is that what you mean?" Hillary glanced at Olivia and Andy. "You two are safe."

"Good." Olivia nodded as if her fine reputation was a given.

"It's against the policy your father put in place when he was chief to talk bad about either of you."

Frankie laughed.

"Nothing bad to say," Olivia said.

Frankie laughed harder and Hillary joined in.

"What?" Olivia glanced at Andy, obviously looking for an ally, but he just shrugged. "What do they say about me? Really?"

"You take risks."

"And?"

"Sometimes that makes us nervous."

"Why should it make you nervous? You're not the one out there. You're just sitting at a computer anyway."

Hillary turned to face her. Was she purposely trying to rile her? Or worse, did she truly think so little of Hillary's job? She recalled Olivia telling her early on that the deputies predicted what kind of night they were going to have based on which dispatcher's voice they heard. So, this was just bravado, maybe for Andy's benefit.

"You're unpredictable." Hillary smiled, deciding to keep the conversation light. "And sometimes you get in trouble and that interrupts my crossword."

They shared a laugh and were spared from further conversation when the server brought their food. As Hillary dug into her eggplant Parmesan, she felt Olivia's fingers brush her thigh under the table. She glanced at Andy, but he was engrossed in twisting strands of angel hair around his fork. She grabbed Olivia's hand and gave it a quick squeeze.

She met Olivia's eyes and felt a flutter in her chest. Affection painted Olivia's expression, and Hillary didn't hide the warmth in her answering smile.

Frankie cleared her throat. "Um, Hillary, did Olivia tell me that your parents moved to Texas a few years back?" Frankie's voice was tight and she flicked her eyes toward Andy.

Hillary glanced at him, and her own stomach tightened in response to the way he stared at Olivia. "Yes, my dad has family there."

Frankie nodded, as if engrossed in the conversation, but she still looked nervous. "It must be difficult to be so far away. I'm glad our families are both still here. Don't get me wrong. I wouldn't mind skipping a Sunday dinner now and then."

Olivia laughed. "No kidding. I'd settle for not having my attendance at church monitored so closely."

"She's just trying to keep us on the straight and narrow," Andy said.

Hillary glanced at Olivia, trying to gauge whether she'd detected the hard edge to Andy's voice. Olivia didn't look worried, so maybe Hillary was hearing things because she was already nervous.

"She's been trying to do that since we were kids. But you and I always found our fair share of trouble, didn't we?"

"We did."

"Once, she left me in charge while they went away for the weekend. I had a party, and by the time Andy invited his friends, too, things got out of control."

"You invited all of your hot cheerleader friends. Of course, I had to call my boys. I gained some cool points that weekend. And it was the first time Frankie and I hooked up."

"What?" Olivia turned accusing eyes on Frankie. "You told me he asked you out to dinner first."

"I may have left out the reason he wanted to take me out."

"Hey, I asked because I'd liked you for a long time. I was just hoping you wouldn't say no *because* we'd already hooked up at the party."

"Are you kidding? That's why I said yes." Frankie winked at him. His answering smile held so much affection that Hillary relaxed a little. Surely a guy capable of that much love for his wife would understand his sister wanting the same happiness.

"And while you two were enjoying your postcoital glow, I spent all day Sunday cleaning the house so Mom and Dad wouldn't know. Between the party and cleaning, I didn't get any sleep that night."

"Well, believe me when I say it was worth it." Frankie kissed Andy's cheek.

"For you, maybe. I spent most of the night trying to keep people out of Dad's office. If anything had been touched in there, he would have known."

"Did your parents ever find out?" Hillary asked.

"I'm pretty sure Mom suspected something, but she never confronted me." Olivia's confident smile reminded Hillary of the girl she'd admired from afar in high school. She'd never been invited to any of those parties.

"And once Dad made sheriff, he wasn't around as much," Andy said.

Andy and Olivia both got quiet. Frankie covered Andy's hand on the table.

"Until we joined the force. Then he was around too much." Olivia laughed.

"I didn't remember that you two started dating during high school," Hillary said.

"Senior year. I caught some flak for dating a sophomore. But I didn't care."

"Because of what happened at that party." Andy gave a cocky grin and nodded.

Frankie shoved his shoulder. "In spite of it."

"That was the night you saw me as someone other than Olivia's little brother."

"Then it's a good thing I was drunk, huh?" Frankie teased him.

"Okay, before we get too far into my brother's sex life, if you'll excuse me, I need to use the restroom." Olivia pushed her chair back.

Hillary wanted to go with her but thought that might be too obvious. However, when Frankie stood and said she would go, too, Hillary wished she had. She'd be left alone at the table with Andy. Now she wanted to grab Olivia's arm and beg her not to leave.

Hillary took a bite of her eggplant, while her mind raced for something neutral to talk about. The silence stretched between them, and he too stared uncomfortably at his plate.

"More bread?" She pointed to the basket, which sat almost exactly between them and as close to his reach as it was to hers.

"No, thank you."

"So, Andy, what do you like to do in your spare time?" Lame, maybe, but she'd panicked a little.

"Frankie and I just bought a house, so I've been working on fixing it up."

"Oh, that's cool. I've always thought it would be neat to rehab a house. Or maybe have one built. I'd like picking out the décor."

"It's an old farmhouse just outside of town on Route 10."

"I think I know the one you mean. It has a gray barn out back."

He nodded. "I'd like to turn the barn into a woodworking shop and make some of the furniture for the house."

When she saw Olivia and Frankie heading across the room, she congratulated herself on surviving the awkwardness.

But Andy apparently didn't check over his shoulder before he decided to open a new subject. "What are you doing with my sister?"

"I'm sorry." Hillary's stomach tightened. She knew he'd been suspicious, but she didn't expect such bluntness.

"You seem nice, and I heard about—well, I understand you needed a friend—"

"Andy." Frankie had just reached the table and tried to interrupt, but he shrugged off her arm.

"But I don't want you to get the wrong idea. Olivia is not gay."

"Damn it, Andy," Frankie said.

Hillary looked at Olivia, who stood behind Frankie with an expression of sheer panic. Hillary waited for her to say something, but she'd apparently found something really interesting about her shoes. They'd talked about this dinner potentially easing Andy toward the truth, but surely Olivia wouldn't let such a blatant challenge go unexplained. Andy made it sound like Hillary wanted to turn his poor innocent sister.

The look of sympathy on Frankie's face was too much to bear. Hillary turned back to Andy, contemplating the fallout of setting him straight herself. But she wasn't the kind of person who outed someone from spite, so she looked Andy in the eye and nodded. "I understand." However, her words were meant more for Olivia than her brother. Whatever she thought they'd been building, Olivia obviously didn't feel as strongly as she did. Otherwise, she wouldn't be able to stay silent. "Would you excuse me for a moment?"

She should smile politely and get through the rest of the meal. And she'd try, but she needed a moment to collect herself before she could manage that. She started toward the restroom, but, almost of their own volition, her feet carried her toward the exit.

"God, I am such an idiot," she muttered as she shoved through the door. She willed back the tears that gathered in her eyes. As she stepped outside, her shoes clattered against the flagstones beneath her feet—those ridiculous shoes.

"Hillary." Olivia called as she followed her out, but Hillary kept moving through the parking lot. "Hillary, damn it, wait."

When Olivia grabbed her arm, Hillary whirled around quickly and Olivia drew up short.

"What? What exactly could you have to say to me right now?" Somewhere between the bar and the front door she'd decided to go on the offensive. She'd thought she could set aside her own feelings, but Andy had cut right through to her insecurities. If she wanted to be with Olivia she had to resign herself to being the best friend in the eyes of everyone else. No matter how much she wanted Olivia—how much she told herself she could—she couldn't do that.

Olivia looked like she'd slapped her. "I—he caught me off guard. What did you want me to say?"

"I don't know. But you could have done something. Instead, I look like the predatory lesbian who's trying to take advantage of his sister." She shook her head. "Damn it, I knew better, and I let myself get swept up. I convinced myself I could handle this because you were different—"

"I am."

"But you're not. You've just proved that."

"I want to come out to them. You know that. I need more time."

"More time implies that eventually you'll get there. But I don't think you will, Olivia. And that's your decision. I just can't live in a bubble with you. I'm not going to lie about who I am, even to protect you. I won't live in the closet. I've done the whole coming-out thing with my family already."

"Then you should be able to understand why this is difficult for me. But then, I imagine it's pretty easy to be out from a thousand miles away."

Hillary blinked, the words stinging as much as a physical blow.

"Shit, Hillary, I'm sorry. I didn't mean that."

Hillary was already backing away from her. "I think you did." She turned and headed for her car without looking back. She thought fleetingly that they'd ridden to the restaurant together but didn't slow her pace. *Let Andy take her home.*

CHAPTER SIXTEEN

Stop!" Olivia rounded the corner and saw her suspect just ahead. She pushed harder, churning her legs, gaining on him. But she didn't close fast enough. He vaulted a chain-link fence like he was running hurdles. Given her height, she couldn't clear the fence nearly as fast, and when she reached it he had enough head start that she opted not to go over. By the time she did, he would be out of sight anyway. "Damn it," she yelled, slamming her hand against the fence. If this was television she could have just shot the guy.

Instead, she returned to the apartment where she'd started the chase. She'd been dispatched on a report of two men fighting inside the apartment. As she'd gotten out of her car, a woman had screamed from the breezeway and a man had run out of the building and taken off. She'd called out, and when he didn't stop she'd followed.

She reached the apartment and cursed under her breath. Sergeant Gilleland had arrived, likely because she'd heard Olivia call out the foot pursuit on the radio. Now, she not only had to return empty-handed, but she'd do so in front of her supervisor.

"Lost him. Damn fence," she said, still trying to catch her breath.

"That's okay. The guy inside knows who he is. Apparently they're buddies. Got in a fight because he loaned our suspect some money and didn't like how he was spending it."

"Well, that's no way to treat your buddy." She went inside the apartment and found the other party seated on his sofa with a towel-wrapped pack of ice pressed to the side of his face. "Do you want to tell me what happened?"

"Sure. I loaned him five hundred dollars. He was supposed to pay me back when he got paid. But he came over today to tell me he didn't have it."

"How does that story end with you getting punched in the face?" The guy wasn't telling the whole story, and Olivia didn't have the patience for detective work today. If he wanted her help, the guy needed to spell it out for her.

"Uh, well, we were out with some friends last night and I saw him spending money—a lot of money."

"So you're mad because he was buying rounds at the bar?"

"Not exactly."

"Listen, man, I don't have time for guessing games. Just tell me what happened."

"We went to a strip club out by the interstate."

"So here's the deal. I can't do anything about the money. That's between you and him. But I can take a report on the assault and you can go get a warrant on him."

"Okay. I'll do that."

She nodded. "Come out to my car and we'll get this report done. Let me give you a little advice for the future. If you want to keep your friends, don't loan money you can't afford to lose. Nothing hurts a friendship more than policing a guy's lap dances."

Olivia grimaced as she took a sip of her coffee. She wasn't especially picky about her coffee, but hazelnut was the one flavor she couldn't drink. She made eye contact with the woman behind the counter and motioned her over.

"This is hazelnut. I asked for a vanilla latte."

"Sorry about that."

"May," another barista called out, placing a cup on the counter.

"What's your problem today, Dennis?" Gilleland asked as she picked up her order.

"Nothing." She should have driven the extra couple of miles to go to Pacey's. Since she only wanted coffee and a quick sandwich, she'd opted for the chain soup-and-sandwich joint for her meal break because it was closer.

"Whatever it is, stop bringing it to work."

"I'm not—"

"You were sullen in pre-shift. You've been snippy with our dispatcher all day. I'll be surprised if she doesn't complain about you."

Olivia bit her lip. She had been short with the dispatcher, but since Hillary was the one behind the console, Olivia didn't expect an official complaint. Her aggravation had been aimed inward for the most part. She'd been so happy to hear Hillary's voice and couldn't have controlled the lift in her mood or the acceleration of her heart rate. Then she remembered that Hillary probably wouldn't be as thrilled to communicate with her. She found herself listening carefully as Hillary dispatched her on her first call of the shift. Her tone didn't carry any extra warmth; in fact, her words were clipped and sparse.

She'd tried to call Hillary to apologize but had gotten voice mail. Her text hadn't been answered either. So she'd backed off, deciding not to try again until she'd made some progress toward telling Andy the truth. Despite what had happened at dinner two nights ago, she still planned to take that step.

When her corrected order was placed on the counter, Olivia grabbed it and headed outside.

"So what is it?" Gilleland followed her to the far side of the parking lot, where she'd parked her cruiser away from everyone else. She'd planned to sit inside the car and eat her sandwich before checking in for the next call. "Woman trouble?"

"What? Why would you ask that?" She leaned against the front of her car, trying to appear more casual than she felt.

May shrugged. "I just assumed."

"That I'm gay?"

"You're not?"

Olivia's first instinct was to lie, but she'd come to trust Gilleland. And maybe she'd been going about this wrong. Maybe Andy shouldn't be the first person she came out to. "I am. But that's not widely known at this time."

"You're not out?"

"I'm in the process. *Very* early in the process."

"Your secret's safe."

Olivia nodded. She unwrapped her sandwich and took a bite, but now the bread tasted dry in her mouth, and it took a lot of effort to chew and swallow.

"So who's the woman?"

A swig of coffee washed down the lump of bread. "I don't think we should really talk about who."

"Is she not out?"

"What?"

"Closeted women can really mess you up. I've been there."

"No. She's not—"

"Then what's the problem? Does she have a girlfriend already?"

"No. But you—ah, you know her." She sighed at Gilleland's expectant look. "Hillary O'Neal."

"Oh."

"Yeah."

After another moment of silence, Gilleland said, "That explains why you aren't worried about a complaint from dispatch."

She shrugged. "That's no excuse."

"You're right. But if you knock it off, I can give you a pass on tonight." Gilleland hesitated, then said, "It's probably not my place, given my history with her. But she's worth it."

"I know." She didn't think Gilleland was fishing for details, and she didn't want to give any. "I hope this won't be—"

"Uncomfortable? No. I have no designs on you."

"I—uh—I actually, meant—"

Gilleland laughed. "I know what you meant. Hillary and I parted on good terms."

"That's what she said."

"Glad to hear it. It's ancient history. Hillary is great. We just weren't *it* for each other."

Olivia recalled Hillary saying something similar while talking about her dating history and wondered if she'd been referring to May. Knowing their relationship had been over for some time and that May now had a spouse didn't stop a twinge of jealousy.

❖

"How are you sleeping?" Stein asked before Hillary had even gotten seated.

"I look that bad, huh?" When Stein didn't respond, Hillary shrugged, lacking the energy to lie.

"Have you given any more thought to a sleep aid?"

"I don't want drugs." She sighed. "I know they help some people. But I want to handle this without them if I can."

"Sleep deprivation is only going to make it harder."

"I don't need it to be easy. I agreed to talk, that's what I'm here doing. I don't want pills," she snapped. She'd functioned on little sleep plenty of times before, and she could do it again. She was afraid if she took sleeping pills she could come to rely on them. And given the varied shifts she often worked, she couldn't afford the dependency.

He shifted back in his chair, rested his elbows on the arms of his chair, and steepled his fingers. She'd come to hate when he did that.

"How was your weekend?"

"Work-wise? Pretty uneventful. Since I'm still not allowed to work overtime, I was off both days." Once a year, the dispatchers rebid for shifts and days off, based on seniority. At the beginning of her career she'd worked weekends and the shifts no one else wanted. But she'd been there long enough to get weekends off on the second shift. Often she grabbed overtime shifts and worked through them.

"How about personally?"

"I'm not here to talk about my personal life."

"We can talk about anything you want to."

"Okay. I went out to dinner—on a date, sort of." She hadn't mentioned her sexual-orientation and had no idea where he stood on the matter. So she decided to test him.

"And how did it go?"

"It wasn't really a date. It's someone I'm thinking about getting involved with, and she wanted me to meet her brother." If he was surprised at her use of the feminine pronoun, he didn't show it. He waited expectantly and she didn't try to outlast him. "I wouldn't call it a success."

"What happened?"

She quirked her lips and tilted her head as if unaffected by the results, when, in fact, the opposite was true. "He doesn't want his sister to be gay."

"What does she want?"

"She says she wants to be with me."

"You doubt that?"

"Given her reaction to his disapproval—I don't know."

"But she's not out and that makes you nervous."

She nodded.

"The world is changing fast. It's getting easier to be out in today's world. But Reinsville is still a small town. And sometimes, no matter where you are, family pressure can be stifling."

"So maybe it's not just work that's keeping me up at night." Despite her joking tone, she was certain he picked up on the underlying truth to her words.

Olivia pushed open the door to Andy's favorite boxing gym. When she'd texted him earlier insisting they talk, he told her to meet him here and to wear something to work out in. As she stepped inside, she inhaled the distinctive smell of sweat and canvas. She followed the steady rhythm of gloves against a speed bag and found Andy in the far corner.

She'd first worked out with him here while she was in the academy. After the first time one of the other guys in her class put her on her back while learning defensive tactics, she'd begged Andy to help her. So he'd brought her here and taught her to fight. She'd built on his lessons with those her instructor had given her.

She'd come here again—the day after that tequila-drinking crackhead slammed her against the wall—and pummeled a heavy bag until her fists were raw, but she still hadn't managed to chase away the memory of her world going black. Andy had shown up, bandaged her hands, and sparred gently with her until she couldn't lift her arms. As siblings they hadn't always agreed or even gotten along, but he'd been exactly what she needed that day. Maybe he could do it again.

"The ring is free," he said as soon as he saw her.

She nodded and followed him to the center of the room. She dropped her bag, and then they taped each other's hands, pulled on gloves, and climbed into the ring.

He raised his hands, guarding his face, and danced backward away from her, obviously expecting her usual aggressive attack.

She lifted her hands, intent on working off some anxiety before she approached the reason for her visit. But when she looked at him, she had to know right now that they would be okay. She needed his support because her heart told her that the worst was yet to come, and she couldn't get through telling their parents without him.

"I'm gay."

He stopped bouncing, dropped his arms to his side, and stared at her. "Did Hillary—"

"No. This isn't about her."

"You weren't gay before you started hanging out with her."

"Yeah. I was. I just didn't have the guts to tell you."

"So why are you telling me now?" He acted like he didn't want to know. Like if she said she took it back, he would accept it and pretend she hadn't said anything.

She shrugged. "I'd been trying to work up my nerve to tell you— all of you. But being with Hillary—"

"*With* her? So you're already—"

"I'm—I want to be with her, Andy. I—I maybe love her."

He stared for a moment longer, and when he spoke his voice was cold. "You maybe love her? Enough that you're willing to destroy your family for her?"

His words hit a tender spot in her heart, and a blast of pain nearly sent her to her knees on the canvas. "Andy, I need—"

"Not to mention how the guys on the force will treat you?" He raised his hands again and assumed a fighting posture.

She only cared about one guy, and right now he was letting her down.

He moved to her right, and she adjusted her guard. "Does Frankie know?" He pushed out a left that bounced off her gloves.

"She's known since high school." She answered with a tentative jab, but her heart wasn't in it and he blocked her easily.

He whistled. "I didn't realize she could keep a secret that long."

"She's always supported me. And I need that, from you, too, if I'm going to tell Mama and Daddy."

"You think that's a good idea?"

She ducked a jab and blocked a cross. "Maybe it's ambitious, given our parents. But I want what you have. I want to bring someone home for Sunday dinner and have my family know what they mean to me. And yeah, maybe I want to get married and have kids someday."

"Are you prepared for them to not accept this?"

"I guess I should be. If you can't, they surely won't."

He shrugged, and she wished she could find anger instead of heartache. She wanted to scream at him, but she had to funnel all her energy toward not crying instead.

Was she willing to risk losing her family, the only anchors she'd known in her life? She dropped her hands thinking of Hillary. Yes. She was worth that risk.

Distracted, she reacted a second too late to Andy's movement, and her head snapped back with the impact. Even with his gloves on, the quick jab was hard enough to bring tears to her eyes. She stepped back immediately, the sharp, coppery taste already threatening to gag her. She tucked her left hand under her right armpit and jerked off her glove.

"Oh my God. I'm so sorry. Are you okay?" He pulled his own gloves off and reached for her face.

She could only nod as she caught a stream of her own blood in her hand. "Get me something to stop this, will you?"

He hopped out of the ring and grabbed a towel, then rushed back and shoved it into her hand. She pinched her nose, and when she sniffed at the sudden shot of pain, she had to swallow more blood. She tried not to think about whether the towel was clean as she pressed it to her face.

He helped her out of the ring and sat beside her on a bench until she got the bleeding under control.

"Dude, you can't beat the gay out of me." She longed to hear him laugh, but he sat stiffly next to her and stared at the floor.

"I'm sorry."

"Yeah, I know." But she didn't. Was he sorry for the punch or that he refused to accept who she really was?

"There's a chance Dad will react very badly to this. I hope you're not expecting Mama to stand against him."

"I should know better than to expect anything from any of you." Still clutching the towel to her face, she awkwardly grabbed her things and left the gym. She didn't look back even when she heard the heavy sound of him hitting a bag—hard. She hoped he hurt his hand.

Chapter Seventeen

"What are we doing out here?" Jake asked as he got into the passenger side of her car and closed the door.

Hillary picked up a CD from the center console. "I need to listen to this."

"I'm giving up my lunch break so you can listen to Kelly Clarkson's latest?"

She swatted his shoulder. "Don't be an ass." She handed over the disc so he could read the date and incident number written on the front.

"Ann made this for you? That's a move I wouldn't expect from her."

"Why's that?"

"Because it implies more insight than I'd have given her credit for."

"She didn't do it."

"Then who?"

"Olivia."

"Impressive."

"Are you going to listen to it with me or not?"

"Of course."

She turned the key to the accessory position and pushed in the disc. Right away she heard her own voice dispatching two deputies to an injury accident. She'd dispatched thousands like it in her career, most of which ended with an incident report and a referral for the parties involved to call their insurance companies.

Officer down. I have an officer down, struck by a truck. Dispatch, send me an ambulance. Signal ten.

Hillary sucked in a breath as adrenaline shot through her, the same as it had that day. The deputy had been so panicked he didn't identify himself, and she'd had to check his radio identifier to determine which of them had made the transmission. She'd called out to the EMS dispatcher and had an ambulance on the way in seconds. She'd given the location to any other deputies that could assist.

Give me an injury code.
Jesus, get that ambulance down here. He's pinned under this truck.

"Are you okay?" Jake covered her hand, which had been trembling against her thigh.

"Yeah." She squeezed his hand and held it as the audio rolled on. She didn't let it go until the incident reached the point of routine notifications.

She felt like she was sitting in that chair again. Only, on that day she'd been working on instinct and training. Today she was able to listen more objectively. She'd handled everything according to policy. Of course, she'd known that already because, as with any on-duty death, an after-action report had evaluated every aspect of the incident.

"Couldn't have done it better myself," Jake said.

"Thanks." She released his hand and ejected the disc.

"I mean it. You did everything right. You know that."

"I know. I didn't realize how much hearing it again would help."

"I guess Olivia knew just what you needed."

Hillary nodded. She didn't doubt that Olivia knew what she needed better than anyone she'd met in a long time. That's what made staying away from her so hard. But Hillary had vowed to do just that, because Olivia had made it clear that knowing something and being able to deliver it were two different scenarios.

❖

Olivia leaned against the front bumper of the Jeep and waited for Hillary to come out of Five-C. When she saw a handful of people exit the front door, nerves tightened her stomach and she reached into her pocket for her keys. She didn't want an audience. If someone saw her here and thought—

She stopped that line of thinking, realizing this was exactly the kind of paranoid reaction Hillary objected to. So she stayed where she was and waited. The group dispersed to separate cars as they made their way through the parking lot. Olivia had parked next to Hillary's car, directly under a streetlight, and she saw a couple of dispatchers glance her way, but she kept her head up and her eyes on Hillary. She knew the moment Hillary noticed her by the stiffening of her posture and the hesitation in her step. Hillary glanced at Jake, and judging by his expression, he seemed to be checking if she wanted help. She gave him a subtle shake of her head and continued toward her car.

"I think I'm having some problems with my cell service. I've been texting you, but your replies aren't coming through."

"You should call someone about that." Hillary opened the door to her car.

"Someone besides you, huh?" Olivia pushed off the car and approached. She grabbed the top of the door and held it open.

Hillary looked up and did a double-take, obviously seeing Olivia's face for the first time. In addition to the bloody nose, Andy's punch yesterday had left her with bruises around the inside of both eyes. She reached toward Olivia's face, then caught herself and let her hand fall to her side.

"What happened?" Though she tried to act unaffected, Olivia heard concern in her tone.

"I told Andy I'm gay. He socked me in the nose."

"Because you're gay?" Hillary looked outraged.

Olivia smiled and, encouraged, took a step closer. "I might have left out some things in between. We were working out—sparring. I dropped my guard and he got a shot in. I think he expected me to block it in time."

"You think?" Hillary narrowed her eyes.

"He did. He wouldn't take out his anger with violence."

"Was he angry?"

"Yeah. And shocked and worried." Olivia took another step, effectively trapping Hillary in the triangle of space between the car and the door. "And not at all supportive."

"I'm sorry."

Olivia shrugged, forcing nonchalance. Truthfully, she hoped Frankie could get through to him. Last night, she'd decided to give him some space to get over his shock. But she wasn't confident he'd ever truly accept her.

Hillary touched the bridge of Olivia's still-swollen nose, and she flinched.

"This is the part where you kiss me," Olivia whispered.

"What?"

"In your romance novels, this is the convenient plot device that brings us together, and when you touch me, you're overwhelmed by the urge to kiss me."

"For someone who makes fun of me for reading them, you seem to know an awful lot about them. But this isn't a book." Hillary planted a hand in the center of her chest and pushed her back. "And I don't need a plot device to know that right now I'd rather slap you than kiss you."

Olivia laughed, which only made Hillary angrier.

"You could have been seriously hurt."

"I was sparring. By definition I can only sustain a minor injury."

"You take too many chances."

Olivia narrowed her eyes. "I can't argue with that. But that's not what this was."

"So your plan is for me to kiss you, right here in the parking lot of Five-C?"

"How's that for taking chances?" Olivia smiled. "Or, you could follow me to my place."

"For a kiss?"

"I thought I'd start with that apology I've been trying to initiate for two days. But we can see where it goes from there."

❖

Olivia hurried inside ahead of Hillary and moved around the room quickly, assessing and straightening. She'd never updated the mismatched sofa, chair, and coffee table she'd purchased secondhand when she first moved out of her parents' house. She couldn't find a reason to when she so rarely had guests over. Her place was her solace, where she could be herself. Frankie was the only person who really knew her, and Olivia ignored her complaints about the décor.

Her apartment was slightly bigger than Hillary's but not nearly as quaintly decorated. Suddenly, she wondered what Hillary saw when she looked around. It wasn't much, but it was home, and it was the one place where no one could tell her what to do.

"You look uncomfortable. I can go if—"

"No," she blurted, then sighed. "No. I just—I don't have many guests. Or any, really."

"Then I'm honored. But what am I doing here, Olivia?"

"I—I came out to Andy."

"You said that." Hillary's voice had an edge that Olivia didn't like.

"Okay, sit down." When Hillary glared, she added, "please," but Hillary crossed to the window instead. Olivia forged ahead. "I'm sorry. I should have stood up for you with Andy. I panicked, and rather than admit the truth, I let him put it all on you."

Hillary kept her back to Olivia, but she could tell by the shift in her posture that she'd crossed her arms.

"I told Andy. My parents are the next step."

"Given Andy's reaction, you're still planning to tell them?"

"Yes." She sighed and threw her hands up in frustration. "Look, I showed up at your work tonight without caring who saw. Doesn't that show good faith?" She took a step closer. "Hillary?"

Hillary spun around, slammed her hands against Olivia's shoulders, and shoved her against the opposite wall. She took Olivia's mouth fiercely, while her hands clutched Olivia's shirt. Olivia grabbed Hillary's waist and pulled her closer, reveling in the press of Hillary's breasts and thighs against hers. As Hillary deepened the kiss, pain radiated from Olivia's nose.

"Ow."

Hillary broke the kiss and rubbed her thumb across Olivia's cheek, under her eye. "Sorry."

"Are we stopping?"

"I wish I could. I wish I could hate you for making me want you so badly." The vulnerability and self-reproach in Hillary's eyes nearly broke her heart.

"But you can't, because you know I feel it, too." She wanted to be strong enough to back off—to let Hillary keep her ideals. Then, Hillary nodded and gently laid her palm against Olivia's cheek, and any resolve she might have gathered evaporated.

"You've hated yourself enough for both of us," Hillary whispered.

Olivia sighed and rested her forehead against Hillary's. Hillary had a way of seeing things in her that she kept hidden from everyone else. She'd spent her entire life being someone else, and she now realized she stood on the precipice of opening up completely. And for a moment that thought scared her to death.

"Are you okay?" Hillary trailed her fingers along Olivia's jaw and grasped her chin.

"Yes." The warmth and concern in Hillary's eyes soothed her apprehension. "Absolutely. I've never felt better than I do right now."

"Have you—I mean, we haven't talked about, whether you have—"

Olivia laughed.

"You seem nervous and I—never mind. You don't have to tell me. I might not want to know."

"You want to pretend you're my first."

"It doesn't make a difference. But you already know I have."

"If I say I've never done this before, will you be gentle with me?"

"Okay, stop laughing at me." Hillary hid her face in Olivia's shoulder.

Olivia slid her hand into the back of Hillary's hair and tugged lightly. "I don't want you to be gentle. I don't want you to hold anything back. I want you to give me everything."

Hillary moaned and kissed Olivia, nipping at her lower lip. "You're so used to me telling you where to go and what to do."

"Every shift." Olivia smiled. "So, where do you want me to go?"

Hillary pushed her toward the bedroom. "In there."

Olivia stopped beside the bed and waited. She knew what she wanted. She'd been thinking about touching Hillary for weeks. But the idea of Hillary leading her through their first time together aroused her in a whole different way.

Hillary pulled her T-shirt over her head and dropped it on the floor. Olivia stared at the beige cups holding Hillary's breasts and fought the urge to touch them. Hillary stepped closer, a challenge in her eyes as if she could tell how much restraint Olivia was exercising.

She grasped Olivia's wrist and brought her hand to her breast. Olivia stroked Hillary's pebbled nipple through the satiny fabric. Hillary wasn't far off when she'd asked if Olivia had done this before. She hadn't. She'd been with a couple of women, but those stolen, shame-filled trysts were nothing like this. She'd never been this free to enjoy the sensation of a woman giving herself to her. And as much as she might enjoy their game, she didn't want to wait for direction from Hillary. She wanted to give and to take, endlessly.

She unfastened Hillary's pants and pushed them down her hips. Hillary didn't protest the change of pace, maybe sensing Olivia's need. She stripped them each of their clothes, guided Hillary down on the bed, and lay next to her. Hillary rolled onto her side toward her, and Olivia slid her hand into the hollow of her lower back. When Hillary arched into her, she closed her eyes and savored the feel of Hillary's breasts and stomach against hers. If not for her need to explore further, she could be very happy right here for the rest of her life.

Olivia kissed Hillary's neck and whispered words that weren't nearly strong enough to describe her emotions, "God, you feel good."

She eased Hillary onto her back and moved over her. She kissed her collarbone, then down the center of her chest, before pulling one nipple between her teeth. Hillary gasped and jerked so quickly that Olivia lifted her head and met her eyes.

"Too hard?"

"They're sensitive."

Olivia nodded, taking another moment to enjoy the flush on Hillary's cheeks and the heavy arousal in her eyes before bending her head again. This time she worked her nipple more gently with her tongue. When Hillary buried her hands in Olivia's hair, the scrape of her fingers against her scalp sent a shiver through her. Hillary tugged, and a sharp pull of pleasure echoed between Olivia's legs.

She squeezed her thighs together and remained focused on Hillary—on every reaction. She moaned when touched here, and she arched when stroked there. When Olivia's mouth ghosted over her abdomen, Hillary's fingers tightened and she pushed her head down farther. Olivia wrapped her arms around Hillary's thighs and pressed her tongue tentatively between her folds. She explored the taste and texture of her, circling slowly until she reached the firm prominence of her clitoris.

"Olivia." Hillary gasped.

No one had ever said her name with such unguarded desire. She dipped her tongue farther, licking and sucking and discovering what Hillary liked. When Hillary rose into her, Olivia pulled back, not wanting this to end yet.

Hillary grasped two of Olivia's fingers and squeezed, and Olivia took the hint and eased them inside her. As she started to thrust, she lowered her mouth again. She let Hillary's hips set the pace, slow and deep, and every time Hillary pressed down onto her, she sucked her hard.

"Oh God, please don't stop." The desperation in Hillary's voice kept Olivia's mouth working against her. She would never stop if that's what Hillary asked for. Hillary panted in rhythm with the erratic drive of her hips.

Hillary cried out, dug her heels into the bed, and arched, pushing toward the head of the bed, but Olivia stayed with her. She pulled her knees up under her and moved farther into the vee of Hillary's thighs, holding firm, deep pressure with her fingers while Hillary trembled with aftershocks.

When Hillary relaxed, Olivia carefully withdrew, then moved up her body, dropping kisses across her skin. She would happily do that all over again right now. As if reading her mind, Hillary playfully pushed her to the side just as Olivia's mouth reached her collarbone.

"Slow down, hotshot. I need to recover."

Olivia huffed and flopped onto the bed on her stomach beside Hillary, turning her face toward her. Hillary's eyes were closed and a small smiled graced her lips. Olivia's heart swelled with the pride of putting that look of satisfaction on her face, chased by another emotion. She'd said "maybe" when talking to Andy about loving Hillary. But she had no doubts, especially not in this moment.

Hillary opened her eyes, and Olivia flicked her gaze away in case Hillary could see the truth in them.

"Everything okay?" Hillary caressed her cheek.

"Yes." Everything was better than okay. Right now, everything was amazing, and she would deal with the rest later.

Hillary kissed her, then pulled back, smiling. "You taste like me."

"That was new." Maybe it was bad form to talk about past experience while in bed with a woman, but she wanted Hillary to know what this meant to her, even if she wasn't ready to say the words.

"You've never?" Hillary traced a finger along Olivia's lower lip, suddenly acting shy.

"It always felt too intimate." She'd never let herself consider a relationship outside of sex. Holding back with everyone else had begun as self-preservation and become a habit she couldn't break.

"Was it okay, for you?" Hillary asked.

"Absolutely. And you?"

"You couldn't tell?" Hillary threaded her fingers through the hair at Olivia's temple and stroked her head.

"I may have picked up on something." She closed her eyes, content to enjoy Hillary's touch.

Hillary rose up, moved over her, and lay along her back. "You didn't think we were going to sleep before I got my hands on your body, did you?" The rasp in Hillary's voice combined with her warm breath against Olivia's ear to ensure she wouldn't be sleeping anytime soon.

Hillary pressed her hips into Olivia's ass. Olivia groaned, and as she pushed back against her, Hillary took the opportunity to slide a hand under her and cup her breast.

"I've been waiting my whole life to touch you."

"Your whole life?" Olivia smiled into her pillow.

"It feels like it. I remember watching you in your cheerleading uniform. Do you still have that thing?" She rolled Olivia's nipple between her fingers.

Olivia laughed, enjoying the need that roughened Hillary's voice almost as much as the feel of her hands on her. "Now I wish I did."

"I went to the games just to see that tight little shirt ride up when you raised your arms. If I'd ever questioned my sexuality, your abs would have convinced me."

"What if reality doesn't live up to fantasy?"

"Honey, it already has. Where were you a few minutes ago?" Hillary bit the shell of her ear, inspiring a new tingle of pleasure. "Besides, I saw you in bike shorts and a sports bra weeks ago. I wanted you so bad that day, and I still thought you were straight then."

Hillary released her breast and skated her hand down Olivia's stomach. When she slipped it between Olivia's legs, Olivia's ability to continue their banter disappeared. She was still so hard from making love to Hillary, that when Hillary touched her clit, her hips jerked. Hillary alternated gentle passes with firm strokes and soon had Olivia thrusting desperately against her hand.

"Not yet." Hillary slowed her hand, and rolled her hips into Olivia's ass. Then she moved to lie alongside Olivia. When Olivia started to turn over, Hillary planted a hand between her shoulder blades. "Stay there. I just want to watch you."

She slid her hand down to the back of Olivia's hips, her other hand still buried between Olivia's legs. She slipped a finger inside her, and Olivia's moan vibrated in the back of her throat. She closed her eyes for a second, enjoying the sensation, then forced them open, watching Hillary watch her. As Hillary pulled out and slid back inside, adding another finger, Olivia spread her legs to accommodate her. She bit her lip and held Hillary's eyes, hoping she could see how good she made her feel.

Olivia adjusted her angle so she could thrust her clit against the heel of Hillary's hand with every stroke of her fingers inside her. Tendrils of pleasure spread out through her body, connecting her hardened nipples with the sensitive flesh between her legs.

"Can you come like this?" Hillary flicked her eyes down Olivia's body, then back up.

"Yes." Right now she could. Right now her body surged toward that peak, as out of control as her thrusts were becoming. She planted her elbows on the bed and arched her back, finding the leverage to ride Hillary's hand over the edge. She squeezed her eyes shut as her body seized, then released in waves. She kept her eyes closed, enjoying the transition into a slow throb and the way Hillary now traced soft circles on her back.

"I've set a bad precedent here." Hillary's voice dragged her back to consciousness, and she realized she'd been about to drift off.

"How so?" The pillow muffled her voice, and she found the energy to turn her head more to the side.

"You show up, say you're sorry, and not only do I cave, but I take you to bed."

"And you call that bad?"

"Not for you, I guess."

She poked Hillary gently in the side. "I seem to remember you having a good time, too."

"I had a very good time." Hillary gave her a slow kiss, a languid caress that flowed through her like warm caramel.

She rolled to her back and Hillary shifted to her side, resting her head on Olivia's shoulder and draping her arm across her stomach.

Olivia pulled the covers over them both. "Stay?"

Hillary smiled and kissed her chest. "Yes."

After a few quiet minutes, she felt Hillary relax in her arms as she fell asleep. But Olivia wasn't ready to drift off yet. She rested her cheek against the top of Hillary's head and smiled as Hillary burrowed closer to her.

She'd meant it when she said she'd never felt better. She'd let fear rule her life for too long. Coming out to Andy had been the first step in breaking that pattern. And while she still worried about telling her parents, she could finally imagine a future for herself that included a true and honest partner. She didn't have to resign herself to a life of loneliness, hoping that her family would fill the void.

She recalled Hillary's words about hating herself and swallowed the thick feel of tears in her throat. She would not cry after sex.

CHAPTER EIGHTEEN

Hillary rolled over, awakened by her phone signaling a text message. From the other side of the bed, Olivia's phone vibrated against the nightstand. Hillary squinted at the screen of her phone, then set it back on the nightstand without opening the text.

"There's no way he could know yet," she mumbled.

"Who?" Olivia's phone buzzed again.

"Jake." She rubbed her hand across Olivia's warm, firm stomach. "He's going to be so jealous." She propped herself up on her elbows and traced a lazy finger along Olivia's collarbone.

"Did you plan to tell him?"

"That I bagged the hottest deputy on the force? The one no one else could get close to? Absolutely." Hillary grinned to let her know she was joking.

"Last night was amazing."

"And this morning?" Only a few hours ago, Olivia had teased her into consciousness, running her fingers down her back and over her hips. They'd made love again, and then Olivia had pulled Hillary against her and they went back to sleep.

"This morning, too."

"For me, too. Whatever else happens, it meant something to me." She didn't know why she'd said that except that she hoped Olivia didn't have morning-after doubts. If so, letting her go would be even more difficult now.

"Nothing has changed." Olivia traced her finger along Hillary's jaw and smiled. "Or everything has. It means something to me, too."

Olivia kissed her tenderly. When her text alert beeped twice, one after another, Olivia picked up her phone. "What's going on? Why are both of our phones blowing up?" She swiped the screen and her expression grew serious. "Can you turn on the television?"

"Missing your favorite morning show?"

"A Nashville police officer shot someone."

Hillary sat up, grabbed the remote, and turned on the television. She gathered the sheet around her waist and watched with growing dread as the situation in Nashville escalated. Officers responding to a robbery confronted a suspect who ran into an apartment complex. While attempting to apprehend him, the officer's Taser misfired. The suspect went for a gun and several officers shot him. He was rushed to the hospital but didn't survive surgery. A crowd had gathered outside the hospital and threatened to get out of control.

"We're going to need coffee." Olivia slid out of bed and headed for the kitchen.

Hillary let herself enjoy the sight of Olivia walking around her house naked before she faced the seriousness of what she'd just seen. The reporter flashed three different photographs of white male officers who had all fired their guns, though it was unclear at this time which ones had hit him and where. The robbery suspect was a young black man. His accomplice, reportedly a woman, had escaped. Hillary winced as the reporter went on what could only be termed an opinionated rant about a situation he couldn't possibly know enough about. This early in an incident, law enforcement tended to hold back many important details while the investigation moved forward, leaving the media with nothing to go on but speculation. The less-responsible members of the press would take that speculation and run with it.

"Seriously?" She tugged on an oversized T-shirt and strode down the hall.

Olivia already had the television on in the living room and stood in the archway to the kitchen watching it while she waited for coffee to brew. She stepped back to the counter and filled two waiting mugs.

"Why are the police always automatically the bad guys?" Hillary took the mug Olivia handed her. "Thank you."

Olivia shrugged. "I guess because sometimes we are."

"I thought you, of all people, would be outraged at a false accusation."

"We don't know it's false, yet." Olivia sipped her coffee, more calmly than Hillary would have expected. "Yes, I know how it feels to be on the wrong end of an investigation, though mine was nowhere near this scale." Olivia sat on the couch. "But I took an oath to serve and protect, as did every law-enforcement officer out there. Sometimes an investigation is the only way to know that oath isn't abused."

"That's a mature way of looking at things."

Olivia laughed. "You mean a *more mature* way than you expected."

"Well, it's not exactly congruent with your reputation."

"It's a little easier when I'm not quite so personally involved. I've lost my temper, some. I admit it. And I probably will again."

"I know." Olivia wasn't mean-spirited. She had a quick fuse, but more than that, she put on a show of bravado because she felt she had to in order to be taken seriously. Olivia's behavior wasn't even novel. Hillary had seen plenty of gangly or short male officers compensate in the same way.

"My time at Five-C wasn't all bad." Olivia cupped the back of Hillary's neck and pulled her in for a coffee-flavored kiss.

Hillary set her coffee on the counter so she could wrap her arms around Olivia's waist. "Yeah?"

Olivia smiled. "I got all of those free lunches."

Hillary shoved her away, smiling while Olivia laughed at her.

"This looks like it's going to get messy." Hillary gestured to the television where a line of police officers struggled to contain a mass of angry citizens.

"We've seen a lot of that lately." Several high-profile cases had garnered media attention in recent weeks. One had gone the way of the officer involved, but the jury was still out on the other—specifically the grand jury. "This is all going in the direction of body cams."

"The technology is there. But I've heard some of our own deputies say they don't want them."

Olivia shrugged. "If I'm not doing anything wrong, a camera can only help me. As a matter of fact, it *might* have helped me. Besides, like you said, it's technology. Everyone has cameras on their phones, though I'd much rather be exonerated by my own video. But these cases make it harder for the rest of us."

"I can imagine."

"The majority of people cooperate. You know as well as I do, this job isn't as dramatically charged as primetime television wants us to think. But when the public doesn't trust one of us, some people don't trust any of us. So we get attitude and grandstanding and *are you going to shoot me, too* and *I know my rights.* It can become a lot harder just to do our jobs."

"I know what you mean. I can't even count the number of times in nine years that someone has told me their taxes pay my salary. I want to tell them that I need a raise, because if my salary was the only thing motivating me to do a good job we'd both be in trouble."

❖

"One-thirty-seven."

Olivia couldn't help but smile every time she heard Hillary's voice, even when she was calling her on the radio to give her work.

They'd spent more nights together than apart in the past two weeks, and Olivia couldn't be happier. As long as she didn't think too much about revealing their relationship to the rest of her family. Frankie apparently intended to force Andy to come around. She'd made him have dinner with Olivia and Hillary last weekend. He'd acted aloof but polite, and Frankie had only had to glare at him a couple of times, which Olivia chose to count as a small victory. She would have to deal with telling her parents soon, but for now she and Hillary lived in a pretty little bubble of fun and sex.

"One-thirty-seven, go ahead."

"And one-thirty, be direct. Thirty-seven is my only unit available for an open line on 9-1-1." Since she would typically dispatch two deputies on this type of call, she had to let the sergeant know there was no one to back Olivia up. "We're still on the line and can hear a man yelling and a kid crying." Any time someone dialed 9-1-1, operators stayed on the line, even if the person wasn't able to actively converse with them. They listened and updated the call with any pertinent information.

"One-thirty, I'll go with her," Sergeant Gilleland said.

Hillary acknowledged her transmission and gave them both the address over the air, as well as sending it to their laptops.

"Why do I know that address?" Olivia murmured. She glanced at her computer screen and the location clicked in her head. "Manuel." She pushed her foot harder on the gas.

She arrived before Gilleland. As she got out of the car, instinct pushed her toward the door, but halfway up the walk she slowed down. She glanced around the outside of the house but didn't see anything to indicate what was going on inside. Since the last time she'd been here, a hasp had been affixed to the door and frame. A broken padlock lay on the porch, and she nudged it aside with her foot.

She knocked on the door. "Police, open up." When she didn't get a response, she pounded harder. The door still didn't open.

She leaned over and looked in the window at the front of the house. She could see through to the eat-in kitchen. Manuel sat in a chair at the kitchen table, his expression sullen and stubborn. His father paced the room around him, looking like he was on a rant. Manuel fiddled with something tucked under his leg. She leaned closer. Was that a cell phone?

She keyed her radio. "Do you still have that open line?"

"Yes. We can't make out what the man is saying, but from his tone, he's angry."

Manuel lifted his head and looked his father in the eye. She couldn't hear what Manuel said, but she jumped when Manuel's father backhanded him across the face. She sucked in a quick breath, fighting to maintain control.

"Sarge?" she said into her shoulder mic.

"Go ahead."

"Signal ten." Trying to keep her voice even, she gave the code that let Gilleland know she needed to hurry. Unfortunately, she also alerted Hillary that she was having trouble on her call.

"Ten-four. Hold what you have. I'm five minutes out."

Ignoring Gilleland's request to wait for her before proceeding, she headed back to the door and pounded again. But this time she didn't wait for an answer. After quickly assessing the door, she kicked, planting her foot just below the doorknob. She had to hit it twice before it swung inward violently.

As she eased into the kitchen, Manuel's father yanked him out of the chair and pulled him close like a human shield. She stopped in the archway between the living room and the kitchen. She didn't see a weapon, but that didn't mean he didn't have one concealed. His dark hair was greasy-looking. Sweat covered his skin and dampened an arc on the front of his T-shirt and circles under his arms. His eyes were wild with something more than anger. Meth? Or something else?

"You okay, Manuel?"

"Yeah." His voice trembled and his father's arm tightened around his neck. The side of his face had reddened and swelled already.

"You think you can keep him from me? He's my son. I will always find him."

She silently cursed DCS for not protecting him.

"You're weak. You thought you could hide him. Just like you thought you could keep me out of my own house." He laughed, almost maniacally.

"Let's talk about this. You haven't done anything you can't walk away from yet."

"I don't want to talk. I need you to leave me and my son alone." Manuel winced as his arm tightened again.

"Your son is right there with you." She took a step forward. He jerked back and Manuel whimpered. She held her hands up in front of her just above waist level, hoping to portray surrender though she remained alert and ready to react. "But I know you don't want to hurt him. I can see how much you love him."

His hands eased, but he didn't release Manuel. "Let us leave."

"You know I can't do that."

"I'm not going to prison."

"This isn't the way to go about that. Get yourself an attorney and fight the charges."

He shook his head vehemently. "We're walking out of here. Now." He moved toward the door, but she took a step to the right and blocked any path he might have to the front door.

He looked at the knife block on the counter, then back at her. She gave him her best warning look and rested her hand on her Glock.

"What are you going to do, bitch, shoot me? And get your cop friends to cover it up?"

"I can't let you leave with him." She clenched her jaw and moved her hand into a stronger position over her gun.

He reached for the knives, and the snick of the blade pulling from the block coincided with the slide of her gun out of her holster. He angled the knife against Manuel's throat, and she fought to keep her temper in check. She wanted to put a bullet in him and was pretty certain she could do it.

"Put the knife down."

He didn't comply.

Footsteps sounded behind her. "Put it on the counter." Gilleland's order was calm and controlled. She moved into position beside Olivia, her gun drawn as well. She keyed her radio. "Dispatch, give us the air. We have one at gunpoint." While advising Hillary what they had, her transmission also alerted the other deputies not to tie up the radio channel in case things went bad on them. Several of them would be on the way to help as soon as they heard the nature of the situation.

"Get out of my way," he yelled. His face turned red and spittle flew out of his mouth. When Manuel started to cry, he shook him. "Stop crying. You're not a baby."

"I saw you at the range awhile back, Dennis." Gilleland spoke evenly despite his raised voice, causing him to quiet down to hear her.

"Huh?" Olivia kept her eyes and her gun trained on him, while trying to figure out where Gilleland was headed.

"You emptied an entire mag and every shot was dead-on. Are you always that accurate?"

"Yes." She adjusted her stance, keeping her hands firm but relaxed on her gun. She stared at him and directed her next question to both him and Gilleland. "Do you want to see?"

"You won't shoot with the kid in front of me." He obviously tried to be hard, but he sounded nervous.

"I'm not going to hurt him." She projected more confidence than she felt. "But I can't make any promises about you." She tilted her head toward Sergeant Gilleland but didn't take her eyes off him. "Sarge, this may have to be a head shot. That kid is kind of tall. That okay?"

He tried to duck down behind Manuel. She didn't think he was going to hurt Manuel, so she'd decided to take a gamble. But she didn't know how she'd live with herself if she was wrong.

"Do what you have to do, Deputy."

"One more chance. Put the knife down." She pushed because the longer this went on the less likely it would end safely. If they didn't talk him down soon, most likely Gilleland would make her pull back and wait for negotiators. She didn't know how she would leave Manuel alone in this room with him.

His hand flexed around the knife handle and she raised her gun, aiming at his head. She met his eyes, trying to see through his drug haze. She flicked her eyes to Manuel but had to look away from the fear on his face. She wasn't sure she could take this shot. But this guy wasn't leaving the room unless he did so in handcuffs or on a stretcher.

"Papa, please." Manuel whimpered.

His face softened for a moment, the anger easing at his son's fearful tone. He pressed the side of his face against the top of Manuel's head and whispered, "I'm sorry." Then he released him.

But Olivia didn't let down her guard and wouldn't until he was in custody. She'd seen the hard edge still in his eyes. Manuel ran to Olivia, blocking her path to his father for just long enough for him to rush her. She shoved Manuel toward Gilleland and squared up. He telegraphed his next move, swinging his knife in a huge arc and giving her enough time to react. She ducked to the side and struck out with her non-gun hand, knocking the knife from his hand. They grappled for only a second before she got hold of his arm and pulled it high behind his back. Using her leverage, she forced him to his knees, then prone on the ground, and shoved her gun into the base of his neck.

"Stop resisting," she ground out, hoping she wouldn't have to shoot him in front of his son.

Gilleland moved in with her cuffs. When he tensed up beneath her, Olivia applied more pressure to his arm and he cried out.

"Stop, or I'll break it." The image of the knife against Manuel's throat flashed through her mind and she dug the barrel of her gun deeper into his spine. She leaned down and growled in his ear, "Test me and I'll make you a quadriplegic without a second thought."

"Dennis, I got him." Gilleland reached in front of her and snapped a cuff on one of his wrists. When she tried to nudge Olivia aside, she didn't budge. "Stand down. I've got him." She squeezed Olivia's shoulder.

Behind Gilleland, Olivia caught sight of Manuel cowering in the doorway. She handed the suspect over to Gilleland, stood, and holstered her gun. Gilleland cuffed him and Olivia helped her haul him to his feet.

She keyed her radio. "Suspect is in custody. You can have your air back."

"Ten-four." Hillary's voice trembled.

"I'll have one of the other guys transport him. We'll have to wait for Crime Scene to get here. And we're going to have a shitload of paperwork to do," Gilleland said as she walked him toward the front door. She nodded toward Manuel. "Does he need an ambulance?"

"I'll take him to the hospital and have his caseworker meet us there." The injury to his face needed to be looked at and documented by a doctor for his state file.

She got Manuel settled in the backseat of her car, then made the call to DCS before getting behind the wheel.

"Your case worker will meet us there." She looked over her shoulder.

He looked even smaller in the big backseat of her cruiser. He bowed his head, clenched his hands together between his knees, and stared at the floor. "I don't want to go to the hospital."

"Sorry, bud, it's procedure. I'll wait with you there until your case worker gets there. She seems nice." She pulled out of the driveway. "Where did you go last time? Did they find you a foster home?"

"I was staying with my grandma."

"Did your father pick you up from there?" She glanced at him in her rearview mirror.

He shook his head. "She lets me play in the park across the street from her house. He came there."

Maybe ten was old enough to go to the park by himself. She wasn't a parent and didn't know. But Manuel looked much younger, and unfortunately, even Reinsville wasn't the same small town she grew up in. She didn't want to judge his grandmother when she didn't know the circumstances, but she did plan to pull the DCS worker aside and ask a few questions when she arrived.

❖

After Olivia finished at the hospital, she returned to the scene. The Emergency Department had been blessedly slow, and the doctor had seen Manuel right away. While he examined Manuel, Olivia talked to the caseworker, who promised to investigate the situation at his grandmother's before returning him there. She took Olivia's contact information and said she'd let Olivia know where he ended up so she could check on him. There were still some advantages to small-town living.

By the time she got back to the house, the crime-scene tech had arrived and should be almost done processing the inside of the house. Because the suspect had pulled a knife and Olivia had fought with him, they would be collecting the knife and photographing the scene. She and Gilleland would decide what charges to add to his pending drug offenses. Olivia was prepared to stack on as much as she could. She wanted him behind bars until Manuel was old enough to fend for himself.

"Get the kid all settled?" Gilleland asked as she exited the house and met Olivia halfway down the walk.

"He's with his case worker. She's going to keep me updated on him."

"That kid has been through a lot. He could use a cop in his corner."

She nodded, considering for the first time that she could be a lasting influence in Manuel's life. He could easily get lost growing up in the system, and then he'd be aged-out at eighteen. But if she kept in touch with him, checked on him, and helped him, maybe he'd have a better chance.

"Good work, Dennis. But I think I asked you to wait for me before going in."

"You did." She met Gilleland's eyes without apology.

"I would have done the same. But when I say back off, you need to do that."

"Yes, ma'am." She'd shown her hesitation in that house, and Gilleland might have interpreted that as distrust. It wasn't, but she couldn't explain what it was right now. Emotionally, she couldn't go back to the place where all she could think about was hurting that guy.

"I'm not going to ask if you could have stopped yourself if I hadn't been here."

"If he hadn't resisted anymore, I—"

"I said I'm not asking. Are you ready to head to booking and start the paperwork?"

She grimaced. "Sure. Would you mind if I stop by Five-C on the way there?"

Gilleland raised a brow. "Yeah? She never struck me as the type to need reassurances."

"She's not. But she's had a rough couple of months—we both have."

"Make it quick."

"Got it, Sarge."

CHAPTER NINETEEN

Olivia pulled up to the front of Five-C, saving time by parking illegally. She wouldn't be here long. She hurried through the door and down the hall toward the dispatch center. She paused in the doorway to scan the room. Hillary was at a console on the other side of the room, with her back to her.

"That was crazy, huh?" She barely glanced at the other dispatchers; her only thought was of reaching Hillary. Hillary turned and seemed to crumble when she saw Olivia, as if she'd been holding it together until this moment. Without thinking, Olivia gathered Hillary against her. "Hey, I'm okay. I'm okay." She whispered into Hillary's hair, repeating the words until she felt Hillary's breathing slow down.

She caught Jake's curious look and that of another dispatcher. But instead of pulling away, she held Hillary closer. Jake's eyes flickered between Olivia's face and her hands rubbing Hillary's back. She saw understanding come over his expression. She returned her attention to Hillary, not caring at that point what assumptions were made. She eased back only enough to meet Hillary's eyes but kept her arms around her.

"Better?"

Hillary nodded.

She smoothed her hand over Hillary's hair and pressed a kiss to her temple. "Good."

"What are you doing here?"

"I came to check on you. But I can't stay long. I have to go do a bunch of paperwork with your ex."

Hillary pushed her away playfully. "Then tell her I said hello."

"Sure. We talk about you all the time."

"Smart-ass."

"Can I see you after shift?" she asked, not comfortable with how much she wanted Hillary to say yes.

"Of course. My place?"

"See you then." She didn't try to hide her smile as she walked out. When Jake gave her an inquisitive look, she tossed him a flirty wink.

Hillary couldn't erase the goofy grin from her face as she watched Olivia disappear through the door. Olivia seemed to have known that Hillary wanted to see her after being shaken up by the earlier incident. The only positive she could draw from the experience was that she hadn't panicked when she heard Olivia ask for May to hurry to the scene. Sure, she'd been worried, but she'd stayed in her seat and seen it through. Not that she could have handed over her radio until she knew Olivia was safe. She'd never been more relieved than when Olivia advised that they had him in custody.

Later, she might be interested in hearing more about what had happened out there, but for now she was just happy it was over and Olivia was safe.

"You've been holding out on me." Jake stretched his headset cord as far as it would go to get around the corner of the short cubicle wall that separated their workstations.

"A little bit, maybe."

"A little bit? She came up here to see if you were okay."

She shrugged, playing indifferent. "You know we're friends."

"Don't even." He held a hand up in front of him. "Truth. How long have you been keeping this from me?"

"A couple of weeks."

"What? How could you?" He pressed his hand to his chest in what she assumed was mock-indignation.

"It's new. I wanted to keep it to myself for a bit."

"And?" He inclined his head, and when she didn't respond, he said, "Is she as good as she looks?"

"That's personal." Just thinking about Olivia got her hot all over again.

"What? You always tell me. You told me how it was with Ann."

"This is different."

"Game changer?"

She nodded.

"Since today was the first hint she isn't straight, can I assume she's another closet case?" Disapproval saturated his tone.

"She wasn't out, but—"

"I know I was all for you being the one to crack her façade. But, please, don't do this. I don't care how hot she is."

"She came out to her brother."

"Come talk to me when she's had a sit-down with daddy dearest." He returned to his side of the partition.

She understood his point, and she couldn't say she wasn't nervous about how things might play out. Though Andy had been a jerk at dinner that first night, he'd shown improvement since. And Olivia had Frankie's support, which meant Andy would come around. Her parents might be different. She'd met Sheriff Dennis only a couple of times professionally and the one time at dinner, but he didn't seem like the kind of guy who bent his beliefs, even for his children. She didn't want to ask Olivia to choose between them. But she'd already drawn her line regarding hiding her relationships. Granted, lately, she'd sort of been straddling that line. But after touching Olivia, not crossing it completely could be a struggle.

❖

"I'm going to regret asking this, but how much did you not tell me about that call today?" Hillary planted her hand in the center of Olivia's bare chest. They'd made it through a couple of slices of reheated pizza before ending up naked in bed.

"It wasn't bad at all. I had it under control pretty much the whole time." She covered Hillary's hand and stroked the back of her wrist.

She'd been purposely vague about the details of the call, not wanting to upset Hillary.

"Your answer doesn't inspire confidence. You typically don't have to hold someone at gunpoint if you're the one in control."

"I said *pretty much* the whole time."

"I knew I was going to regret it. I'm not equipped for another bad call right now, least of all one you're involved in."

"You handled it," Olivia said.

"Because the situation didn't go *really* bad."

"Because I was in control." Olivia smiled. She lifted Hillary's chin until she met her eyes. "You are a very good dispatcher. One of the best. Needing a little help now and then doesn't change that. In fact, I think helping each other out is part of the job description when it comes to public safety. For all of us."

"You're getting good at the speeches. Where's the Deputy Dennis who earned her reckless reputation?"

"Still here." Olivia covered Hillary's hand that rested on her stomach and slid it up to her chest. "She showed up for a bit today. Kicked in that door like a badass. You should have seen it."

"Yeah?"

"Got into a good old-fashioned stand-off with that guy."

"You sound a little too excited about that, considering how hard my heart was pounding at the time."

"Back to my original point, I stormed in there. But things might have gone very differently if I hadn't had backup."

"So, May saved your ass."

"Hey, I didn't say that." She wasn't about to admit she'd needed Gilleland's help in there. At least not while she was in bed with Hillary. No, right now she wanted to feel powerful and bulletproof. "It was all me. She just supplied the cuffs."

"I'll be sure to thank her the next time I talk to her."

"How often do you talk to her?" The thought of Hillary and Gilleland chatting over coffee irritated her more than it should.

"Aw, jealousy is so cute on you." Hillary tweaked her nipple playfully. "Are you worried it won't be the first time I've thanked her for handcuffs?"

"Shut up." She feigned anger and pushed Hillary's hand away. "Seriously, how often?"

Hillary shrugged. "Once a week, maybe. And we text sometimes when I'm assigned to your channel. You'd probably like her if you gave her a chance."

"As much as I hate to admit it, I do. She's a good supervisor. She supports us without stifling us."

"Translation, she lets you run a little wild but pulls you back before you get into trouble." Hillary tugged on her earlobe.

Olivia stared at her.

"What?"

"I don't think I could have described today any better if I tried."

"I'm glad."

"You're glad?"

"Yeah, I like you a little wild. But I want you safe. Other than maybe Andy, there's no one out there I trust to do that more than May."

Olivia rose and moved over Hillary's body. "Let's stop talking about your ex."

"Okay," Hillary murmured. "What else do you want to discuss?"

"No more talking." Olivia covered her mouth, silencing any further conversation.

❖

"Wait here," Olivia said as she climbed out of her patrol car.

Hillary glanced around at the neighborhood they'd parked in but didn't recognize anything. Why was she riding around in Olivia's patrol car? Olivia strode up the walk to the house she'd parked in front of, looking very sexy in her uniform. Hillary had never been one to chase badges, but Olivia's swagger made her knees weak.

Olivia kicked in the door to the house, but a second blast followed the splintering of the doorframe. Olivia's body flew backward as if propelled by some unseen force. Hillary shoved open the car door and rushed to her side. Olivia gasped for breath and struggled to sit up.

"Olivia, lie down, you're hurt." A cluster of holes had been ripped in the front of her uniform shirt.

"Shotgun blast." She fumbled open the front of her shirt. "My vest caught them all."

"We should call the paramedics to check you out." Given what she knew about the spray of a shotgun blast, Olivia had to be injured somewhere and not realize it. Hillary reached for the radio mic on Olivia's shoulder, but Olivia pushed her hands away.

"I told you to wait in the car." She stumbled to her feet and pulled her gun. When she made a move toward the house, Hillary grabbed her arm.

"Come back to the car and wait for backup."

"It's okay. Sergeant Gilleland will be here soon. Send her in when she gets here."

"Wait for May, please."

"Stay here." Olivia shook her off and ran through the front door.

Hillary stared at the door, trying to decide if she should follow Olivia inside. She couldn't leave her alone in there. But without a gun, would she be a liability? She ran to the car, glanced at the radio, and instead grabbed her cell phone. With shaking fingers she scrolled through her contacts for May's number and dialed. As soon as May answered she shouted the address into the phone and begged her to hurry. She ignored May's attempts to calm her down.

Several long minutes later, May's car screeched to the curb. She shot out of it and called, "Where is she?"

"Inside. Please, May—" Hillary's words were drowned in the tears she'd been holding back.

"I'll get her."

May disappeared inside the house and, left alone, Hillary tried to control the hysteria she had been holding back. She stared at the door, willing them to come out. She cursed Olivia under her breath for going inside, for having a dangerous job, and for not waiting for backup. Why did she always have to be so headstrong?

The sharp report of a gunshot jolted her awake. She stared at her bedroom ceiling, panic still pounding in her chest. Olivia. What had happened to Olivia?

"Is something wrong?" Olivia rolled over and touched her arm.

"I—just a dream." She willed her breathing to slow. *Just a dream. She's here. She's okay.*

"Come here." Olivia held out her arm, inviting Hillary into her embrace. Once Hillary had settled there, she stroked her head and kissed her forehead. "Do you want to talk about it?"

She shook her head. She'd become accustomed to nightmares in the past couple of months. But most of them featured faceless officers in trouble or some crisis in her own life. She wrapped her arms around Olivia, searching for solace in Olivia's solid warmth. *She's okay.*

"Whatever it was, it's just a dream."

"I know."

"What can I do?"

"Just hold me for a minute."

"I can do that." Olivia held her tighter. "I guess I haven't gotten any better at chasing away the bad dreams. Why *are* you keeping me around?"

"Hmm, well, the sex is good." Hillary said, feigning concentration.

"So, I have that going for me." Olivia squeezed the place on Hillary's hip that drove her crazy. Hillary hadn't even known she would like the possessive way Olivia handled her. But Olivia had discovered that spot on their second night together.

"Yes, you do." Hillary shivered as Olivia's fingers in the hollow of her hip sent a tingle through her. "Maybe you can't stop the dreams, but you can sure distract me from them."

"Let's see what I can do about that." When Olivia moved over her, Hillary wrapped her arms around her and pulled her down so she could feel her weight on her. She ran her nails over Olivia's back and felt Olivia's breathing quicken against her face. She'd picked up a few of her own tricks in the past couple of weeks.

Olivia grabbed her hands and pinned them to the bed next to her head. "I think I'm the one doing the distracting here. You don't touch."

"Touching you distracts me."

"Yeah, it distracts me, too. And I'm focusing on you right now. You won't hear me say this very often, but the only thing you need to do is lie there."

Hillary laughed. She lifted her head and kissed Olivia. As soon as she did, Olivia melted against her, stroking her tongue inside her mouth.

"No." Olivia spanned her hand under the edge of Hillary's jaw and eased her head back into the bed, firmly but not with enough pressure to hurt her. Olivia met her eyes and Hillary could see in them that she knew exactly how each touch affected her. Giving that power to Olivia didn't bother her. Olivia didn't hold anything back with her, and Hillary loved seeing her embrace her own arousal because she'd stifled it for far too long.

As Olivia mapped out all the sensitive points on her body, Hillary immersed herself in every stroke and tender brush of her lips. She closed her eyes and let Olivia's hands and mouth chase away the remnants of the dream that flashed behind her lids. Her climax swept over her, carrying away everything but the intimate space between them. She pulled Olivia to her, cupped the back of her neck, and rested their foreheads together.

"God, I love what you do to me," she whispered before she could stop herself.

"Just what I do to you?" Olivia met her eyes, but in the darkened room, Hillary couldn't read them.

She trailed her fingers from Olivia's neck along the underside of her jaw. "Are you really prepared for me to answer that?"

"Yes."

"This isn't just physical for me. It hasn't been for a while now."

"You said yourself you've had a crush on me since high school. I'd understand this being an extension—"

"Are you preparing yourself for disappointment?"

Olivia started to pull away, but Hillary held her close.

"I admitted to the crush. You were hot, and adolescent-Hillary didn't stand a chance." Hillary smiled. "But the time we've spent together—I'm not just admiring you from afar now." She framed Olivia's face and angled it toward her. "You are beautiful, and strong, and amazing. And you've made me fall in love with you."

Olivia smiled. "I made you?"

"You're kind of a bully that way." Her heart pounded as the force of what she'd just said crashed over her. Olivia professed to want openness with her family, and Hillary would give her space to get there. "Listen, I'm not pushing you. I just—that dream threw me and the way you—you being here, it makes everything better. I got caught up."

"Did you mean it?" Olivia's expression had grown serious, but Hillary still had no idea what she was thinking or feeling.

"I did."

"Then say it again."

"I'm in love with you." Hillary laughed when Olivia swept her up and pebbled kisses on her neck. "I love you." Hillary rolled them both over, landing on top of Olivia. She covered Olivia's mouth with hers and palmed one of her breasts, trumping further conversation.

Chapter Twenty

I'm glad you had an opening for me today," Hillary said as she followed Stein inside his office.

"We were supposed to check in later this week, so we bumped it up a few days. Sit." He waved toward the chair she usually chose during their sessions. "What's going on?"

She started with a brief account of the call to Manuel's house that she'd sent Olivia and May on. She told him how she'd reacted when she knew Olivia could be in danger. She heard the pride in her own voice when she described keeping her seat and seeing it through.

"It sounds like you handled the incident well."

"I guess."

"How did you sleep last night?"

"Why did you ask me that?"

He shrugged. "You seem confident that you did what you were supposed to. Sometimes these things can re-aggravate past stress. Based on experience, your brain processes stress through dreams." He leaned back, laced his hands together, and rested them on his stomach. "When you first came to me, you exhibited several symptoms of post-traumatic stress. I told you then, and I'll repeat it now. There is nothing definitive about this and we can't treat it as such."

"But I was doing better. Hardly any dreams. I'm not reliving the incident anymore. No irritability and my temper has been—"

"And yesterday an officer on your radio, one to whom you have an emotional connection, got into trouble. Everything turned out fine, but I would still expect it to be stressful."

She nodded. "Since you brought up that emotional connection, there've been some developments along that vein."

"I thought as much. First, tell me about the dream. I suspect that'll explain what I need to know about the two of you."

She briefly described the dream, but she didn't gloss over the details, even the ones that would cue him in to her feelings for Olivia.

"I can see why that may have shaken you up. And May? You called her Sergeant Gilleland when you talked about the actual incident, but when you described your dream, she was May."

"She's Olivia's supervisor. And an ex of mine."

"That's complicated."

"Not really. She's a good person. We're—amicable."

"That's polite. There's not a lot of mystery in this dream. You worry about Olivia's safety. She has a reputation for being reckless." He smiled when she gave him a surprised look. "Yes, Deputy Dennis's reputation precedes her. I'm guessing May is known for dependability and level-headedness, professionally and personally."

"Yes. When we were together, I knew I could rely on her. We split because we weren't meant to be, not because of dishonesty or betrayal."

"You don't trust Olivia?"

"I've known May longer." She grasped the first logical explanation she could think of. But his expression indicated she couldn't get away with the vague response. "I want to. But professionally, I think she puts the job above her own safety and too often lets her need to prove she's strong enough rule her actions."

"And personally?"

"I know she wouldn't purposely hurt me. I trust that. But she hasn't faced her parents yet, and I know what their approval means to her. She's spent her entire life striving for it."

"Do you believe her feelings for you are strong enough to override that?"

"I don't think I have a right to ask for them to be."

"Isn't that her decision?"

"I don't like it when you do that."

"Do what?"

"Ask me a question that you already know the answer to just so I'll have to admit you're right."

He smiled. "They are *her* parents. So let's leave that relationship to her for now. Regarding this latest incident, you did your job. And she's safe. But as a deputy, she could face danger again. You should stay vigilant about how that affects you." He stood, indicating their time was up. "And remember you can come back and see me any time."

"You're cutting me loose?"

"I released you back to work weeks ago. We've reduced our sessions, and this one was a checkup, really. Don't hesitate to call if something changes or you just need a refresher."

She shook his hand. "Thank you for all your help." As she walked out, she was surprised to realize she meant it. She'd been involved in tough calls before, but that accident had been by far the worst. She'd always told herself she just wasn't the therapy type. But the truth was, she'd been afraid that admitting she needed help showed weakness. Yes, she knew she'd had a textbook reaction and that she wasn't the first in public safety to feel that way. Which is why guys like Stein could build an entire practice around just treating cops, firefighters, and the like.

"Mama," Olivia called as she opened the back door to her parents' house. "I brought the cheesecake from that bakery you like." The kitchen was empty, so she slid the white box into the fridge, then headed for the living room. Andy sat in her father's chair with his feet up on the ottoman with a bowl of potato chips resting on his stomach. "Where's Mama?"

"She's at the nursing home doing her volunteer work."

Olivia shook her head. "If she was going out, why did *I* have to go by the bakery?"

"Bakery's on the other side of town."

"Dad?"

"He went to pick her up." He glanced at his watch but still hadn't looked at her. "She got done a few minutes ago."

"What are you doing here? Don't you have a television at home?" She gestured to the flat-screen. "What is this anyway?"

"*Die Hard* marathon. Frankie's hosting some kind of baby shower for one of her coworkers. Too much estrogen for me."

"All right. Tell Mama her cheesecake is in the fridge." She turned toward the door, but he stopped her.

"Hey, sit down for a minute."

She searched his face for some clue about his mood, then dropped down onto the couch.

"How are things going with Hillary?"

"Do you really want to know?"

"Give me a break. You were raised by the same guy I was. Surely, you can understand why I have trouble with this."

She shot off the sofa. "So, I was wrong to hope you were more evolved than him."

"I want to be. You're my big sister and I don't want to see you get hurt. He's going to disown you."

"She loves me." She turned and met his eyes, registering the flash of surprise in them. "This isn't going away because none of you approve."

"You'll choose her over us?"

She didn't need to consider her answer, but she took a moment anyway. "Yes."

"I can't believe—"

"Tell me you wouldn't choose Frankie, if it came down to it."

"I would never have to make that choice."

"Then you're luckier than I am," she said quietly.

He sighed heavily.

"It won't be easy, but I can keep my friendship with Frankie without seeing you anymore."

She made it as far as the front door before he spoke again.

"She said she loves you?"

"Yesterday." She turned, her hand still on the knob.

"You say it back?"

She looked away.

"Why not? It's all over your face."

"I wasn't sure it was fair to say it until I'd told them." She nodded toward her parents' wedding photo on the wall behind Andy.

"Feels good, huh?"

"Amazing."

"Good." He pointed at the screen. "Watch this. It's the best part."

She laughed and settled into the couch. The entire exchange was a perfect example of their relationship. Supportive but not too emotional.

Sometimes, a little time with Andy proved just what she needed. She loved Frankie, but she would have wanted to talk this moment to death. With Andy, things were usually straightforward. He took after their father in that way. Apparently, Andy had landed on the side of acceptance. That's where she expected their father's path to diverge.

She stayed until the credits rolled. They exchanged good-byes, but as she turned toward the door, her father's voice stopped her.

"Sit down." It was an order, not a request. He walked into the room, slowly and stiffly. Her mother followed, her eyes darting between Olivia and her husband.

Olivia swallowed, knowing her poker face was failing her now, but she complied, retaking her seat on the sofa. She might be having that conversation with him sooner than she'd thought. "What's going on?"

"Is there something you need to tell me?"

She glanced at Andy, but he shook his head, subtly indicating he hadn't told him.

He didn't wait for an answer before he went on, "I got a call today from a captain I used to work with. It seems there are some rumors going around the department about your personal life."

"This isn't how I wanted you to find out."

He clenched his teeth so hard the muscles in his jaw danced. "So it's true?" he asked tightly. "You're gay." He twisted the word as if it disgusted him to even say it.

"Dad—"

"How exactly did you want us to find out? Because I can't imagine there's a good way to hear that your daughter is going to hell."

She flinched as if he'd slapped her.

"Andrew, maybe we could listen—" Her mother tried to interject something, but when he gave her a hard look, she didn't say anymore.

Olivia's heart fell as she realized this was about to play out exactly like she'd feared. Her father had made up his mind, and her mother wouldn't stand up to him. Even though she'd predicted some sort of rejection, the reality hurt more than she'd expected.

"I wanted to tell you myself. I've been trying to figure out how." She hated how small her voice sounded.

"I wish you'd spent more time deciding how to spare us the heartache." Without waiting to hear anymore, he strode from the room.

"Mama." Olivia turned toward her mother, but she was already steps behind her husband.

The door clicked shut behind them, but it might as well have slammed, given the silence in the room. She leaned over and rested her elbows on her knees, fighting nausea and a sharp pain in her chest.

❖

Hillary shifted her grocery bags to one hand and knocked on the door to Olivia's apartment with the other. As soon as Olivia opened the door, Hillary knew something was wrong. Olivia's eyes were red, and her hair looked like she'd been worrying it with frustrated hands. Before Hillary could reach for her, Olivia turned and walked away.

"What happened?" Hillary followed her to the kitchen. She'd promised Olivia she would make her dinner after shift, and she wanted to get the asparagus in the oven soon so she could start working on the steaks she'd brought.

"My father—he—they know." Olivia paced the small area between the counter and the breakfast bar.

"What? You told them?"

"Someone beat me to it." Olivia's tone was flat, almost expressionless, but agony reflected in her eyes. "Apparently, it's all over the department."

"Oh honey, I'm sorry." She took Olivia's hand and led her to the living room. "Here, sit down. I guess he didn't take it well."

"Unless you consider him telling me I'm going to hell and storming out a good outcome—"

"Wow."

Olivia had barely settled on the couch before she shot back up and crossed the room. She shoved her hands into her dark curls and squeezed her head. "I knew—deep down, I knew how he'd react. I—I didn't want to do this. But I let you talk me into it. You pushed me and I—"

"I did what?"

"You—"

"No. Don't say it again." Hillary surged to her feet, pain slicing through her chest. "I didn't push you into anything. I told you where I stood and you made your decision."

"Well, look where that's gotten me." Olivia's dismissive tone grated on Hillary.

"Damn it." Hillary shook her head. "I believed you. I'm such an idiot."

"What are you talking about?"

"You promised me after Andy that you wouldn't do this again. But I should have known better. Your instinct will always be to side with them."

"It's not you against them."

"It shouldn't be. But right now it is."

"Hillary, I love you, but—"

"Oh, now you can say it?" Her anger built like steam driving a train, and she couldn't seem to contain it. "What's the end of that sentence? I love you, but not enough to stand up for us. I love you, just not as much as I want to be the good little sheriff's daughter."

"Hillary—"

"No." Her eyes welled up, which only made her madder. "You don't get to say that to me right now."

"Well, then when, exactly, should I say it?"

"When you can finish that sentence with I love you *and* I want to be with you no matter what." When Olivia just stared at her, she nodded, her tears falling freely now. She paused at the door on her way out. "Good-bye, Olivia."

"Hillary." Olivia took a step forward, but Hillary forced herself through the door before she could give in to the part of her heart that cried out for her to go back.

Chapter Twenty-one

Olivia stared at the back of her mother and father's bowed heads. She should be praying along with them, but she didn't think God would help her with what she wanted right now. Trying to earn some points with her mother and father, she'd arrived at church early and sat in their usual seats. But when they walked in, they barely glanced at her before sitting in the row in front of her.

Andy looked torn until Frankie dragged him into the pew beside Olivia.

"How are you holding up?" Frankie whispered.

"Okay."

"Are you coming to dinner?"

Olivia nodded as Pastor Dan took the pulpit. She spent the first part of the service thinking about her family. Neither of her parents acknowledged that they knew she was there. If they, good Christians, could treat their daughter that way in God's house, why should she try to maintain a relationship with them at all? And when was the last time she'd really been happy with the status quo? Since high school she'd been suppressing some part of herself for the comfort of everyone around her. And now, when she needed them to consider her comfort and happiness, they were unwilling.

She was still mulling this all over when Pastor Dan said something that got her attention. "I know many of you are just as crestfallen as I am to witness the advancement of the gay agenda in the national news this week."

Olivia snapped her eyes to the front of the chapel and saw him glance at her father, then at her. She stared back, refusing to be the first to look away. He scanned the congregation. "But though the government is content to let this abomination become commonplace, we should not accept it in our own communities. We must continue to fight to keep our family and friends on the path to righteousness."

For the next ten minutes, Olivia endured a barrage of scripture and the pastor's own idea of righteousness. She caught several curious looks. Clearly, the latest development in her life had gotten around just as quickly as news of her suspension had. As she sent her own surreptitious glances across the room, she also saw a couple of sympathetic faces. One was a man she'd gone to high school with, and she'd suspected even back then that he might be gay.

When the service was over, Olivia launched out of her pew and strode down the aisle. She glared at anyone who bothered to look at her. She shoved through the doors and went down the steps so fast, she practically fell down them. She didn't look back at the church she'd grown up in—that she didn't think she'd ever be able to enter again.

She reached her car and stopped with her fingers wrapped around the door handle. Her hands were shaking, and she felt light-headed. She had to calm down before she got behind the wheel. She pressed her palms hard against the hood of her car, and the trembling moved up her arms. She hung her head and pulled in several deep breaths. When she felt someone come up beside her, she jerked her head up, prepared to flee. Frankie put an arm around her shoulders and turned her away from the people spilling out of the church. Most of them would linger on the steps for a while, but she wanted to be out of the parking lot before they made their way over.

"Do you want to ride to dinner with us?" Frankie asked.

"I'm not going." Olivia straightened and yanked open her car door.

"You have to."

"No. No, I don't." She spun toward Frankie, not caring who heard her raised voice. "Were you not in there? I have no doubt where that sermon came from."

"Maybe. But running away from it won't help," Andy said as he joined them.

"What am I supposed to do? I've screwed up my relationships with everyone in my life at once. I'm done. With everything."

"Stop feeling sorry for yourself and do something about it." Andy softened his words with a hand on her shoulder. "Frankie and I are standing beside you. I don't know if he'll come around. But do you want to go back to hiding who you are?"

"No."

"Then go over there and have it out with him."

"And if he doesn't change his mind?"

"That's his loss. I can't say I'm thrilled about the whole thing. But as sister-in-laws go, Hillary's a pretty good one."

"Whoa, slow down."

"Slow down? You're the one who told me you love her."

"What?" Frankie's exclamation echoed across the parking lot. She leaned closer to the two of them. "You love her?"

"Damn it, Andy." Olivia glared at him, then turned to Frankie. "Maybe. But right now, it's a secret." Frankie smiled and hugged her. "Okay, okay. Let go of me." Olivia pulled free and slid behind the wheel of her car. "I need to take a drive. I'll meet you guys over there."

"Do you want me to go with you?" Frankie rested her hand on the still-open door. Frankie was trying to be a good friend, but she probably also wanted to see that Olivia showed up.

"I'm good. See you there in a bit. I promise."

As she left the parking lot, she saw her father holding the car door open for her mother. She drove with no particular destination in mind and with that picture lingering in her mind. Her father was a tough man, a merciless disciplinarian—with his children and with his deputies. But he'd always cherished their mother. In fact, he'd shown Andy how to treat a lady and Olivia how she should be treated. By whom? Her future husband? That had always been the expectation.

Her father had heard the rumors and she'd confirmed them. She couldn't unring that bell. So what else could she do now? Pretend she'd changed her mind? That she could marry some guy and live the way her father wanted her to? Maybe he would even pretend to believe her. Is that how she wanted the rest of her life to go? Her whole family pretending she could ever be happy? Hadn't she confidently told Andy that she would choose Hillary? Now was the time to prove it.

She'd wanted to tell them even before she met Hillary but had never had the guts—or the motivation. Then Hillary had made her feel like she could have the partner she'd always wanted—that she deserved a chance at happiness. She'd asked Hillary for trust and patience, and then, at the first sign of resistance, she'd turned on her. First with Andy and now with her parents. No wonder Hillary didn't trust her; she wouldn't trust herself either.

"Shit." She slapped her palm against the steering wheel.

Driving pretty much on autopilot for fifteen minutes had gotten her two towns over, near the regional airport. She pulled over, getting her bearings before heading back. Outside the largest hangar, a man walked around a small, private plane on the tarmac. She didn't know what kind. She'd only been on a handful of commercial flights in her life. She didn't know shit about private planes. But she watched him complete what she assumed was a preflight inspection. When he climbed inside, she put her car in gear and pulled away. Wherever he was going, it'd probably be a lot more pleasant than what she was about to walk into.

"Hello, dear," her mother said as she entered the kitchen, her tone as agreeable as if Olivia had just gone out for milk. The pretense had started already.

"Hi, Mama."

"The ham is almost ready."

Olivia nodded. She wouldn't be staying for dinner. She strode into the living room, where her father sat in his favorite chair watching football; he didn't even look at her. Andy and Frankie shared the couch. She could sit down and watch the game and pretend nothing was wrong. Maybe he would eventually stop freezing her out. Yes. She could beg for his attention and approval. But right now, all she really wanted was Hillary's arms around her.

"What am I doing here?" she muttered.

"Olivia." Frankie scooted over and patted the cushion beside her. Olivia shook her head.

"I can't do this." She turned to go, but her father's voice stopped her.

"Did you say something?"

She froze in the doorway. His smug tone practically dared her to walk out. She turned back toward him. He stared at her, clearly expecting her to fall in line. Suddenly, she didn't care if she wiped that expression off his face.

"Did you ask Pastor Dan to talk about homosexuality?" She took a little bit of satisfaction in the narrowing of his eyes.

"I confided in my pastor that I was in crisis." He'd resurrected that tone of voice from his days as sheriff. She'd never dared argue with it then, but now it only fueled her rebellion.

"*You* were in crisis?"

"How else would you describe my only daughter purposefully engaging in sinful behavior?" He surged from his chair and faced her in the center of the living room. She tilted her head to look up at him, fighting the sensation of being a little girl intimidated by her father.

"I would say your daughter is trying to be happy."

"Depravity often makes the sinner think they're happy."

That shot rocked her. She took a step backward as if absorbing a physical blow.

"Olivia. Dad." Andy stood and stepped between them. "Let's just sit down and talk about this calmly."

She glanced at Andy, trying to ignore the fear in his eyes, then made the mistake of looking at Frankie, which made her eyes brim with tears. But when she turned back to her father her resolve hardened again.

"We don't have anything to talk about right now."

"We're family. We can work this out."

"Maybe. Someday. But not today, Andy." She knew the moment that her father understood she wouldn't grovel. "I have other fences to mend first." She paused at the archway between the living room and kitchen. "I know this was a shock. It's not what you wanted for my life. But I'm your daughter," her voice broke, but she drove on, "and you're supposed to love me, unconditionally. When you're ready to do that, well, I bet you can guess where I'll be."

She paused as she passed through the kitchen. Her mother held a dish towel to her nose and mouth, and tears streamed down her face. Olivia looked for compassion, but her mother wouldn't meet her eyes.

"I'm your daughter," Olivia whispered as she pulled open the door and left the house.

❖

As she descended the front steps she pulled out her cell phone and dialed, but her call went to voice mail. When she got in the car, she didn't think she could go home. What would she do there? Sit and stare at the walls of her empty apartment. Her father's reaction had hurt her, but if she had no one to go home to, ultimately, that was on her. And fixing it—well, that was her responsibility, too.

So instead of going home, she drove to Hillary's apartment. Her car wasn't in the parking lot, but Olivia went to the door anyway. As she expected, Hillary didn't answer. She got back in her car and headed for Five-C. Hillary had been cleared for overtime, but since she'd been spending her free time with Olivia, she hadn't pulled any extra shifts. No doubt, though, Hillary was also hurt and confused, and Olivia guessed she'd turn to work for distraction.

Seeing Hillary's car in the lot at Five-C didn't bring an ounce of gratification. In the lobby, she grimaced when she saw Holt behind the desk. Apparently, this guy was never going to get reinstated, and he didn't seem to care.

"Dennis, you here to see your girl?" He probably thought that stupid wink made him look smooth.

"What?"

"I heard you were hooking up with that dispatcher. O'Neal, right?"

"Who told you that?"

He shrugged. "I don't know. One of the dispatchers. They were wondering if you're going to be any friendlier now that you've become a dyke."

"That's ridiculous."

"Yeah, yeah, I know. It's not a choice." He made finger quotes around the word choice. "I've got a cousin that's a fag."

She stared at him, not knowing which redneck thing to correct first. Could he be more clueless? His eyes shifted over her shoulder and a slimy smile spread across his face.

"There's your girlfriend now."

She looked around to find Hillary standing in the doorway. Judging by the apprehensive look on her face, she'd been there long enough to get the gist of their conversation.

She wished Holt would just shut up, but apparently Hillary's appearance didn't deter him. "If you want some advice—"

"I don't, actually." She clenched her jaw and kept her eyes on Hillary, who looked like she expected Olivia to deny their relationship. Olivia's chest ached. *I've done that to her.*

"Women don't go for that stone-cold attitude." He kept talking like he hadn't heard her. "They want you to be all warm and fuzzy and shit."

She glared at him, wondering if he was purposely being an ass or if he was just that dumb. She glanced once more at Hillary and tried for a reassuring smile, but Hillary's eyes remained cold. So she turned back to Holt. "Really? It's been my experience that women don't mind a little mystery. Maybe it's the mustard stains that are hanging *you* up." She gestured to the trail of yellow spots down the front of his shirt. He looked down and his smug smile faded.

"You really are a bitch, you know." His face twisted in anger.

"I know." When she turned back toward the dispatch center, Hillary was gone. "Have a good night, Holt," she said over her shoulder as she walked away.

"Hillary," she called as she turned the corner and saw her at the end of the hallway. She kept walking, and by the time Olivia entered the dispatch center, Hillary had already taken her place at a radio console. When she reached her, she said quietly, "Can we talk?"

"I'm working." Hillary's eyes stayed on the computer in front of her. She answered one of the officers on her channel.

"You can't even look at me now?"

Hillary's fingers froze over the keys, but she didn't turn her head.

"I want to apologize."

"I don't want your apologies."

"My dad, he—"

"I said, I'm working." Now she did snap her eyes to Olivia, but they were colder than Olivia would have thought possible.

"Hillary, please—"

"I think she asked you to leave." Ann moved between them.

Instead of backing off, Olivia took a step closer. "I bet you're loving this, aren't you?"

"Just looking out for a friend." Olivia couldn't decide which pissed her off more—Ann's arrogant smirk or her playing protector to Hillary. "Are you going to leave or do I need to call your sergeant?"

Olivia stared at her. Did she know who Olivia's sergeant was? That was just one more painful twist of the knife. She pushed past Ann, purposely bumping her shoulder.

"Can't get away from your damn exes," she muttered as she passed Hillary. By the way Hillary stiffened, she was sure she heard.

❖

"Everyone is buzzing about Olivia's standoff with Ann." Jake slid into the chair across from Hillary.

"Everyone should mind their own business." She'd come to the break room seeking peace from the prying eyes of her coworkers. She pushed her food around in the plastic storage container. She'd lost her appetite even before she'd reheated it.

She hadn't appreciated the way Ann had acted like she needed a white knight but hadn't decided whether to speak to her about it or ignore it. She didn't want to encourage such personal interactions with Ann, but she had trouble letting it go.

She'd heard Ann's comment about Olivia's sergeant and had no doubt she'd purposely referred to May Gilleland. Ann knew about her history with May and that their split had been much more amicable.

Jake shook his head and whistled. "Olivia Dennis. When you bring the drama, you really bring the drama. Sheriff Dennis is going to go through the roof when he hears—"

"He already knows."

"And?"

"Like you said—through the roof."

"So is that what she was here trying to apologize for?"

She dropped her fork and looked up at the ceiling before replying, "It's a long story and I'd rather not go into it right now."

He nodded. "You'd better watch yourself, friend. Sheriff Dennis and Sheriff Martin are buddies. If Dennis decides he wants you gone because of this—"

"He wouldn't."

"You're probably right. A devout Christian, Southern daddy who just found out his daughter is a dyke wouldn't hold a grudge against the woman she's sleeping with."

"Please, don't call her that." She usually didn't get torn up over labels, but on the heels of hearing Holt refer to her the same way, the term made her stomach turn.

"That's what you took from that?"

"My job's not in danger. Civil-service protection is just one of the perks of government employment."

"What about that confrontation out there? You don't think Sheriff Dennis could paint that as conduct unbecoming."

"That's a stretch." She knew Olivia's father might not be thrilled about their relationship, but she hadn't seriously considered that it could have professional ramifications for her.

"Maybe. But he'd have Ann on his side. She'd do it just to get to Olivia."

"I guess I'll worry about that if it happens." She picked her fork back up and tried to summon the desire to eat something. They sat silently while she took several small bites. Then she sighed and replaced the lid, giving up.

Jake reached across the table and covered her hand. "I'm sorry."

"For what?"

He shrugged. "It's clear you have feelings for each other. So I'm sorry if it's not going to work out."

She nodded. "Thanks."

"Sounds like she maybe wants another chance."

"Yeah, well, that would require me to believe things could be different." The exchange she'd witnessed in the hallway with Holt flashed through her mind. He'd been brash and insulting, but for the most part, Olivia had seemed to let it roll off her. Yet as soon as she considered that Olivia might have changed, she heard Olivia saying that Hillary had pushed her into telling her folks.

That simply wasn't true. Whether she knew it or not, Hillary had recognized steps toward Olivia's coming out since the day she'd admitted to Hillary that she was gay. She'd been headed in this direction, with or without Hillary. But she wouldn't allow Olivia to blame her for the demise of her family and resent her later. Not being with Olivia was ripping her apart. She had to keep reminding herself that she couldn't enter a relationship with that anvil hanging over them.

Chapter Twenty-two

Olivia pulled her Jeep into a parking spot and jumped out. She circled to the back and unfastened the straps holding her bike on the rack. As she turned and set it on the ground, she caught sight of a familiar car at the other end of the parking lot. Judging by the distance, she guessed the lone occupant in the driver's seat could see her clearly. She tugged off her T-shirt, leaving only her sports bra and bike shorts. She braced her hands against the Jeep and leaned forward, pushing one leg behind her, and stretched. She continued working through a series of stretches.

She put on her helmet and climbed on her bike. She pedaled a couple of times, then coasted toward her usual route. As she entered the path, she cut through the grass and circled toward the far side of the lot, approaching the car from the blind side. When she heard the engine turn over she picked up her pace. At the last minute, she swerved to the left and pulled up on the driver's side of the car.

"Well, this time I do think you're stalking me," she called through the open window.

Hillary paused with her hand on the key. "You knew I was here?"

Olivia nodded. She searched for some indication in Hillary's expression that she might be happy to see her. She was here, after all. But Hillary's face gave away nothing.

"And that little show by the side of the Jeep was for my benefit?"

"That depends."

"On what?"

"On whether you enjoyed it?" Olivia winked and was encouraged by the quirk of Hillary's lips and the spark in her eyes.

"Have a nice ride." When Hillary reached for the gear shift, Olivia put her hand on the edge of the window.

"Wait. Take a walk with me?"

"I don't think so."

"Then what are you doing here? You were just going to watch me take off on my ride, then leave?" She climbed off her bike and leaned it on the kickstand next to the car.

"Maybe."

"Can you meet me halfway here? You came down here for something."

"I missed you."

"I'm right here." She reached for Hillary's shoulder, but Hillary leaned away.

"I thought maybe if I saw you—physically saw you, it would be easier to, I don't know—not see you, I guess."

"How's that working out for you?" She bent down and met Hillary's eyes, not hiding her loneliness. "Because it's killing me."

Hillary's gaze softened and she tightened her hand around the steering wheel. Olivia let herself believe Hillary wanted to touch her. Maybe lay her hand against Olivia's cheek in that tender way she did. And the fact that she found the strength to restrain herself nearly broke Olivia's heart.

"Please, take a walk with me. For old times' sake." She shamelessly used her most plaintive tone.

Hillary sighed. "Okay."

"Great. Just let me put my bike up." She swung her leg over the bicycle.

"I'll meet you over there." Hillary put the car in gear.

"You're not going to wait until I ride over there and then drive away, are you?"

"No."

Olivia lifted her chin in the direction of her Jeep. "You go first."

Hillary rolled her eyes and drove across the parking lot, and Olivia rode behind her. When they reached the Jeep, she dismounted and loaded her bike onto the rack. Hillary waited while she stowed her helmet and pulled her shirt back on.

❖

Hillary walked next to Olivia and tried not to react when their shoulders brushed. She hadn't seen Olivia since Ann chased her out of Five-C six days before. Hillary had become consumed by whether Olivia struggled as much not to text or call as Hillary did. By Saturday, she'd convinced herself that seeing Olivia from afar would strengthen her resolve. She was an idiot.

"Do you want to sit?" Olivia indicated the same bench they'd been sitting at when Olivia had first invited her to the Dennis home for dinner.

"I'd rather just walk." She couldn't relive the nervousness and excitement of that moment.

Olivia nodded and they traversed farther down the path. The only sounds were their footfalls and the distant chatter of kids on the playground. Hillary's breath caught when Olivia's hand brushed hers and she felt Olivia's fingers curl as if trying to hold hers. She stopped in the middle of the path as emotion threatened to drown her.

Agreeing to talk had been a mistake, and she searched for a way to escape the pain of being so near Olivia. "I can't—"

"I love you—"

"Please, don't lead with that."

Olivia gently took Hillary's shoulders and guided her to the side of the trail. She waited while another couple passed them. "I love you and I want to be with you. *And* I don't care what anyone else thinks about it."

"How's your family?" Hillary ignored her declaration, hoping a few extra minutes would keep her gullible heart from believing those words.

"My parents aren't exactly speaking to me. But, on the upside, my Sundays are free. And I'm not real keen on hanging out with them right now, either."

"I never asked you to—"

"I didn't do it for you. Well, not only for you. I did it for me." She returned to the path and began walking again. Hillary followed. "Every Sunday I used to sit at my parents' table coveting what they have and what Andy has found with Frankie. I'd given up trying to convince myself that I could be happy alone. But there was no scenario in which my father could accept me being with a woman. Even knowing that, when I told him, he said—" Olivia's voice cracked.

The loneliness Olivia described pulled at her, and, giving in to the need to comfort her, Hillary took Olivia's hand. She didn't say anything, focusing instead on their hands swinging loosely between them.

"I was hurt and looking for someone to blame. And I—I chose wrong."

They came to another bench, this one more secluded, and Hillary pulled Olivia to it. "How does anyone get any exercise on these trails if they put a bench every hundred yards?"

After they sat down, Olivia angled toward her and grabbed both of her hands. "Since that first day at Five-C, you've been the one person I could count on. And I repaid you with mistrust and accusations. I'm so sorry."

When Olivia caressed her cheek, Hillary couldn't help leaning into the touch and closing her eyes. "No fair. You know I'm weak when you touch me."

"Well, then we have that in common."

The blatant vulnerability in Olivia's eyes melted the final trace of Hillary's anger, leaving her at the mercy of love and forgiveness. "I'm sorry, too. I should have tried harder to understand how difficult this was for you. I'd been hurt by straight women before, and I shouldn't have put their actions on you. I was afraid of getting my heart broken."

"Can we start over?"

Hillary shook her head, then kissed Olivia. She flushed when they drew a curious look from a passing jogger. "I'd much rather pick up where we left off. It took you over a month to come out to me, and I don't want to go through that again." She stood and pulled Olivia to her feet. "Let's go someplace more private."

Olivia threaded her arm around Hillary's and pressed close to her. "You know, given who I am, you should probably just get used to the idea that I'm occasionally going to have to come crawling to you with an apology."

Hillary tried to suppress a smile. "You think so?"

"I promise to try to make only the small mistakes. Can you live with that for the rest of your life?"

"The rest of my life?" She bumped her hip against Olivia's. "Is Olivia Dennis proposing a committed relationship?"

"I wouldn't use the word *proposing*?"

"Too much, too fast?"

"Committing to me probably comes a little more naturally to you, considering you've been obsessed with me since high school."

"I wouldn't say obsessed. Plus, during a number of years in between I distracted myself with other women."

"Good Lord, can we go one day without talking about your exes?"

Hillary laughed. They'd returned to the trailhead and Olivia pointed to Hillary's car.

"Do you want to follow me to my place?"

"Sure."

Olivia opened Hillary's car door. "So you did like the stretching?"

"If that's what you want to pretend it was." Hillary smiled as she got behind the wheel. "Okay. Yes. I haven't exactly hidden my appreciation of your body."

"So I *am* just a physical specimen to you." Olivia feigned hurt.

"A near-*perfect* physical specimen, if that makes you feel any better."

"It does. At least I know I have that over Ann."

"Don't be mean." Hillary rolled her window down and pulled the door shut. "But you're right. You're definitely hotter than Ann."

Olivia smiled as if vindicated, swaggered over to her Jeep, and climbed in. Hillary waited for Olivia to back out of her spot, and then she followed her out of the parking lot. When her phone rang she glanced at the display.

"Miss me already?" she asked after pushing the call button.

"You didn't say I was hotter than May."

"You're out of cheese dip. There are chips left but no cheese dip," Andy said as Olivia backed out of her new fridge holding two beers.

She'd talked Hillary into the fancier model while they were furnishing their new house. Of course, they had to buy the matching appliances. Hillary had put up token resistance, but she suspected she'd been just as excited about the double ovens in their new range.

"But we have plenty of beer." Then she pointed at a bowl on the counter. "And there's hummus. Use the chips in that."

"I don't even know what that is."

Olivia shook her head. "This is why I didn't want to invite straight people to this party."

"Hey, I wouldn't miss this. It's not every day my big sister moves in with her lesbian lover."

"Ass."

"So, less than six months and you guys are U-Hauling," Frankie said as she came into the kitchen. "You've really embraced the whole lesbian thing, huh?"

"Okay. Enough with the lesbian jokes." Olivia adopted an irritated tone, but she knew it was their way of showing her they accepted her. She only needed to look across the room at Hillary to not care how many jokes they made. Hillary stood among a group of female deputies. Between them, they made up three couples, including May Gilleland and her spouse.

"It's all out of love, my friend." Frankie wrapped her arm around Hillary's waist. "You know I like Hillary."

"Yes. I do. In fact, I think you're almost as in love with her as I am."

Frankie shrugged. "She's great."

"You were the one person whose loyalty I could depend on, even against Andy. Now, I think you'd side with her in a fight."

"Treat me right and you won't have to find out." Hillary threw her arms around both their shoulders. She kissed Frankie's cheek, then grasped Olivia's chin, turned her face, and kissed her lips. "For example, is one of those mine?" She lifted a beer from Olivia's hand.

Frankie punched Olivia's shoulder lightly. "Don't worry. I'm still your friend first. And to prove it, I'll let you take me to lunch tomorrow."

"Actually, Mom invited me to meet her for lunch before shift."

"Really? That's great," Frankie said.

"She made a point of letting me know Dad will be out fishing with Sheriff Martin. So I guess her going behind his back is a baby step, huh?"

"Any time she goes against his wishes is more than a baby step," Andy said. "Come on, Frankie. We should go socialize with Sarge."

"I can't believe you made me invite Gilleland," Olivia said after they'd gone.

"*And* her wife."

"Yeah, yeah. She's got a wife. So what? It's bad enough I have to play nice at work knowing she's seen you naked, but now she's in our home."

"You said you like working for her." Hillary grabbed the waistband of Olivia's jeans, pulled her close, and gave her a slow kiss that made Olivia wish they could kick everyone out. That would probably be in bad taste, given the party had just started an hour ago. "Besides, you said it—our home. You're the only one seeing me naked now."

"It is a great house." Olivia looked around, seeing not only the charm and Craftsman woodwork she'd fallen in love with, but also the potential for them to fix it up further. This place was the first one they'd looked at. As soon as she'd walked in the front door, Olivia could see them there together and would have bought it that day. But Hillary had made her look at several more so they could be certain they didn't miss a better place.

The house had been just one more major change in her life. Frankie had been joking about moving fast, but nine months ago, while she was miserably attending Sunday dinner every week, Olivia wouldn't have predicted she'd be here now. The rumors had flown around the department and some of the guys had treated her worse, but many either didn't seem to care or let her know they accepted her.

They'd taken a trip to Texas and Olivia had met Hillary's parents. There she found the kind of warmth and acceptance she could only hope for with her own.

She hadn't been back to her parents' church and likely wouldn't. She hadn't given up on God, but until she found a different place to worship, she'd settle for her private prayers and the often-spiritual experience of an early morning bike ride through the park.

"Go with me tomorrow?"

"To lunch with your mother? I don't think so."

"Why not?"

"You don't have to do this. I know you want to prove a point to me—"

"The only point I have to prove is to my mother. I'm not going to grovel for a relationship with her. If she wants to see me, she has to see all of me. And that means the part of me that is in love with you."

"I get that. But she's made a gesture that seems to indicate she's adjusting to her new definition of you. Maybe now isn't the time to rub it in her face."

"I didn't say we were going to make out at the table. I want you beside me."

"I'll make you a deal. You go alone tomorrow. Give her a chance for a private conversation. Then if there's a second lunch, or dinner, or whatever, I'll go with you."

Olivia wanted to argue. She couldn't remember the last time she'd had a genuine conversation with her mother. But maybe that was as much her fault as her mother's. She could hardly have a sincere, intimate conversation when she'd been hiding a pretty big part of who she was. She would do it Hillary's way and not get ahead of herself.

She would love to someday take Hillary to lunch and have her mother—maybe even both parents—treat her as much a part of the family as they did Frankie. But as she looked around the room at their friends and Andy and Frankie, she realized that if that never happened she still had a pretty rich family life.

"Speaking of private conversations, when do you think all of these people will leave?" Olivia kissed Hillary's neck.

"Not for a while yet, so cool it." Hillary brushed away Olivia's wandering hands. "Let's mingle and I'll make it up to you later."

"Ten-four, ma'am. I go where you tell me to." Olivia caught Hillary's hand and let her lead her into the living room.

Hillary put on her dispatcher voice. "Don't forget it, Deputy."

About the Author

Erin Dutton is the author of nine romance novels: *Sequestered Hearts*, *Fully Involved*, *A Place to Rest*, *Designed for Love*, *Point of Ignition*, *A Perfect Match*, *Reluctant Hope*, *More Than Friends*, and *For the Love of Cake*. She is also a contributor to *Erotic Interludes 5: Road Games and Romantic Interludes 1 & 2* and revisited two characters from one of her novels in *Breathless: Tales of Celebration*. She is a 2011 recipient of the Alice B. Readers' Appreciation Award for her body of work.

When not working or writing, she enjoys photography, playing golf, and spending time with friends and family.

Books Available from Bold Strokes Books

Deadly Medicine by Jaime Maddox. Dr. Ward Thrasher's life is in turmoil. Her partner Jess has left her, and her job puts her in the path of a murderous physician who has Jess in his sights. (978-1-62639-4-247)

New Beginnings by KC Richardson. Can the connection and attraction between Jordan Roberts and Kirsten Murphy be enough for Jordan to trust Kirsten with her heart? (978-1-62639-4-506)

Officer Down by Erin Dutton. Can two women who've made careers out of being there for others in crisis find the strength to need each other? (978-1-62639-4-230)

Reasonable Doubt by Carsen Taite. Just when Sarah and Ellery think they've left dangerous careers behind, a new case sets them—and their hearts—on a collision course. (978-1-62639-4-421)

Tarnished Gold by Ann Aptaker. Cantor Gold must outsmart the Law, outrun New York's dockside gangsters, outplay a shady art dealer, his lover, and a beautiful curator, and stay out of a killer's gun sights. (978-1-62639-4-261)

The Renegade by Amy Dunne. Post-apocalyptic survivors Alex and Evelyn secretly find love while held captive by a deranged cult, but when their relationship is discovered, they must fight for their freedom—or die trying. (978-1-62639-4-278)

Thrall by Barbara Ann Wright. Four women in a warrior society must work together to lift an insidious curse while caught between their own desires, the will of their peoples, and an ancient evil. (978-1-62639-4-377)

White Horse in Winter by Franci McMahon. Love between two women collides with the inner poison of a closeted horse trainer in the green hills of Vermont. (978-1-62639-4-292)

The Chameleon by Andrea Bramhall. Two old friends must work through a web of lies and deceit to find themselves again, but in the search they discover far more than they ever went looking for. (978-1-62639-363-9)

Side Effects by VK Powell. Detective Jordan Bishop and Dr. Neela Sahjani must decide if it's easier to trust someone with your heart or your life as they face threatening protestors, corrupt politicians, and their increasing attraction. (978-1-62639-364-6)

Autumn Spring by Shelley Thrasher. Can Bree and Linda, two women in the autumn of their lives, put their hearts first and find the love they've never dared seize? (978-1-62639-365-3)

Warm November by Kathleen Knowles. What do you do if the one woman you want is the only one you can't have? (978-1-62639-366-0)

In Every Cloud by Tina Michele. When she finally leaves her shattered life behind, is Bree strong enough to salvage the remaining pieces of her heart and find the place where it truly fits? (978-1-62639-413-1)

Rise of the Gorgon by Tanai Walker. When independent Internet journalist Elle Pharell goes to Kuwait to investigate a veteran's mysterious suicide, she hires Cassandra Hunt, an interpreter with a covert agenda. (978-1-62639-367-7)

Crossed by Meredith Doench. Agent Luce Hansen returns home to catch a killer and risks everything to revisit the unsolved murder of her first girlfriend and confront the demons of her youth. (978-1-62639-361-5)

Making a Comeback by Julie Blair. Music and love take center stage when jazz pianist Liz Randall tries to make a comeback with the help of her reclusive, blind neighbor, Jac Winters. (978-1-62639-357-8)

Soul Unique by Gun Brooke. Self-proclaimed cynic Greer Landon falls for Hayden Rowe's paintings and the young woman shortly after, but will Hayden, who lives with Asperger syndrome, trust her and reciprocate her feelings? (978-1-62639-358-5)

The Price of Honor by Radclyffe. Honor and duty are not always black and white—and when self-styled patriots take up arms against the government, the price of honor may be a life. (978-1-62639-359-2)

Mounting Evidence by Karis Walsh. Lieutenant Abigail Hargrove and her mounted police unit need to solve a murder and protect wetland biologist Kira Lovell during the Washington State Fair. (978-1-62639-343-1)

Threads of the Heart by Jeannie Levig. Maggie and Addison Rae-McInnis share a love and a life, but are the threads that bind them together strong enough to withstand Addison's restlessness and the seductive Victoria Fontaine? (978-1-62639-410-0)

Sheltered Love by MJ Williamz. Boone Fairway and Grey Dawson—two women touched by abuse—overcome their pasts to find happiness in each other. (978-1-62639-362-2)

Asher's Out by Elizabeth Wheeler. Asher Price's candid photographs capture the truth, but when his success requires exposing an enemy, Asher discovers his only shot at happiness involves revealing secrets of his own. (978-1-62639-411-7)

The Ground Beneath by Missouri Vaun. An improbable barter deal involving a hope chest and dinners for a month places lovely Jessica Walker distractingly in the way of Sam Casey's bachelor lifestyle. (978-1-62639-606-7)

Hardwired by C.P. Rowlands. Award-winning teacher Clary Stone, and Leefe Ellis, manager of the homeless shelter for small children, stand together in a part of Clary's hometown that she never knew existed. (978-1-62639-351-6)

No Good Reason by Cari Hunter. A violent kidnapping in a Peak District village pushes Detective Sanne Jensen and lifelong friend Dr. Meg Fielding closer, just as it threatens to tear everything apart. (978-1-62639-352-3)

Romance by the Book by Jo Victor. If Cam didn't keep disrupting her life, maybe Alex could uncover the secret of a century-old love story, and solve the greatest mystery of all—her own heart. (978-1-62639-353-0)

Death's Doorway by Crin Claxton. Helping the dead can be deadly: Tony may be listening to the dead, but she needs to learn to listen to the living. (978-1-62639-354-7)

Searching for Celia by Elizabeth Ridley. As American spy novelist Dayle Salvesen investigates the mysterious disappearance of her ex-lover, Celia, in London, she begins questioning how well she knew Celia—and how well she knows herself. (978-1-62639-356-1)

The 45th Parallel by Lisa Girolami. Burying her mother isn't the worst thing that can happen to Val Montague when she returns to the woodsy but peculiar town of Hemlock, Oregon. (978-1-62639-342-4)

A Royal Romance by Jenny Frame. In a country where class still divides, can love topple the last social taboo and allow Queen Georgina and Beatrice Elliot, a working class girl, their happy ever after? (978-1-62639-360-8)

Bouncing by Jaime Maddox. Basketball Coach Alex Dalton has been bouncing from woman to woman, because no one ever held her interest, until she meets her new assistant, Britain Dodge. (978-1-62639-344-8)

Same Time Next Week by Emily Smith. A chance encounter between Alex Harris and the beautiful Michelle Masters leads to a whirlwind friendship, and causes Alex to question everything she's ever known—including her own marriage. (978-1-62639-345-5)

All Things Rise by Missouri Vaun. Cole rescues a striking pilot who crash-lands near her family's farm, setting in motion a chain of events that will forever alter the course of her life. (978-1-62639-346-2)

Riding Passion by D. Jackson Leigh. Mount up for the ride through a sizzling anthology of chance encounters, buried desires, romantic surprises, and blazing passion. (978-1-62639-349-3)

Love's Bounty by Yolanda Wallace. Lobster boat captain Jake Myers stopped living the day she cheated death, but meeting greenhorn Shy Silva stirs her back to life. (978-1-62639-334-9)

Just Three Words by Melissa Brayden. Sometimes the one you want is the one you least suspect. Accountant Samantha Ennis has her ordered life disrupted when heartbreaker Hunter Blair moves into her trendy Soho loft. (978-1-62639-335-6)

Lay Down the Law by Carsen Taite. Attorney Peyton Davis returns to her Texas roots to take on big oil and the Mexican Mafia, but will her investigation thwart her chance at true love? (978-1-62639-336-3)

Playing in Shadow by Lesley Davis. Survivor's guilt threatens to keep Bryce trapped in her nightmare world unless Scarlet's love can pull her out of the darkness and back into the light. (978-1-62639-337-0)

Soul Selecta by Gill McKnight. Soul mates are hell to work with. (978-1-62639-338-7)

The Revelation of Beatrice Darby by Jean Copeland. Adolescence is complicated, but Beatrice Darby is about to discover how impossible it can seem to a lesbian coming of age in conservative 1950s New England. (978-1-62639-339-4)

Twice Lucky by Mardi Alexander. For firefighter Mackenzie James and Dr. Sarah Macarthur, there's suddenly a whole lot more in life to understand, to consider, to risk…someone will need to fight for her life. (978-1-62639-325-7)

Shadow Hunt by L.L. Raand. With young to raise and her Pack under attack, Sylvan, Alpha of the wolf Weres, takes on her greatest challenge when she determines to uncover the faceless enemies known as the Shadow Lords. A Midnight Hunters novel. (978-1-62639-326-4)

Heart of the Game by Rachel Spangler. A baseball writer falls for a single mom, but can she ever love anything as much as she loves the game? (978-1-62639-327-1)

Getting Lost by Michelle Grubb. Twenty-eight days, thirteen European countries, a tour manager fighting attraction, and an accused murderer: Stella and Phoebe's journey of a lifetime begins here. (978-1-62639-328-8)

Prayer of the Handmaiden by Merry Shannon. Celibate priestess Kadrian must defend the kingdom of Ithyria from a dangerous enemy and ultimately choose between her duty to the Goddess and the love of her childhood sweetheart, Erinda. (978-1-62639-329-5)

The Witch of Stalingrad by Justine Saracen. A Soviet "night witch" pilot and American journalist meet on the Eastern Front in WW II and struggle through carnage, conflicting politics, and the deadly Russian winter. (978-1-62639-330-1)

Pedal to the Metal by Jesse J. Thoma. When unreformed thief Dubs Williams is released from prison to help Max Winters bust a car theft ring, Max learns that to catch a thief, get in bed with one. (978-1-62639-239-7)

Dragon Horse War by D. Jackson Leigh. A priestess of peace and a fiery warrior must defeat a vicious uprising that entwines their destinies and ultimately their hearts. (978-1-62639-240-3)

For the Love of Cake by Erin Dutton. When everything is on the line, and one taste can break a heart, will pastry chefs Maya and Shannon take a chance on reality? (978-1-62639-241-0)

Betting on Love by Alyssa Linn Palmer. A quiet country-girl-at-heart and a live-life-to-the-fullest biker take a risk at offering each other their hearts. (978-1-62639-242-7)

The Deadening by Yvonne Heidt. The lines between good and evil, right and wrong, have always been blurry for Shade. When Raven's actions force her to choose, which side will she come out on? (978-1-62639-243-4)